HONG KONG GOTHIC

Other **Hong Kong Writers Circle** anthologies:

Haunting Tales of Hong Kong (2005)
Sweat & the City (2006)
Hong Kong Whodunnits (2007)
Love & Lust (2008)
Hotel China (2009)
Measurements: Sketches from Hong Kong (2010)
As We See It: Hong Kong Stories (2011)
Of Gods and Mobsters: Classic Tales Retold in Hong Kong (2013)
Another Hong Kong (2014)

www.hkwriterscircle.com

HONG KONG GOTHIC

Edited by

Kate Hawkins, Edmund Price and Marnie Walker

HONG KONG GOTHIC

Individual stories © 2015 the Authors
This collection © 2015 Hong Kong Writers Circle
ISBN 978-988-16858-5-8 (paperback)
ISBN 978-988-16858-6-5 (e-book)

Published by The Hong Kong Writers Circle
Flat 2B, Block 2, La Serene, 2 Serene Avenue, Discovery Bay, Hong Kong
http://www.hkwriterscircle.com

Typeset in Adobe Garamond by Alan Sargent
Cover art © 2015 Michel Guy

Printed in Hong Kong, the UK and the USA
First printing January 2015

Contents

A casement sunders . . .

. . . the candle snuffs

Introduction

THE EDITORS OF THE Hong Kong Writers Circle anthology are tasked each year with selecting a theme that inspires the writers' imaginations and offers variety from past collections. Asking contributors to relate the idea of Gothic culture to the city of Hong Kong posed a unique challenge. For most of us, the term denotes tales of old world romance: beautiful damsels and chivalric heroes lured to crumbling castles in the remote corners of Europe, where madmen and monsters lurk in the shadows. Meanwhile, 'Asia's World City', as the Tourism Board likes to call it, is characterised by modern skyscrapers, neon, crowds, shopping and unbridled capitalism.

As this anthology demonstrates, Hong Kong is also very rich in Gothic inspiration. From the perilously steep streets of Sheung Wan to the dark subterranean world of the MTR and on into the jungle wilderness of the New Territories, this collection slithers, climbs and haunts the vast network of the city and beyond. Love, greed, pride, and sorrow mingle with madness and the supernatural. Characters encounter monsters that prey on lust, ghosts suffering from loneliness, and demons that come to collect the doomed. You will find that Hong Kong streets can be as sinister and mysterious as the foggy lanes of Jekyll and Hyde's London, its architecture as labyrinthine as a Transylvanian castle, and its people as romantically perverse as the broody vampires and vengeful she-devils that have been seducing readers for over a century.

We have divided the collection into four parts, along the concepts of comeuppance, mystery, uncertainty and closure. We do trust that within the overall collection you will find stories that delight, inspire, surprise and, we hope, frighten you. And so, gentle reader, we invite you to enter the pages of *Hong Kong Gothic,* if you dare. . . .

Kate Hawkins, Edmund Price and Marnie Walker
Editors

Acknowledgements

The editors would like to thank everyone who contributed to, or otherwise helped to bring about, this anthology. In particular, the authors themselves, without whom there would be no collection; Michel Guy for the cover art; Alan Sargent for the layout; Chameleon Press for the printing; Simon Berry for the style guide; SCC Overton and Melanie Ho for the additional story reviews and Melanie Ho, the Chair of the Hong Kong Writers Circle, for her assiduous support of the entire process.

A door slams . . .

The Girl Above
Ian Greenfield

I AM ON THE POINT OF SLEEPING when the sound of an explosion tears through me. I shout out and my heart races as the glass in my bedroom window shakes. I creep towards the window but suddenly stop. I can hear noises that scare me even more than the explosion. Movement in the flat above that could be the scraping of a chair, then a hint of singing, snatches of the same chorus in Cantonese that has been haunting me over the last few days. I don't know what the words mean but they send a shiver down my spine; a cliché I didn't think happened until recently.

After moving to Hong Kong nearly a year ago, still drunk on the flight after celebrating England's World Cup Final victory over West Germany, I'm still not fully used to the claustrophobic feeling of living in a building where silence is a luxury seldom present. Sounds from the apartments around mine and traffic on the streets outside are a far cry from the solitude of the farmhouse I'd grown up in where the nearest human neighbours were a five-minute walk away. After many months, though, background noise has become little more than an annoyance.

Only the sounds I can hear from above create a different feeling, one of unsettling dread, because they should not be there.

'Has someone new moved into the apartment above?' I asked Mr Chow, my landlord, with only minor concern, two days after first hearing noises.

Chow shrugged. 'Still the girl. But she disappear. No come back. No pay rent. She owe me money.'

'So were you in there moving things? Getting ready for a new tenant?'

Chow shook his head. 'Why you ask?'

'I just heard things.'

'Maybe girl come back. I go check. Maybe get my money.'

Only I know that the girl can't have come back.

But if the flat above is empty, who is making the sounds? Maybe the landlord really is up there this time? But at this time of night? And what about the singing? I am rooted to the spot, straining to listen even though I don't want to hear it. I am trying so hard that everything else is shut out until the rest of the world suddenly comes crashing back in as sounds from the street increase in volume; someone screaming, random shouting and the whine of approaching sirens.

Peering outside, I see fire leaping out of a window on the opposite side of the street and people beginning to mass below, fleeing the building within which the fire rages. Many of the people look shocked and are turning in circles as if unsure where to go. A convoy of emergency vehicles arrives: an ambulance, two fire engines and, more telling, several police cars and vans, men streaming out of them wearing black riot helmets and carrying wicker shields.

These are dark days in Hong Kong and the excitement I felt after arriving as a fresh-faced teacher is fast fading. It isn't just the riots – clashes begun by leftist Chinese wanting to stake their claim for freedom from the clutches of a dying British Empire – but the way my life has spiralled out of control in recent weeks. And how I am struggling to cope.

It is a long night as the police and fire services deal with what has happened opposite, maybe expecting violence to erupt around them. But nothing further happens.

Even more comforting, there are no further noises from the flat above.

I awake with a pounding headache and sweat soaking my pyjama bottoms. I cannot hear the fan on the wall, but I'm sure I left it on last night. Pressing my palms against my temples I sit up slowly. It feels as if getting out of bed to switch the fan on is too much of an effort but the heat and humidity are oppressive. I struggle to my feet and cross the room. After pulling the fan's cord I take several tottering steps back towards the bed and let myself fall into its embrace. I probably should have opened the window as well but for now it is enough to let the air blow against my damp body, sending a chill across my naked chest.

As I lie there, I think back on the events of last night, wondering if they were part of some lucid dream. There had been rioting on my street two days ago but that had been little more than a large crowd of youths at one end shouting at the gathering of police that faced them. I'd been about to step outside my building when an old man came rushing in waving his arms. 'Don't go out. Don't go out. Fighting.'

The man lived on the third floor and this was the first time he had ever spoken to me. The fear in his voice was obvious. There was no fighting, though, only a few thrown rocks amidst the verbal sparring.

Last night was more than just macho posturing, though. Was anyone hurt? Had the bomb – I am sure that's what it was – been intended for a specific target or was it a random act of violence? Am I really safe in my own home? Unlike some of my colleagues, I haven't taken advantage of the summer holidays to take the long journey home to England but I'm now thinking that getting out of Hong Kong might not be such a bad idea.

For several reasons.

My doorbell rings.

I jump. Such an innocuous sound but one I am not expecting. I seldom have visitors. Maybe John from work has heard about the explosion and is checking on me. Although why not telephone? John hasn't gone travelling, saying there is more than enough to give him a good time in Hong Kong. He's several years older than me and my mentor with respect to the pleasures Hong Kong can offer but I have avoided seeing him in the last two weeks since. . . .

I close my eyes and shut the thought out.

Again the bell rings.

'Coming,' I shout, slowly getting to my feet.

The only reply is a further ringing of the bell.

I must have risen too quickly because stars swim around the outskirts of my vision. The next thing I know I am falling, tripping over the bed sheets tangled on the floor. My head strikes the floor and I swear loudly.

By the time I reach the door to my apartment the bell is no longer ringing. I peer through the spyhole and freeze. I can only see her back as she turns the corner in the corridor but that's enough for me to recognise her. It's the girl from the floor above.

Only it can't be. I must be imagining it.

Like I've been imagining all the noises I keep hearing from her apartment?

Maybe I should open my door and follow the fleeing figure, just to confirm that it isn't the girl from upstairs. Because she's dead. Her body nothing more than rotting meat. Only I am too shaken to let common sense prevail. I move away from the door, heading into the kitchen and pour myself some milk.

It is only as I sip from the glass that the significance of that act strikes me. As I child I was petrified of ghosts, or rather one ghost in particular. That of my grandmother. She'd died in my bedroom when I was five, a heart-attack one night whilst reading me a bedtime story. She had just reached the part of the tale where the witch died a ghastly death drinking her own poison when my grandmother clutched at her chest and keeled over. At first I thought she was merely acting out part of the story as she often did, but when she didn't move I started shouting for my parents.

The next time I saw my grandmother was the night after she was buried. She was standing at my bedside, holding a book and smiling. That first night I actually listened to half the story before my brain told me that she couldn't really be there. I closed my eyes, but could still hear her speak and upon opening my eyes again she remained there until my parents came running into my room in response to my screams. I spent the rest of that night sharing my parents' bed but almost every night after that I saw my grandmother again, each time reading a different story. And each time it happened my mother would try to calm me with a glass of milk. It got so bad that my parents moved house and I never saw my grandmother again after that. I also never drank milk again at night because it always seemed to leave a sour taste in my mouth.

It takes me nearly an hour to calm down, by which point I am rationalising what has happened more clearly. It could not have been the girl from upstairs because that's impossible. After all, I had only seen her from behind and fleetingly at that.

There's a bang from the ceiling. I flinch. I need to get out of here.

I hear no more noises from above but what else might follow? Yes, there is surely an explanation but now is not the time to dwell on that. I go down two flights of stairs to reach the lobby of the building, ignoring the lift which is currently on the floor above. I fear that if I call it down I'll find the girl waiting inside, her neck twisted at an obscene angle.

My intention is to walk to a nearby café for lunch and to be away from my apartment. After that I have no idea, although the thought of going to a store to stock up on alcohol is a tempting prospect. The only cold drink in my apartment is milk and I don't want my childhood remedy for night frights to become part of my routine again. Surely if I hear noises again the easiest way to banish them is with a drunken haze?

And if the noises remain then maybe I can blame it on the drink.

One look along the street changes my mind. Less than fifty yards away, where Tai Yau Street stretches northwards to Choi Hung Road, a large group has gathered, blocking the way. There are no signs they are about to become violent but given last night's explosion I'm not prepared to head that way to find out. Halfway down the street, positioned near where the explosion took place, is a group of police-men dressed in khaki uniforms.

Shouting erupts from the people at the end of the street. I cannot understand what is said but I catch the word 'gweilo' and realise their attention is on me. I look towards the police then towards the crowd, the shouting intensifying. Several people break away from the group, moving closer. One of them throws a bottle in my direction and it smashes into the wall beside me.

There are shouts from the police and I wonder whether they are also moving in my direction. Only I don't want to turn away from the five men who have now come to a standstill only a few feet away, gesticulating wildly and hurling what is certainly abuse.

I edge back towards the door to my building, no longer hungry. The food and beer can wait. A policeman now shouts at me, asking me to go inside.

Not that I need telling.

Looking out of my apartment window, there are no further signs of aggression from the crowd but there is also no indication of them moving away. More police have gathered but no attempts are being made to disperse the crowd other than a couple of messages via megaphone. It seems to be little more than a waiting game. Despite not wanting to stay here I don't want to go out, either. Only sooner or later I will have to. There is little in my apartment to eat and the way my nerves are frayed, I'll need something stronger than milk to get me through the night.

The doorbell rings and once again my heart begins racing. This is plain stupid. In all likelihood it is a neighbour knocking or maybe one of the policemen, perhaps checking I am okay after the minor incident outside. I don't really expect it to be some ghost tormenting me, do I?

Shaking my head I walk across the room as the bell rings again.

'Who is it?' I call out.

There is no answer and that freaks me out a little but not enough to stop me from opening the door without looking through the spyhole.

The door swings wide open and there she stands.

The dead girl.

Dressed in a thin white dress that shows a bulge in her belly but with a deep red stain spreading across it. I look into her rounded face and the eyes that flicker towards me before darting away.

I step away from the door, trying to still my trembling hands.

'Mike.' Her voice is little more than a whisper.

'No,' I mumble. 'No, no, no.' I push the door hard, hearing it rattle in the frame as it slams shut.

'Not there, not there,' I mutter to myself.

Only the doorbell rings again. I place my hands against my head.

It isn't enough to shut the noise out.

Yes, as a child I believed in ghosts, but not now.

Now I am a sane, rational adult and those childish fears should not exist anymore. Maybe it is just my guilt playing tricks with my mind but can I really have imagined all the noises that have plagued me over the past few days?

Another ring on the bell and this time she screams out my name. . . .

I had not meant to get romantically involved with the girl from upstairs. On the rebound from a relationship at work that had turned sour, I'd hit the drink heavily for five consecutive nights, struggling to wake the next morning and barely making it through the days on two feet. I'm sure the students must have smelled the alcohol on my breath and noticed I wasn't really focused but no one said anything. Maybe they felt some sympathy for me because everyone had known that Margaret Wilding and I were an item and that something had gone wrong. Most of the students probably knew before my colleagues, as a group of seniors had been in the restaurant when Margaret slapped me across the face and upended her glass of wine in my lap. News like that spreads like wildfire.

By Friday night I was in no fit state, mental or physical, to be out drinking again but that hadn't stopped me. The evening had started in the company of John Harrison but at some point we'd argued about Margaret. Violently. My temper got the better of me and I'd stormed off leaving John with a split lip. The girl from upstairs was coming home at the same time as me. I didn't know her name and had exchanged little more than a smile and a small greeting on the odd occasion when we happened to be exiting or entering the building together. In fact, I thought I'd seen her earlier that evening but had probably got my days mixed up as she was dressed differently, wearing a lust-enhancing red dress. I tried holding the door open for her but stumbled, almost knocking her over in the process.

'You need help?' she said.

I nodded despite feeling frustrated at my helplessness.

She was a small timid thing but was stronger than she looked. Together we managed to get into the lift and she helped me to my door.

'Let me,' she said as I fumbled for my keys. 'I'm Wei-ling. I live upstairs.'

I can't remember anything else that happened that night but in the morning when I woke, Wei-ling was beside me. There was an embarrassing silence as she stirred and the only word she uttered before collecting her clothes and leaving was 'bye'. Two weeks later she rang my doorbell, only this time I was sober. I'd only seen her once during that fortnight but from the lack-lustre smile she offered I'd had the impression she'd been trying to avoid me. Yet there she was.

'Hello, Mike.'

I couldn't even remember telling her my name and at the time I couldn't remember hers.

'Hello.' I paused, a little nervous. 'Do you want to come in?'

Her smile was answer enough and although we talked a little that evening, it was obvious she hadn't come for the conversation.

Several more times we met, but always on her terms. She would come to see me and, although it wasn't formally said, that was clearly the expectation of what was passing for our relationship. There was no invitation to visit her flat and somehow I felt I wouldn't have been welcome.

The relationship seemed to be the physical act of desire and nothing more. Given that I was still hurting from what had happened with Margaret I was happy for things to be that way.

Then nearly three weeks ago, almost four months after that first night, Wei-ling came to me again.

She made no effort to come into my apartment when I opened the door but stood in the corridor. 'Mike, I'm pregnant.'

My shocked silence probably wasn't what she expected.

'What are you going to do?' Wei-ling asked.

'Sorry?'

'What are you. . . .'

'No, I heard what you said. But what do you mean, what am *I* going to do?' She flinched at the anger in my voice and took a step back.

'You need to help me.' Despite her nervousness and some watering around her eyes there was a determination in the way she spoke.

'Me?'

'It's your child too.'

'So what do you want? Money? Is that it?' I must have come across as callous, uncaring, but it was the only way I could react to the shock. Despite my desire for her I didn't love Wei-ling and was sure she felt much the same way about me. In truth, I knew almost nothing about her other than her name and the shape of her body.

'You need to help.' She took a step towards me then and the only thing I saw in her eyes was anger.

'How? You want an abortion?' I'd heard rumours that the United Kingdom was considering legalising abortion with some vote on the cards in the coming months but it wasn't legal yet and I assumed the stance was the same in Hong Kong. What else was she thinking of? Carrying the child to term and then giving it up for adoption? What other options were there?

'What are you going to do?' She jabbed a finger into my chest, moving closer. It was my turn to step back.

'How do you know it's mine?'

She slapped my face.

Three days later I was walking up the stairs to my apartment because the lift had broken down. I saw Wei-ling above me carrying a bag of shopping. I quickly moved upwards, stretching my arm out towards her.

She turned around, confusion and panic etched on her face. 'Don't touch me,' she yelled. She spun her bag in an arc, cracking me on the side of the head.

'Hey!' I shouted out, surprised more than anything else. I instinctively brought my arm up. Maybe she thought I was going to hit her because she swung the bag again. It contained something hard and I felt a searing pain as my nose exploded.

Without thinking I hit out, throwing a punch into the side of her head. She lost her balance, her feet slipping on the stairs, and she tumbled past me. As she fell, her head struck the wall with a thud that echoed up the stairwell. She came to a stop near the corner of the stairs, her neck twisted awkwardly. Dread came over me as I sprinted down the stairs, leaping several steps at a time and almost falling myself.

It didn't take a genius to see she was dead.

The sensible thing would have been to call the police. To have explained exactly what had occurred. Only I was frightened as to the conclusions they would draw. With the alcohol on my breath I dreaded to think what they would assume.

But what else could I do?

I'm not sure what impulse possessed me next but I thought of the hill not far from where I lived, dense vegetation at the bottom of it. Lifting the body I started moving, supporting it as best I could, terrified what someone would say if they saw me.

I got the body down the back stairs and had several seconds of panic before I exited the building through the service entrance to where the rubbish was stored before being collected. From there it was a short walk to the top of the hill. Lifting the body, I dumped it over a short wall and watched as it tumbled down the hillside. Halfway down it stopped and my breath caught in my throat. I thought I might need to climb after the body to ensure it was out of sight, but then gravity kicked in again and seconds later it had disappeared into the undergrowth. . . .

So how can she be screaming my name outside my apartment now?

Holding my hands over my ears I walk backwards away from the door as fast as I can. I bang into the table and a jarring pain sweeps up my back. Moving down the short corridor to my bedroom to escape, I feel a rising panic as the doorbell continues to ring and Wei-ling continues to shout.

How can I make her go away?

Or maybe I need to face this?

And do what?

I pause, then retrace my steps. Once more I open the door, staring at the girl in front of me and wondering how my life has come to this.

'Mike, I need you.' Her hands are clutched to her stomach but she also seems to be holding something. The blood on her dress looks fresh. I cannot remember her bleeding on the night she died – on the night I killed her – but the symbolism isn't lost on me. In killing Wei-ling I had also killed her child. Our child.

The blood drips to the floor as she stands there and I am hypnotised by the motion.

'This is your fault, Mike. You made me do this.' The earlier pleading tone in her voice has been replaced by something tinged with both anger and regret but with a harder edge that makes me look up. She has moved her hands away from her stomach and I can now see that she holds a knitting needle drenched in blood.

She steps towards me, lifting the needle and waving it in my face.

'This is for you, Mike. This is for you.'

I move backwards, stumbling in panic and falling to the floor.

Wei-ling bends down, thrusting the needle at me. 'Look, look.'

I can't do anything *but* look, the red-tipped point edging closer to my eyes.

I don't know what to do. I don't know what to say. Even the fear of looking down the stairs at Wei-ling's dead body didn't compare to this wild-eyed spectre bending down over me, brandishing a blood-soaked needle only inches from my eyes. I feel a warmth spreading across my legs as I lose control of my bladder.

I fully expect that needle to poke into my eyes, jab through the jelly and pierce my brain. And although she moves no closer, I cannot gain the strength to crawl backwards or thrust myself to my feet.

'I had to do it. I. . . .' She suddenly wavers, unsteady on her feet, and it breaks the spell I am under.

I scramble away and slowly start to rise.

Wei-ling drops the needle, stretching her arms out to the side, leaving blood stains on the walls.

'I can't do it. I can't do it by myself.' Tears are rolling down her cheeks. 'She's gone. Still gone and I can't do it on my own. I needed you, Mike. I needed her.'

She sinks to the ground sobbing.

Wei-ling suddenly seems so pathetic that my fear dissipates. I find myself able to speak again.

'I'm sorry, Wei-ling. I'm sorry about what happened.' But what can I do? There is no way back for me, no way back for us.

'It's too late now.'

'Is there anything I can do? Anything to. . . .' To what? Send this spirit away?

'If Mei-ling was here she could help. . . .' She is a broken, crying pile on the floor, blood continuing to pool around her.

'Mei-ling?' I ask. 'Who's Mei-ling?'

Wei-ling looks up at me then, shaking her head with no sign of her cries abating. 'I killed my baby, Mike. I killed my baby.'

'Mei-ling? Is that what you were going to call it?'

Wei-ling weakly shakes her head. 'Mei-ling is my sister. My twin sister. She would have helped me but she disappeared two weeks ago.'

'Sister? I didn't know you had a sister.'

'We kept it quiet. Mei-ling rents the flat. It was a secret that I lived there too. Mei-ling says that if the landlord thought there were two of us living there he would want more money. Now Mei-ling has gone and no one can help me. That's why I . . . why I. . . .' She looks at the blood around her, pressing her hands between her legs.

'You need to get to a hospital,' I say. 'Let me help. Let me. . . .'

'My baby,' she wails, only her voice is weak, her strength sapping away. 'No, no, no. . . .' she mutters.

This time there is no hiding and I have to help her out. I have to do for her what I did not do for her sister. Maybe the difference is that this time there is someone I can save.

I follow Wei-ling to the hospital, coming home late in the evening, pleased to notice there are no people outside my building and no police presence. Wei-ling is going to live but I have no idea what will happen to her next, only that she will need to remain in the hospital for a couple of days.

And myself? I have no certainty about my own future. Someday soon, Mei-ling's body will be discovered and what then? In all likelihood nothing will come back to me but how can I know for sure?

I'd known that I would need to leave Hong Kong and never return but had thought it would arouse suspicion if Mei-ling's body was suddenly discovered. Now the reality of the situation is finally hitting me.

Fear of discovery, fear of the dead and fear of the riots have all gripped me but I am beginning to wonder whether the riots will work to my advantage. Here is a reason for leaving Hong Kong, for returning to England and trying to starting afresh. An opportunity to leave those fears behind.

Only can I really leave it all behind?

It is in the early hours of the next morning that I wake, disturbed by a noise. More rioting?

I try turning over and going back to sleep but there is a noise like the scraping of furniture that seems to be coming from my own apartment. I slowly get to my feet and walk tentatively down the corridor.

Someone is there. In my living room.

The figure turns, features caught in the light filtering in from the streetlights outside. A face so familiar but with her neck twisted at an unnatural angle, a finger raised and pointed accusingly.

The Taxidermist

Sophia Greengrass

A GREASY OLIVE-GREEN FEATHER floated down and landed in a droplet of acid on the workbench. Moon pushed back her glasses and fitted the glass eye into the empty socket. Having previously scraped all the remaining flesh from the skin, she was adding the finishing touches to the newly repurposed Chinese Bulbul. Its outer body was now a cleaned and preserved bag of feathered skin. Next, she had to apply the skin to its new internal form, made of sawdust and wire. With the practice of many years, her fingers tooled the carcass with delicacy and precision. Moon had learned to be a successful taxidermist, beginning as a little girl, no older than seven. Discipline, strong controlled fingers, a respect and spirituality towards the animals' departed souls. There were many stages to preparing a skin for working on, and then yet more to refine it and mount it. Each breed of animal or bird needed slightly different approaches, for scales, feathers or fur, claws, fangs or antlers.

The shop and business was bequeathed to Moon by her grand-father, Albert. Chung Lee Taxidermy had been a family business for over a hundred years, with fine premises among the antique shops in Sheung Wan, one of the oldest areas on Hong Kong Island. Taxidermy was less in demand now than in the days of her grandfather. They'd had to sell the family home and Moon now lived in the space above the shop, and she had also had to find other ways to spend her time.

Once, such splendid animals had come through the door. Moon would sit on the low stool in the corner playing with her pet turtle, Oscar, as her grandfather spoke of the wondrous creatures he had seen in his childhood while watching his own father work. He would describe the animals vividly; it was as if she were watching a wildlife documentary, seeing them alive and sneaking through their habitats. Albert spoke of musk deer and Asian otters, black bears and wolf hares. Large foxes with pointy ears and wild cats with teeth bared; exotic birds, golden pheasants and red-whiskered bulbuls, little egrets and elegant white cranes. Reptiles and snakes had been abundant, the bamboo pit viper with its luminous green skin and the black and white stripes of the many-banded krait. There had been turtles much larger than Oscar, and even crocodiles. Grandfather Albert would always finish with a comment about the destruction that human beings wreaked on the natural world. He said humans and animals didn't mix, that we were destructive, greedy, always thinking about making money at whatever cost to the natural world. It was not the way it was meant to be. He would remind Moon what Chung Lee Taxidermy did to help people to remember the animals that had become extinct, and the ones that died in modern times, by making living models of them so people could see what they had destroyed and remember the cost of progress and complicated living. It was the family's job to respect each living animal by caring for the bodies brought to them for reworking and preservation.

Now the shop lay near-empty, Moon's hands almost idle except for the odd deceased pet poodle, fluffy cat or prized cage bird. These jobs were always difficult, sentimental owners demanded a very high standard, wanted the adored animal to look just as it did when full of life. But of course, once an animal's skin is removed inevitable alterations occur. Some essence is always lost as the soul leaves the body; what you are left with is altogether different.

Moon put a globule of adhesive into the remaining eye socket, and selected the next eye from the tray of various-sized marbles in the drawer of the old apothecary cabinet. She popped it in and wiped away the overspill of adhesive with a tissue. A little heap of organs and muscle tissue were piled up, a red stain spread underneath, as the workbench absorbed the last remaining goo from the bird, as it had many before it. The shop smelled of old school desks and dust and her grandfather. Where for others the smell of baking bread or the aroma of a certain tree in a garden might trigger nostalgia, the smell of formic acid and acetate was a comforting childhood smell for Moon. Floorboards behind the workbench curved downwards and showed a more polished lighter wood, four generations of her family had worn them down, toiling in sensible shoes. Moon fitted the bulbul's skin over the form and worked it in place, making sure the little crescent eye slits matched up with the black marbles. She took her needle and thread and placed tiny, invisible stitches along its lower chest to finish the job.

In addition to the apothecary cabinet, which housed all her tools, chemicals, scraps of fur and leftover bone, there were other pieces of lovingly crafted antique shop furniture. The long wooden workbench that had to be polished and re-stained regularly to prevent the blood and chemicals altering it enough to put off the customers, ran nearly the entire length of the shop. Just like a Chinese butchers or stall, the gruesome activity was on display for all to see. The shop also housed display cabinets. Glass-fronted, these enclosed the middle of the shop on three sides. In these were dogs, cats, foxes and birds, in varying sizes, colours and postures. One of Moon's favourites was an eagle with its wings outstretched, as if ready to claw a fish from the water's surface. She called it Byron. All of the display animals had names. There was Sid the Fox, Peter the Owl and her childhood pet, Oscar the turtle that Albert had stuffed after its death. The largest animal in the shop was a full-height black bear next to the door reared to attack, claws outstretched and mouth gaping to expose what was left of his fangs. His name was Reginald and he held the coats, hats and umbrellas. Many of the display animals were the forgotten animals, brought in and never claimed, so much so that the little shop on Cat Street was like a limbo for departed animals and Moon was their gatekeeper.

Moon's eyes lingered beyond the front window watching the passers-by. It was midday and the shop hadn't been open long. People hurrying by on their lunch breaks already had a glazed look. She could see her reflection in the glass, ghostly and transparent, her short dark hair falling about her pale cheeks in slithers of black. Her apron was a dirty, red-speckled blur. Moon returned her attention to the Chinese

Bulbul. It looked almost cute. The skin fitted the new form and the eyes sparkled as she cradled it in her hands. Its white and olive-coloured feathers felt soft and warm from her touch. Pieces of wire poked out from the claws to attach it to its mount. Moon placed the fist-sized bird into a small cardboard box padded with tissue paper that used to house teacups. She knelt down and put it with the others in the space under one of the worn floorboards. She replaced the board gently just in time to look up and see two policeman disembark at the tram stop across the road and stand at the pavement waiting to cross.

Moon busied herself with her next job, Mr Ng's Chihuahua, Bobo. An occasional customer, Mr Ng had used Moon's skills before, for a poodle, a pug and Bobo's brother, Jing-jing. He assured Moon they all sat on the dresser next to the dining table in good company, with the ancestors' shrine nearby. Mr Ng was a rare breed himself, loyal customers were hard to find anymore. Although there had been new trends in recent years, stag antlers were quite fashionable, and also funny-looking squirrels smoking cigarettes, birds with a bowler hat and briefcase, or gambling foxes, Moon didn't go in for these fads and felt sorry for the poor animals forced to spend their eternity as objects of amusement. She liked working with butterflies for a collection in display cases though, and also insects. Fossils and animal skulls had become popular natural antiquities to furnish houses with. She had done a small amount of work for a fancy clothes shop last year making such decorations.

She bent down and picked up the big bag of salt to return to its drawer. *Ding ding, ding ding.* The old brass door bell sounded out through the dead calm of the shop. The two policemen stood before her. She noticed their guns, she always looked at the guns whenever she passed the police. The policemen were about the same height and build, same black haircut in a short, closely-cropped-to-the-scalp style. She imagined a machine at police headquarters, churning out models of the 2014 policeman, complete with steel-toe-capped boots and no-leak fountain pens. She dumped the salt and struggled to close the heavy bottom drawer with her foot as she turned to face them.

'Hello Miss. I am Officer Wong and this is Officer Sit. Can we speak to the owner and head taxidermist please?' Officer Wong was wearing glasses and spoke with a high-pitched, feminine voice.

'Yes Officer, I'm both. Is there something I can help you with?'

The policemen exchanged looks, before Moon added, 'A deceased pet perhaps, or an antiquity from the display for your home?' Moon pointed to the cabinets. The policemen glanced around them.

Officer Wong spoke a second time: 'We are visiting local taxidermists because there have been some incidents involving stuffed carcasses being left in public places. There have also been strange occurrences in these areas, people being attacked by birds, possibly caused by a new kind of avian flu being transmitted from these stuffed birds.'

Moon furrowed her brow and tilted her head to one side.

'Taxidermy animals are cleaned and prepared so that there is absolutely no danger of contagion of any kind. Some say the birds themselves have cursed us, risen from the grave to wreak havoc on mankind for destroying their habitat. We have gone too far in our crimes against nature.'

'We don't follow superstitious nonsense,' replied Wong. 'Somebody is putting these birds on rooftops and it's causing problems to the bird population and to people. We would like to have a look around your premises and to see your inventory and sales log.'

Officer Sit was staring at a mount of a black king cobra with fangs bared ready to strike. He shifted his weight from one foot to another.

'Of course, I'll help in any way I can. We've only had one bird come through recently, that was Ms Chiu's mynah bird, it was a very dear companion to her, I mounted it in its birdcage. But by all means, have a look around.' Moon motioned with her hands. 'What kind of person would be doing this?'

'Well it would have to be someone physically fit, good at climbing especially, and good at blending in, inconspicuous. A lot of the locations where the birds have been spotted are very difficult to get to, on lampposts and rooftops, difficult to remove.'

Moon bent down under the workbench and pulled out the A4-sized black and red notebook where she recorded all her past work, and the duplicate receipt pad, the design of which had not changed since her grandfather's time. She retrieved her certificates and licence and the name of a supplier in China she sometimes used for carcasses.

Officer Wong set about perusing the book while Officer Sit poked around in the apothecary cabinet.

Moon stood out of the way and pictured the space under the floorboards where a little family of birds lay resting in peace.

After the search and note taking was completed the policemen asked Moon about her competitors and whether she knew of any unlicensed taxidermists or of any kind of black market. She didn't but said she would contact them if she saw anyone or anything suspicious.

The afternoon passed slowly. Moon was occupied by memories of her grandfather. His life's work was finally near completion. Her own father had left for America when she was very young and had never returned. He had found a new wife and told his family to forget about him. Her mother never recovered from the shame and died when Moon was eight years old. Albert became Moon's sole carer. He cooked for her, helped her buy clothes and shoes and the things she needed for school. He brushed her hair and read her bedtime stories. He listened to her and showed her everything he knew about taxidermy and about life. Moon was twenty-four when he died and left her the family business. She wasn't going to destroy his legacy. People were surprised when she told them what she did, but were always happy with the results. A true artist, a commission to restore some of the exhibits at the Museum of History had been wonderful. Some of the old animals were balding and their faces had caved in with rot and age. She repaired them and made them look new again, using parts from newly-deceased animals, like Frankenstein taxidermy. Some of the animals she was working on were extinct or endangered, and she considered it a once-in-a-lifetime privilege.

She fantasised about winning awards for her work and being asked to collaborate with famous artists, to travel the world, to exhibit in art galleries, to meet fascinating and progressive people, and to live a life of freedom where anything was possible. Today she was imagining the wonderful life she might have in London (yesterday it had been

Berlin), building a display of the finest work in a vast warehouse. She dreamed of the galleries, the private clients, the public work, of the hustle and bustle of the world's most forward-thinking and liberated art cities full of beautiful architecture and space. Hong Kong was liveable, but with China as a parent so close, the feeling of control was always there. The city was dirty and crowded. Moon spent many hours on her laptop looking at pictures by artists she loved, one in particular, Hong Kong-raised Bao Zhi. He was a street artist and often showed children in adult situations, shocking and political, as politicians, as aid workers, as soldiers. His work was instantly recognisable because of his style, it was simply painted or stencilled and always with vivid colours and the use of geometric patterns. He often drew animals and incorporated nature, plants and flowers and the issues of environmental damage in his work. There were a few of his paintings still left in Hong Kong, the ones the authorities hadn't painted over yet. The ones too hard to get to.

At ten o'clock, Moon closed the door onto the darkness clinging to the notches of the workbench and dusty cabinets, and walked into the cloak of anonymous night. Outside the air was thick and humid, difficult to get enough of into the lungs. Inside her rucksack, the little bird carcasses gently rose and fell with her steps in their tissue paper coffins. She had changed from her work clothes and into a dark-hooded top, tight black trousers and black running shoes. She slipped into the queue of spent workers walking towards the MTR station. The underground gave Moon the creeps, perverts aplenty lined the trains waiting for their opportunity to brush against an arm, skin on sweaty skin or to look up skirts of those standing from their seats. Groping attacks were not uncommon, and always the staring. In Japan there are special clubs made to look like underground trains lined with fake passenger girls for the men to grope. There were just too many people. Moon sidled into the last empty patch of vertical space and switched her rucksack to her front, pulled out her earphones and blocked out the chatter and noise with bird song. She cradled the backpack protectively, and thought of somewhere else for the journey. She alighted at Tsim Sha Tsui and made her way to the exit, some people pushing to the front of the escalator queue but most wandering like zombies with their eyes glued to smartphone screens. Outside, Moon didn't have far to go. She checked out her target, the Star Ferry pier, and contemplated her planned ascent route, but it was way too early and too busy for her to try to climb up yet. She walked the ten minutes to Kowloon Park and sat near to the imitation pagoda and carp pond. She observed the people practising Tai Chi, and wondered why everything had become so complicated. The city was like an ant colony with everybody walking all over each other. The roads were crazy, the people were crazy, working all day from nine a.m. until ten p.m. and spending a few measly hours doing what you had to do. She wondered who had the better deal, an average worker in Hong Kong with all the modern fluff to make life easier, or a poor fisherman on a Philippine island with bare essentials but surrounded by nature.

Time lapsed and Moon prepared to start. She made her way back to the harbour, to the Star Ferry pier nestled in prime location at the end of the impressive promenade looking out to the iconic view of lit-up skyscrapers. It was home to the light show, a disappointing recipe of lasers and terrible music, and the Avenue of Stars, where Bruce Lee was forever kicking in the light of tourists' camera flashes. Moon ascended the stairs to the top deck. She waited for a few late-night revellers to pass through the turnstiles, then put up her hood, climbed out of one of the windows looking over the sea, and pulled herself onto the roof using pipes as footholds. She climbed well, strong hands, light frame, small feet. On the flat green roof, she carefully made her way to the front of the pier, the harbour side. She drank in the lights in rectangles, angles, curves and colour from her hidden perch above Victoria Harbour. It never failed to stir something in her, standing before the skyline representing capitalism and land-grabbing. There was more to life than this oppressive and synthetic landscape. The huge buildings vandalising the rock underneath were the great pistons of the machine, the city constantly in motion and supporting so much life, good and bad, it was undeniable in its power. From her bird's eye view it looked like a floating fortress of the future.

The black waves below her throbbed with its fallout of progress – a whole lot of rubbish.

Moon removed her backpack and carefully laid the contents onto the hot, hammered metal covering. She took the largest package and slid the sheath away from the inner tray. A fat green and yellow bird greeted her. Taking it out and leaning forward onto the edge of the roof, she let her feet dangle over the side. She used the wire sticking out from the bottom of the claws to attach the Japanese white eye to the pipe running along the roof. The pier looked like a Star Ferry boat itself with its curved green and white exterior, boats that had transported generations of Hongkongers back and forth across the harbour from Central to Tsim Sha Tsui. The seats reminded her of safety bars on old fairground rides. The other two birds took their turn at sitting pretty on the edge, wire stilettos holding them in place, their new eyes staring out at the impressive view. Moon took photos of them from various angles. She tried to imagine the original harbour before the land was reclaimed, and the rocks and hills and woodland before man came and started to build.

'What do you think you're doing?' a hard voice shouted behind her.

Moon jumped, and then straightened up slowly. She glanced around considering options to escape, outrun whoever had crept up behind her. But her work, she needed to finish it. The man, also dressed in dark clothes with a hood up shrouding his face, was not a policeman, no apparent badge, radio or gun.

'I'm not doing any harm, I'm not stealing or destroying anything,' she replied straightening her back, her voice shaky. She gathered her backpack and turned to face the interloper.

'I've read about you in the paper.' A warm colluding smile fixed on his face. 'What kind of birds are they?'

Where this was going? Was he going to mug her? She fondled the handle of the scalpel in her pocket, and ran through the incantation her grandfather had taught her – *Fuhuo ni de linghun.*

'The biggest one, the green and yellow, is a Japanese white eye; you can see the white ring around its eye. That one, the one with olive feathers on its head, is a Chinese bulbul and that one with the crimson throat and the curved beak is a fork-tailed sun bird.'

She felt the tell-tale signs of adrenaline coursing through her body, the pinpricks on her skin, her forehead perspiring unnaturally, her cheeks throbbing red. She could see a crescent-shaped shadow falling across the luminous moon.

'They look like real birds. I like them. I like what you do.' The man seemed confident, unconcerned he was standing on the top of a public building he shouldn't be.

Around them neon lights blinked and pulsed like a science-fiction space station. The noise on the wind whispered the approach of a ferry coughing out its black smoke.

'Yeah well, I'm glad somebody appreciates it. Look, I don't know what you want but I need you to go now.' Moon checked on the newly-positioned bird family, annoyed her ritual had been disturbed.

'Hang on; I want to ask you if you want to do some work with me. Like I said, I like what you do.' The man started to fumble for the zipper on his bag.

'Er, sorry, what do you mean? What work? I don't know you and you need to leave now.'

'I'm an artist too, look.' The man got a small book out of his bag. In it were pictures, drawings of children dressed as political leaders of communist countries, the backgrounds patterned with triangles and squares.

The man smiled and walked towards Moon. 'See?'

Moon swung her right arm with all her force and plunged the scalpel into the man's neck. He stepped back, a look of horror on his face as he grasped for his neck, the blood gushing through his fingers like a hot spring bubbling up through the earth. He fell to his knees groaning. Moon grabbed his shirt and hauled him over the side of the roof, plunging him into the watery darkness below.

Moon knelt down in front of the birds and took out the candle, the vial of her blood and the wooden box containing dust, the crushed skull bones of every animal she and her grandfather and his father had ever worked on.

She made a circle around herself with the bone dust and lit the candle. She lit three joss sticks and set them into the top of the vial of blood. A dark shape crossed the water.

'*Fuhuo ne de linghun. Fuhuo Ne de linghun. Fuhuo ne de linghun.*'

A silence struck the city, she felt as though her head was being crushed. The lunar eclipse was complete, the world turned black, every second felt like an eternity. A wind, freezing cold and smelling of damp earth, rushed past her blowing the hood off her head. It was done. Moon sat cross-legged in her circle and said a prayer to her grandfather. One by one, the dead animals in the museums, her workshop, the hundreds of birds she had placed around the city, blinked their cold glass eyes and began to ruffle feathers and stretch out their boneless limbs. The Chinese bulbul let out a screech as it flapped its wings, shaking off a small green feather which floated down from the rooftop into the fragrant harbour below.

The Tomb

Marnie Walker

'PLEASE, MADÉ, COME OUT WITH ME. The walk will do you good.'
Michael was sure she was going to refuse, but he had to try. She
lifted her eyes from the *Sai Kung Magazine* she was pretending to read
and nodded her head.

'Wonderful!'

A few minutes later they left their village house and stepped out
into the August evening. Michael insisted on holding her hand even
though it was far too warm for touching.

A group of young boys was playing football in the Sha Kok Mei
parking lot. Madé gazed at them as they laughed and wrestled, a
haunted look on her face. Michael led her past them, saying nothing
until they were alone again.

'Just up this way, there's a network of paths,' he said. 'I've explored
them a little, but I can't say I know them well. Let's have a look.'

She narrowed her eyes as if forcing herself to concentrate on him.
She is finally trying, Michael thought. Impulsively, he lifted her delicate
frame and pressed her to him, kissing her lovely mouth. He released
her and she laughed.

They wandered up a paved walkway bordered by a stream, full after
the heavy afternoon rain. They paused to admire how it rushed over
the mossy rocks, spraying their feet from where they stood on the
narrow footbridge. Michael thought there was something precocious
in its fierceness, how it crashed along its tiny bed like a toddler shaking
the bars of its crib.

His heart sank at this thought. Memories of his own child, his son, flooded his mind. He closed his eyes. When he opened them, he felt in control once again. He smiled at his wife.

It had been six months since they had lost the baby. Born twelve weeks premature, he had only survived a few hours. They had named him Liam, after Michael's grandfather. Although haunted by the loss, Michael could now feel some distance from it, could manage the anguish in a way Madé could not. For her, it was happening again and again.

Faced with Madé's depression, Michael thought it best to leave their flat in Sheung Wan and find somewhere else to live. They had been planning to move to the New Territories when the child was a year old, and Michael thought the change would still do them good. He found a three-storey village house with a rooftop garden in Sha Kok Mei. He hoped that living in the countryside would cheer Madé up, remind her of her childhood home in Bali.

They continued walking and came to a grassy field threaded with honeysuckle and morning glories. Dozens of dragonflies buzzed around them as if delighted by their company, their opalescent wings flashing in the golden light. Michael pointed out some fenced-off areas toward the eastern end of the clearing. He knew a few facts about land rights in the New Territories and was pleased when Madé listened attentively to what he had to say. He continued talking as they walked, naming plants and birds he recognised, and she seemed grateful for the endless stream of information, a contended smile on her lips.

This was when he felt at his best, when he could show her things, share his meticulous nature. It had been like this in the beginning. He would visit her in Bali and they would talk and she would ask him questions. They had met in Kuta where she worked the front desk of a large resort. She was originally from northern Bali where her family worked as rice farmers. She was not well-educated, but she was curious and had a quick mind. And she was the most beautiful girl Michael had ever seen.

After a steep climb, the path crested the hill and terminated at a main road. Michael worried she might be getting tired.

'If you like, we could catch the No. 3 bus from Nam Shan Village and head down to Sai Kung. We could have dinner in the square.'

'Can we go on? Just for a little bit?'

'Yes, of course!'

He squeezed her hand, delighted by her enthusiasm.

'We still have a little time before it gets dark. We can explore some of the MacLehose Trail. There's a bit that starts near Ngong Ping Village, which is five minutes up the hill from here.'

Still holding hands, they climbed a series of steep steps. They found the trail, which was overgrown for the first quarter mile. Twilight filtered through the canopy of trees in golden ribbons, as if patterned by stained glass. The space felt magical, protective. Shimmering light danced around them as they walked through the jungle cathedral.

The effect did not last long. It became dark, and they found it difficult not to trip over tree roots and jutting stones. Finally, it was too much. Pleased with their little adventure, they turned back toward the main road.

Madé was holding Michael's arm, laughing as they crashed along, when she slid to a stop, her body rigid.

'What is it Madé?'

She said nothing, just pointed at the dark wash of shadows before them. Michael relaxed. There was no danger. It was just Madé's habit of divining signs in patterns cast away by the world. He sighed and squeezed her arm. She did not move.

A curious twist in the darkness forced him to reconsider. The gloom was thickening, wilfully clumping together into a writhing mangle. The dark shapes split apart into long quivering coils. The forms slithered toward them. He pushed Madé behind him.

'Naga!' Madé whispered.

Now within striking distance, the snakes reared up, hoods flared, hissing violently. The couple backed away. They turned to run but, to their horror, the shadows were also gathering from behind. They were trapped.

'Get off the path!' Michael yelled. Like a tiny deer, Madé jumped up and away. Michael bounded down the hillside behind her.

They made it to a clearing near the base of the hill. It was only when Michael paused to catch his breath that he realised they had been following a faint trail down the mountainside. The path had taken them to a small graveyard, a cluster of U-shaped tombs nestled into the grassy slope that continued downhill for another thirty yards until it was swallowed by the unrelenting jungle. Without the canopy of trees there was enough lingering twilight for them to see clearly. Madé collapsed to her knees on a tomb, breathing heavily. Michael paced in front of her.

'What the hell was that?' he shouted into the jungle as if he could demand an answer from the darkness. 'When we get home, we've got to report this. We could go to the police, or there must be some sort of government wildlife department that will want to know what happened to us. This is not normal behaviour. Those snakes should not have threatened us like that. It was as if they had been trained to attack and who knows? Maybe some arsehole has done just that, made a game of letting loose his pet cobras on hikers while he watches in the bushes getting some kinky thrill out of it. . . .'

He looked over at Madé and stopped talking. She was staring at the small black and white photo on the tomb. It was the face of a young boy. Michael glanced at the dates beneath the picture. The boy had been eight when he died in 1987. Beneath the dates was a Chinese name that neither of them could read.

The boy was very good-looking, with large expressive eyes and a full mouth. Shocked, Michael realised that the boy's features were remarkably like those of his wife. And his son.

His son's face, his questioning eyes . . . Michael wished he could erase the image from his mind. The tiny baby had been fully awake during his few hours of life. He had stared at all of them, his parents, the doctors, with a curious expression, unlike that of a newborn. He never made a sound, just watched, as if he knew his time was brief and he wanted to remember everything.

The boy pictured on the tomb was the same. Those eyes. . . . Michael stared down into them until he could take it no longer and turned away.

Michael knew that Madé was seeing the face of their son in this picture.

He needed to get her away from this place.

'C'mon, Madé,' he called out several times before getting her attention. 'We have to go.'

She looked up at him with a blank, moonstruck face. Her expression cleared and she jumped up. She reached into the side pocket of her cargo shorts and pulled out a small torch.

'I completely forgot I had it. I grabbed it when we were on our way out.'

She handed it to him. They searched around the clearing and found a faint trail leading back into the jungle. Michael fashioned a walking stick from a tree branch. They plunged into the gloom, Michael sweeping the stick in front of them to deter snakes.

After a hundred yards they came upon a well-worn path. They followed it for ten minutes until it terminated at Pak Kong Au Village. From there, they took the bus back to Sai Kung. They walked home in silence.

Exhausted, Madé immediately retreated upstairs. Michael knew they should talk about what had happened, and quickly went up to join her. But it was of no use. She was already lost to a deep sleep.

Dejected, he watched TV for a couple of hours until he got fed up and walked into Sai Kung for something to eat. He went to his favourite ramen place, grateful they stayed open late. It was purely by chance that he glanced up from his bowl of noodles in time to see Madé crossing the street in front of him. She climbed aboard the No. 3 bus, the very bus they had just taken down from Pak Kong Au.

Astounded, he watched as the bus pulled into the street, his wife's profile silhouetted in the back window.

He left some cash on the table and ran across the street to catch the next No. 3. A bus immediately arrived, but he had to wait fifteen minutes before it was full enough to depart. When he stepped off at Pak Kong Au, he almost turned back, thinking he didn't have a torch. Then he remembered Madé's was still in his front pocket.

He walked through the village to the trail. He silently made his way along the hidden path to the graveyard. When he came to the edge of the clearing, his heart sank. Just as he had feared, Madé had returned to the boy's tomb.

Seated with her face toward the boy's photo, she had built a small fire on the tomb's concrete surface. She was chanting, her body swaying to and fro, her hands casting strange shadows as her fingers danced above the flames. Every few minutes, she threw a powder onto the fire that turned the flame blue. Michael lost track of the time as he watched her, and was surprised when he consulted his watch to see she had been carrying on like this for over an hour.

He struggled over what he should do.

He no longer knew how to manage Madé's commitment to the supernatural. At the start of their relationship, he had found her beliefs full of an exciting energy. Her dedication to the spirits, the *canang sari* daily offerings, a custom she continued even after they married and were living in Hong Kong, had seemed poetic, exquisitely remote from his work in finance.

Over time, he realised that so much about her thought was mystical that it was difficult to communicate with her. Her world view was so tainted by magical apprehension that a thing couldn't be just a thing, a fact couldn't gleam with truth.

After the baby's death, Michael had found her beliefs infuriating. She barely listened to the doctor's explanation about heart failure due to extreme prematurity. Instead, she agonised over karmic balance, the vagaries of reincarnation. Michael even went with her to Bali so she could visit the *pelinggih* shrine of her childhood home to address this imbalance.

When none of this had the effect Michael desired, to end Madé's depression, he blew up at her. He said her religion was primitive, idiotic and utterly useless. Later, ashamed of himself, he grovelled, but Madé withdrew into herself. It was only recently that she had shown any willingness to reconcile.

Finally, the ritual was done and with a sweep of her arm, Madé doused the fire with a water bottle. She switched on her torch and made her way back to the trail. Michael crouched down so her beam wouldn't find him. He waited five minutes before following after her.

When he arrived home, she was already in bed, sleeping peacefully as if she had never left.

For the next two nights, Michael trailed Madé to the boy's tomb. Each night she performed the same ritual as before. On the third visit, Madé brought a cloth sack with her. Michael could see something moving inside. When she finished chanting, she reached inside the bag and brought out a small songbird. With one hand, she held the frightened creature over the fire. Its heart-breaking cries echoed in the jungle, which had gone quiet as if it were listening. With a vegetable knife from their kitchen, she stabbed the bird in its heart. She let the blood splash onto the tomb then moved the limp form in a spiralling motion, marking out a pattern in dark drops.

Disgusted, Michael swore under his breath. He vowed he would put an end to this.

The following night, he planned to catch her leaving the house around midnight as she had done before. But she never left. She made none of the usual excuses to isolate herself, and stayed with Michael the whole evening. Her mood was bright, cheerful, and Michael found himself drawn in by her lightheartedness, eager to dismiss all that had happened over the past three nights.

They made love for the first time in months. When they were drifting off to sleep, his arm wrapped around her waist, he felt a surge of relief. They had been tested. He had shown rage, she had acted out with some bizarre behaviour, but they were through it now. They could finally start to live again.

Just after midnight, something wrenched Michael from his sleep. Madé was already sitting up, her eyes wide with terror. A high-pitched wail, like the cry of a wounded animal, was coming from downstairs. Michael couldn't move. He couldn't comprehend the meaning of the mournful cries. The screams changed into an awful cackle, like laughter from behind the doors of a madhouse.

'Who's there?' Michael demanded, scanning the room for some kind of weapon.

As if in response, the intruder began crashing up the stairs. The sound was immense, as if a hooved beast was hurtling itself up to their third-floor bedroom. Michael yanked the lamp from the wall and ripped off the silk shade. With the wooden base slung over his shoulder like a baseball bat, he leapt to the door. He braced his right shoulder against it and locked the deadbolt.

The thing shrieked from down the hall then threw its weight against the door. It clawed at the wood. Petrified, Madé could do nothing while Michael silently held his post.

The creature fell silent. In a falsetto voice, the mocking voice of a boy pretending to be a girl, it cried out:

Mama! Maaamaaa!

Over and over it plaintively wailed until Madé could take it no longer. She covered her ears and screamed.

A siren cut through her screams. There was a pounding at the front door, voices demanding to be let inside.

'We're up here! Help us!' Michael yelled. The thing let out one final cry and then rushed away down the hall.

They heard the sound of the front door being forced open, sounds of police searching the house. Michael was certain they would catch the intruder, forced to either confront them on the stairs or leap from an upper-storey window.

Several minutes passed. The house went quiet. Michael sat with Madé on the bed, his arm around her quaking shoulders. Finally, there was a knock on their bedroom door.

'Mr Taylor? Are you all right? May we come in?'

He cautiously opened the door. A young policeman in a canary-yellow vest and Michael's next-door neighbour, Simon Chang, were standing on the threshold.

'Did you catch him?' Michael asked.

The policeman frowned before responding. 'I'm sorry Mr Taylor. We didn't find anyone in the house.'

'What? Well, he must have jumped out the window. We must go down and see if we can find him!'

'We have people looking outside, sir.'

'And they haven't found him? Look, this guy is violent, probably crazy – you need to catch him!'

Michael pointed at the bedroom door, which was covered in splintered grooves.

'See here, he attacked the door with something. Maybe a knife or a screwdriver.'

'Ah, yes, I see.'

The policeman narrowed his eyes and studied Michael.

'May I please speak with Mrs Taylor alone for a moment? I need to take her statement. Officer Lee will be with me while I question her.'

A female officer stepped into the room.

'Why? Do you think I'm lying?'

'Please, Mr Taylor. I assure you this is standard procedure. If you would go with Mr Chang downstairs, an officer will take your statement there.'

'Michael, c'mon,' Simon called to him. 'He's right, it's standard procedure. Just come down with me.'

Defeated, Michael followed Simon down the stairs.

'I was the one who called the police,' Simon explained. A young lawyer, Simon often worked late hours. He was still dressed in a suit and tie. 'I had just gotten home when I heard screaming.'

Simon made tea in the kitchen while Michael gave his statement to a policeman. He felt drained, his description of the attack robotic. Twenty minutes passed, and finally Madé came downstairs with the officers who had been questioning her. She sat next to Michael who held her hand. She was still shaking.

The officers had a brief conference before turning their attention back to the couple.

'It seems you both believe that there was an intruder in your house. Do you know if he took anything?'

'We haven't really had a chance to look.' Michael replied.

'Okay. You should do this immediately and report to us if anything has been stolen.'

'I really don't think we're dealing with an ordinary thief! This person was violent. He came here to scare us, to hurt us.'

'I understand how you might feel that way, Mr Taylor, given what you have experienced. But these thieves are very clever. They are a real problem for us right now. There might have been two of them, one sent upstairs to scare you, keep you in your room, while the other one searched for things to steal.'

'Two? You couldn't even find the one, and now you think there might have been two?'

'I understand your frustration, Mr Taylor. But these thieves are hard to catch. They are masters of escape.'

The officer left a number to call should they need to report anything as stolen. As the policemen were leaving, Simon's grandmother appeared at the open door. She lived with Simon in his village house. He doted on her. Always very neatly dressed, she was hunched and tiny with a slight palsy in her neck, her deep-set eyes flashing with intelligence. Michael waved her in and she joined them for a cup of tea. She spoke to her son in Cantonese.

'Grandmother was also awakened by the noise. She is very happy to see you are both well.'

They drank their tea in silence. Finally, Madé excused herself to go back upstairs.

'Yes, go on, sweetheart. I'll be there in a few minutes.'

After he heard the bedroom door close, Michael asked Simon if he knew anything about the boy's tomb. He described where it was.

'No, but let me ask grandmother. She has lived here all her life, and she knows a lot about local history.'

As Simon spoke to her, Michael could see a comprehension dawning on her ancient face. She spoke rapidly, pointing at Michael and then toward an open window.

'She wants to know if you or your wife have been to the tomb recently?'

'Yes. We both have. Madé has developed a . . . fascination with it.'

Once Simon had communicated this, the old woman sighed. She spoke again, her grandson occasionally interrupting to ask questions.

'What is it? What is she saying?'

'She says she knew the boy that is buried there. Yuman was his name. He died many years ago. Drowned. He lived in Pak Kong Au, where grandmother has several cousins. Other members of his family are also buried there. But not many. The family abandoned the site because of its bad feng shui. It has brought them terrible luck. She says there is something bad in the ground there. Very old. The geomancer that chose the spot did not know of it.'

'Geomancer?'

'A feng shui specialist who finds auspicious sites for tombs.'

'So what is up there? Does she mean the boy? His spirit?'

Simon shook his head. 'No. She says Yuman was buried properly, with a paak sz ceremony. His soul is at rest. It is something else. A "sai man", a low person.'

'I don't understand what that means.'

'It's an embarrassing part of our history. Not many outsiders know about it. Up until the early twentieth century, many regional wealthy families kept male slaves, sai man. They worked as domestic servants, but they were really status symbols. By the 1920s, most families had abandoned the practice due to its expense. It was hard on the sai man when they were set free. They were unskilled, docile, their families in tatters. Many of them went into the fishing trade. But there was one, a young man grandmother remembers.'

He turned to ask her a question to which she gave a lengthy reply.

'Yes, a boy of fourteen. Everyone called him Ben Dan, a sort of nasty nickname. He was violent, not like the other sai man. He wanted vengeance against the family that had discarded him. He sneaked into their home one night, killed them all in their sleep, even the children. When the villagers found out, they tracked him into the jungle, murdered him. They buried him right where they killed him. The very same place where the boy's tomb rests. The villagers covered it up, which is why the geomancer didn't know about it.'

'And she remembers this?'

'Yes. She was very little when it happened, but her brothers were old enough to remember. She says she saw the boy once in the street, before he committed the murders. He terrified her. He was extremely dirty with matted hair and long brown nails. He screamed if anyone looked at him, and then burst into hysterical laughter if they showed any fear.'

'Really?' Michael said, his heart skipping beats as he remembered the screams, the shrieking laughter from behind the bedroom door.

'Over the years, people have seen strange things after dark on the trails near where he lies. Some have even seen his ghost. Grandmother claims she saw him tonight. Crouching outside your kitchen window before he slithered inside.' Simon sighed. 'I'm sorry, Michael. The last thing you need to hear after your ordeal are ghost stories.'

Michael interrupted him. 'What about snakes? Has anyone ever had visions of snakes near his grave?'

When Simon asked her, she said nothing at first, just narrowed her eyes in a close scrutiny of Michael's person. When she spoke, she accusingly pointed her finger at Michael.

'She says Ben Dan was a sort of snake charmer. He kept a pet cobra in the shack where he lived. And yes, there are those who have seen snakes.'

The old woman interrupted Simon, insistent he ask Michael something.

'I'm sorry, Michael, but she keeps asking me what you have been doing at the tomb.'

Michael swallowed hard before answering. 'It's not me, it's Madé. She has been visiting the tomb after dark, making offerings and I don't know what else. We lost our son, you see, shortly after he was born. And the picture of the boy on the tomb, he looks remarkably like him. Given her beliefs, her ideas about reincarnation, it's only natural she would become fascinated.'

The grandmother became very excited, and started shouting at Michael.

'I'm sorry, Michael. She is getting worked up. I should take her home.'

'No! Please tell me what she is saying.'

Simon sighed again. 'She says the boy who died, Yuman, could not have looked anything like you or your wife or son. She thinks Madé has been tricked by the spirit of Ben Dan. He has been waiting for the right person, someone he could trick into bringing him back. And this person is your wife. Grandmother is angry at you because you are strong, you are the man, yet you did nothing to stop her from doing these things. Now the ghost will not leave until a great sacrifice has been made.'

Michael started to protest when he noticed Simon staring over his shoulder. He turned to see Madé watching from the stairs.

'Madé!' he cried.

She looked directly at him, her eyes eerily peaceful. 'I'm sorry,' Michael turned back to Simon. 'I really must see to her. We can talk again in the morning.'

He went with Madé back up to the bedroom. 'I don't know what you overheard, but its just nonsense from a superstitious old woman. The police are right, we were attacked by thieves, not some sort of ghost.'

'It's all right,' she said, her tiny hand on his lips to silence him. 'I was seduced, just as the old woman said, tricked into using dark magic. I thought the boy was our son from a former life, and I could bring him back.'

'Stop, Madé. It's nonsense. No one has the power to bring back the dead.'

She turned away from him. 'I know you don't like to believe it, but I have been selfish. And foolish. I awakened this spirit, Ben Dan. I must go to him before he hurts someone. I have to, to reset the balance. And to protect you.'

'No, Madé! All of this is real only if you let it be. Please, stay with me. I love you.'

'I love you too.' She kissed him. They lay down on the bed and made love.

Afterward, Michael held the sleeping Madé close, determined to stay awake until dawn. Restless, his mind was plagued with a terrifying vision: Madé running through the jungle to Ben Dan who was crouched in shadow on the boy's tomb, his arms outstretched, his claw-like hands beckoning to her. When the vision became a dream it held him fast, like a spell. Finally, he threw it off and forced himself awake, turning on the bedside lamp.

Madé was gone.

Michael threw on his clothes and ran through Sha Kok Mei, racing along the dark trails until he came to Pak Kong Au village. With only the light of a full moon to guide him, he made his way back to the tombs.

He came to the edge of the clearing. Still in her nightgown, Madé was standing on the tomb with her back to him. Her shoulders were shaking as if she were crying. A dark figure was standing directly in front of her, enveloping her, his grubby arms clasping her close to his chest, his long, brown nails digging into the visible flesh of her back.

'Madé!' Michael cried. A cloud blocked the light of the moon, and for a moment, all was darkness. When the moon reappeared, Madé was gone.

Michael rushed up to the grave, desperate to find some sign of her. But there was nothing. He moaned and collapsed to his knees. Weeping, he glanced up at the picture of Yuman. No longer was it the boy with the huge, questioning eyes of his son, the full mouth of his wife. It was someone else entirely.

Like a castaway on a dark sea, Michael sat alone on the tomb. He begged the night to swallow him, to take him in exchange for his beloved Madé who, ever devout to nature's secret magic, was so deserving of life. He closed his eyes, reached out his arms, and felt the jungle close in around him.

The Flatmate

Sharon Tang

H E WOKE TO THE SOUND of his mother pounding on his door. 'Get up, GET UP! It's *twelve o'clock Benjamin!*'

His girlfriend had gone out with her girlfriends last night, so he had gone home and stayed up until four in the morning playing computer games. Then spent the next hour looking through porn and masturbating before finally passing out on his bed.

'Ugh,' he grunted.

'What? What did you say?' *Pound pound pound pound.* She couldn't come in because he'd locked the door. 'You good for nothing boy! You've wasted half the day, if you keep doing this you'll end up wasting away your life!'

When was this constant nagging ever going to end? He was nineteen now for fuck's sake.

'Open the door NOW!' *Pound pound pound.*

'All right, all right,' he shouted. He got up and turned the key in the lock.

Mum burst into his room. 'It's lunch-time now for God's sake,' she shrieked. 'What is the matter with you? Get up and get dressed! And your room *stinks!* Take a shower!'

He stumbled out of his room as Mum ushered their maid in to perform a decontamination.

'I'm really going to move out,' he muttered to himself several times in the shower, and several times more loudly so that Mum could hear.

'Well, why don't you?' Mum yelled at him when he came out. 'Then you'll see what the real world is like out there instead of spending all your time playing your bloody stupid computer games!'

'All right I will! I got myself a girlfriend didn't I?' he yelled back, and was rewarded with a thwack on his head.

'I want to move out,' he told Lily in the canteen at uni. They'd started going out a few months ago. It was nice having a girlfriend. Before her, he normally ate lunch on his own.

'You want to move away from your parents?' she asked, cocking her head. 'Where to?' Lily was really quite pretty, and straightforward. She was from the Mainland, but spoke good English. Ben, on the other hand, did not speak really Chinese. Apart from the odd word, picked up from when Mum would yell at him in Cantonese about whatever. He and Lily communicated solely in English.

'Yeah,' he said, looking at his phone. 'It's my mum. She's a cow.'

Lily tutted. 'You should not call your mother names. She just wants you to be independent. Like me.' She lived in student accommodation in Pok Fu Lam. Ben couldn't get in to student accommodation because even though he considered himself to be from the UK, his parents lived in Hong Kong and he was treated like a local. Typically Hongkongers lived with their parents until their thirties or forties, or until they got married, whichever happened first.

'I tried looking for places to move out to before, I just couldn't find anything.'

'Did you look on the university website?'

'All the ads are placed by nutters or are fake,' he said.

'Fake? Why?'

He shook his head. It had surprised him, half of them didn't reply to his phone calls or messages. Most of those who did told him the room wasn't available. Even one time when he had seen the notice going onto the website just minutes before. And then there was the remaining one per cent where when he did manage to go see their flats, invariably they turned out to be dives.

They were walking through the campus, passed the noticeboard, and stopped to take a look. Someone had stapled about twenty of the same flyer for a pop concert right across the whole board, covering half of it and all the messages underneath. Ben turned away, but Lily patted his arm.

'Look, Ben, I think this one is new!' Unenthusiastically he turned back and looked.

It was on a small scrap of paper, fluttering in the breeze.

> Flatmate wanted. University student with a flat in Sheung
> Wan looking for a flatmate. Available immediately.
> Phone or text Cassidy Cheung: 28156063.

'Cassidy, is that a girl's name?' Ben said.

Lily looked at the note thoughtfully. 'Could be boy's name.'

'Cassidy,' he muttered, as he jabbed at his iPhone.

He dialled the number and waited. It went to voicemail. He tapped out a text.

Hi Cassidy, I am looking for a room to rent and saw your ad at HKU, please get back to me thanks Ben

It was a pleasant afternoon, and inspired by the note they went for a wander around Sheung Wan after classes. They walked past the dried herbs and sportswear shops up to Hollywood Road. At the antique shops Lily got really excited and forced him to go in with her. He couldn't see the appeal, it looked like clutter on clutter, sometimes you had to squeeze through a small gap in the junk just to get your foot in through the door.

'Wow, look at that!' she kept saying, pointing out stuff. She got really worked up over paintings, saying how they looked just like some Chinese artist he'd never heard of. 'Perhaps one of them might even be real,' she said.

'Yeah, fantastic,' Ben said, and he looked up from his phone. 'Woar, look at that. That's like something from *Assassin's Creed.*'

It was a battle axe, propped up against the wall. The head was large, curved, glinting dully. The handle was carved with patterns all down it.

Lily looked at it with interest. 'Maybe it was used to fight in battles many hundreds of years ago.'

'Looks like it weighs a ton.'

A beaming shop assistant came up to them. He spoke to them in English. 'Genuine antique. Exquisite, yes?'

Lily nudged Ben. 'Look at those!'

'Wah.' There were five awesome swords on display. 'Are those real?'

'Of course, real swords, genuine antique, genuine. You want to see?' He went over and took one off the wall, and then dropped it. Lily and Ben both gasped, as the samurai sword missed the man's toes by about an inch.

'It's okay, it's okay,' he said. He thrust it into Ben's hands.

Ben was impressed. He pointed at another one. 'How about that one?'

'Ah yes, this one is very special,' the man said. 'Look at this,' he said pointing out engravings on the blade.

'What does it say?' Ben asked.

Lily leaned into look at the words, muttering to herself as she tried to decipher them.

'Very old Chinese characters, from ancient times,' the man said earnestly. 'It was a sorcerer's sword, for fighting evil spirits.'

Ben's eyes were like saucers. 'Evil spirits . . . like . . . what?'

'Evil spirits,' the man raised his arms and waved them around.

'What, like a bear?'

'So you interested? Very cheap!'

'Yeah? How much?'

Ten thousand.'

'Ten grand?' Ben handed it back to him.

'Okay, for you, nine thousand. Look at the beautiful pattern on the sword, real magician sword! From ancient times, look.'

'Yeah, very nice. I go check my bank account and see if I have money,' Ben said, pushing Lily out the door in front of him. The Chinese grammar was contagious.

'We take credit card!' the man called out after them as they walked off down the street.

'It was a beautiful sword,' Lily said as they walked away. It was just beginning to get dark.

Ben's phone hummed and he whipped it out of his pocket.

Hi you can come look at the room tonight if you are free, Cassidy

'Wow,' Ben said. 'I don't believe it, I actually got a reply about the room, says I can go look at it tonight.'

'That's good!' Lily said, pleased. 'We can go now, we should be close.'

'You think so?' Ben said, looking around.

'Sheung Wan is very small,' Lily said, 'and near to the university. It's perfect.'

A short while later they were ringing the bell in an old residential building. The door was opened by a wide-eyed Chinese guy.

'Uh . . . Cassidy?' Ben said.

'That's right, you must be Ben.' So Cassidy wasn't a girl. 'Hi, glad you found this place okay.' Cassidy looked at Lily.

Pause. 'This is my girlfriend Lily,' Ben said.

Lily nodded.

It was a very small flat, the tour of it took about two minutes. The hallway/living room held one wooden settee, one square table pushed into the corner and a full-sized fridge.

He showed them the bedroom, which was surprisingly big, and held a double bed with a desk and a small television. 'Wow, this isn't bad.' Ben said.

'That's my room,' said Cassidy, pointing at a closed door next to the bathroom, without offering to show them it. He shrugged. 'It's a mess, nothing special.' His English was fluent with a very mild Hong Kong accent.

Cassidy asked Ben if he was from London and said he had gone to boarding school in the UK. He was supposed to go to university in London, but instead did a gap year travelling around Europe and decided to return to Hong Kong.

'Where did you go in Europe?' Ben asked. After his A-levels he'd spent the summer at home with the TV and his various entertainment systems before coming over to Hong Kong and starting uni straight away. Why didn't he think of doing some sort of travelling beforehand?

'It was almost a year, so I went all over. I loved Scandinavia. I spent months in Eastern Europe too, so raw.'

'Wow,' Ben thought that going to Paris on his own was a bit adventurous.

'And your parents? Are they happy with you going to university in Hong Kong?' Lily asked.

Cassidy smiled. 'Nope. Plenty of arguments at home. That's why I'm living here on my own.'

'Yep,' Ben said. 'I know what you mean.'

He moved in over the next week, bringing with him his beloved electronics. On his first night he brought back food he'd bought from the 7-Eleven downstairs. Instant noodles, so much better than the bland healthy stuff the maid cooked at home.

Humming a K-pop tune, he opened the fridge and paused. It was empty apart from a thermos flask and a couple of bottles of Coca-Cola in the door. Cassidy must eat out a lot.

Ben knocked on Cassidy's bedroom door. 'Cassidy?' There was no reply. He knocked again, and then turned the door knob. It was locked. He must be out. Ben went to bed around three a.m., but as far as he could tell Cassidy didn't return before he fell asleep.

Ben adjusted to life in his new accommodation. He attended his classes, saw Lily, lived off char siu fan and instant noodles, and played his computer games.

'So how is it with your flatmate?' Lily asked him as they walked back to Ben's place. Earlier on the sun had been searing, but it was cooling down with dusk around the corner.

Ben shrugged. 'Fine. He's never around actually, I see him sometimes in the evenings for five minutes, and then he goes out.'

'He goes out every night?'

'Yeah. I never see him come back, or in the mornings. Maybe he sleeps in really late.'

'He goes out with friends maybe?'

'Yeah, dunno.'

Lily gave him a pained look. 'Why don't you ask him? You are flatmates.'

Ben shook his head. 'Dunno.' A couple of other times after seeing Cassidy leave, out of curiosity Ben tried to have a look in Cassidy's room. But it was always locked, which annoyed Ben as there was no lock on his door.

He opened the door to the flat, and conditioned air poured out. It was a bit dim inside so he flipped the light switch on.

'Is Cassidy home?' Lily whispered.

They stopped to listen. Nothing, other than buzzing from the fluorescent lights and fridge.

'He might be in his room,' Ben said. They looked at his door. It remained impassively closed.

Lily took out some food to deposit in the fridge, looking around the shelves as she did so. 'What is this?' she said, taking out an old takeaway box.

Ben looked out from his room door. 'Oh yeah. That's mine. It's old. You can throw that away.'

She took out another box. 'This is disgusting, I am going to throw all this bad food out.'

'Well, don't throw out Cassidy's food though.'

'Then come here and tell me which ones are yours,' she commanded.

They ended up clearing out almost the entire fridge.

'Does Cassidy not eat? What is *this?*' Lily took out the thermos flask. She opened it and peered inside, creasing up her nose in distaste. 'Herbal medicine?'

'That's not mine.' Ben looked, but with the lighting it was hard to see properly. Some kind of dark liquid. It smelt metallic.

'Must be Cassidy's. Put it back.'

Lily put the flask back, then gasped. Ben turned around. Cassidy was standing at his bedroom door, looking at them.

'Uh, hi,' said Ben.

'Hi,' Cassidy said.

'I didn't realise you were in.'

'Ah.' Awkward pause, then, 'Well sorry I can't stay to chat, but I've got to head out.'

'Where are you going?' Lily asked, looking at him keenly.

'Where am I going?' Cassidy said. 'Uh, Wan Chai.'

'Perhaps . . . we can go out for dinner one time, all three of us?'

Cassidy hesitated. 'Yeah. Okay. Yeah. Should have done this sooner. How about this Saturday?'

'Yes! Saturday we are free,' Lily beamed.

'Only I can't do dinner, but why don't we go to a bar for drinks?'

After Cassidy left they ate their takeaway dinner, and Lily went to take a shower. Ben was playing his latest game on his Xbox when Lily bounced in, smelling like flowers. She threw herself onto the bed, holding a couple of books in her hand. 'There's no mirror in the bathroom.'

'What are those?'

'I saw these on the table outside. They must be Cassidy's.' She flicked through them. 'Manga. Oh my God, wow, very violent.'

The page she was on depicted a blow-by-blow scene of a girl being attacked by a vampire. It showed her head being torn off, after which the vampire held it up and gulped blood out of it with lascivious pleasure. The skill of the artist made looking at the cartoon even more vivid and grotesque than if they'd watched the scene play out for real. Ben flicked through the rest of it. It was like vampire porn.

'It's kind of cool actually. Any more like it outside?'

Lily hit him. 'It's horrible.'

Ben picked up the other book. *'The Rough Guide to Eastern Europe.* I'd like to go one day.'

'What is there to see there?'

'Uh, not sure really. Just heard it's different.'

Lily was reading through a newspaper she had picked up from the lobby. It was a thin scrap of a thing, the kind that was more ads than content. All in Chinese, which Ben would never bother to pick up.

'Anything interesting?'

Lily shook her head. 'Always about rape and murder. It says two people were found murdered in Wan Chai.'

'Really? I thought Hong Kong was safe.'

'It has a dark side,' Lily said, which Ben found funny.

'How would you know that?'

'I know.'

Ben shrugged. Sometimes Lily could be a bit strange. It was probably a Mainland thing. He put a movie into the DVD player and flopped back onto the bed.

That Saturday they met up with Cassidy in Wan Chai. He took them to a bar close by the red light district, so hidden away in the basement of a dark building that Ben was surprised that anybody else was there. It was dark and a little seedy, only lit with red and blue neon lighting up on the walls, and staffed with weary-looking Filipinas. It was not their usual scene, which was more well-lit cafés and cheap and cheerful student-friendly diners. He was surprised that this was the sort of place Cassidy frequented. Ben glanced at Lily, worried she'd hate it.

'It smells here,' she whispered to him. But she sat down with them at a table.

Ben had a beer, Lily had a girly alcoholic drink from a shiny bottle, and Cassidy was drinking some brew from a tumbler.

Lily had only had a couple of sips of her drink through a straw, and she was already looking pink.

'So, this is my regular spot,' said Cassidy, 'I come here for the drinks.' He lifted up his tumbler.

'What is it?' Lily asked.

'Special brew,' he said with a quick flash of a smile. 'Chinese herbs and stuff. But keep it on the down low, you know? It's not completely legal.'

'What, you mean like snake venom or something?' Ben said.

'Uh, yeah. Snake venom and all that. Very good,' Cassidy took another swig.

They ended up staying at the bar longer than they thought they would. Ben had a second beer, Cassidy had another one of his drinks. Lily became giggly after consuming a third of her drink.

'She doesn't drink much,' Ben said. 'Not that I do that much either, I mean, I don't really go out drinking.'

'How old are you both?' Cassidy asked.

'We're both nineteen.'

'Actually, I'm still eighteen until next month,' Lily piped in. 'How old are you?'

'Twenty-one. I know, ancient. I started university late.'

'Right, 'cos of your travelling,' said Ben.

'Well, I know going to pubs or bars is not really a local custom. But, I figured since you were from the UK.'

'Oh no, I don't mind going to bars, I just don't go much. I'm sort of on a budget.'

'Yep, me too, I shouldn't come here that much really. My parents are pretty strict with the cash flow, so I really appreciate your rent money.' He looked at Lily, who had ordered some food to try and alleviate her alcoholic haze. 'But I bet you're one of those Mainlanders with filthy-rich parents aren't you?' he half-joked.

Ben smiled.

'I'm only living in student accommodation,' Lily muttered.

'So how did you find this place,' Ben said, 'it's pretty hidden away isn't it?'

'Friend introduced me. What do you think?'

'It's a bit . . .' of a dump, was what he wanted to say, '. . . dark.'

'Yes. But I like that.' Cassidy looked at him with an intense expression on his face. He couldn't explain why but Ben suddenly felt uneasy. 'Why don't we come back here next week?'

'Uh. . . .'

'Hello there!' A robust Filipina boomed, appearing at their table. She'd come to place Lily's order of chips down on their table. Cassidy's nostrils flared. 'My name is Mimi! Are we having a good time here?' she winked at Cassidy. She was wearing a glittery blue tube top and a miniskirt, both of which were too small for her. Lily whacked Ben's arm, and he tore his eyes away from Mimi's cleavage.

'Well, if you need anything else just let me know!' Mimi sang out, and tottered off in stiletto-heeled sandals that she just managed to stay on.

'Are you okay?' Lily asked Cassidy.

'Huh, me?' He was looking slightly green. 'Actually, I've got a bit of a headache.'

'Oh, perhaps we'll leave after we finish the food?'

Cassidy stood up abruptly, 'No, no . . . no, no, I'm fine. You two stay and have fun, I'll see you at home,' and with that he just left.

'Okay,' Ben said. 'That was weird.' He looked at Lily's chips. 'Those smell good, did they add something to those? Cheese?'

'Mmm, garlic chips, delicious,' said Lily, tucking in. 'Maybe this is the only good thing about this place.'

A couple of days later in the university canteen, Lily came up to Ben looking worried, and took him by the arm. 'I want to show you something.' She held up a newspaper, open to one of the back pages.

It was a story of another murder in Wan Chai, with a grainy photo of a beaming Filipina on the page.

'Is that. . . ?'

'We saw her, this woman, at that bar with Cassidy.'

'Blimey,' Ben blew out a breath. 'That is totally weird.'

'Have you seen Cassidy since that night?' Lily said in hushed tones.

'No, but I hardly ever see him anyway.'

'Why is that? He is supposed to attend classes here, but I have never seen him once. Have you?'

'I guess I haven't.'

'Don't you think that is very strange?'

Ben shrugged. 'A bit.'

'I think he is very strange.'

'I don't think he's that strange.'

'He's out all night, we never see him at the university, he doesn't eat, the one time we go out with him he takes us to that horrible place and drinks strange things . . . and now this woman is dead in the newspaper.'

'It's just a coincidence.' He took his Coke out of his bag.

'No, Ben, there is something not right about him.'

'How do you know?'

'I just know.'

'Does it say how she died?'

'It says, "gory murder" and "ritual killing".'

'Well, it was a *very* dodgy place. Plus she looked a bit, well . . . you know. Dodgy. Too.'

'It says *"the blood was drained from her body"*.'

'That's like an episode of *CSI* I saw.'

'Do you remember that comic book in your flat?'

'So? I've got a copy of *Twilight* in my room.'

He opened his drink and took a swig. Then with a massive retching noise he spat it out on to the ground. Part of it was gelatinous, and glooped out of Ben's mouth more slowly as he tried to expel it. The liquid glistened dark brown-black on the ground, and smelled . . . really, really bad.

'What is it?' Lily shrieked.

'I don't know, I don't know,' Ben yelled, there was thick brown liquid residue around his mouth. He started spitting vigorously, then ran off to the toilets to rinse his mouth out.

Lily was waiting for him when he came out.

'That was utterly vile, it tasted like . . . like. . . .' Did he swallow any of it? Ben felt nauseous.

'Where did you get this from?' She asked him, holding the bottle between two fingers.

'I don't know, 7-Eleven. Yesterday. I took it out of the fridge this morning.'

'Is it Cassidy's?'

'Well, I bought this one though, oh wait, did I?' He looked at the bottle closer. On closer inspection it looked like an older bottle which had been reused a few times. 'Shit, it's just the same as my one, what the f—'

'I'm going to test it,' Lily said.

'What? Test it how?'

'In my lab, I know someone who can help me to find out what it is.'

'Who?'

'Family friend, he happens to be working in the university. Do you want to come with me?'

'You know, I don't feel really well. I think I'm going to go home.'

Lily grabbed his arm. 'Don't Ben! Don't go to that place!'

'What? You think Cassidy's going to do something to me? I'll be fine.'

They were interrupted by Lily's girlfriends. Giggling they jostled up to her. 'Hi Lily! Are you coming to class?'

'Actually. . . .'

'It's okay,' Ben said to her. He was dying to get away, at least so that he could go scrub his mouth out. 'I left some of my books at the flat. I have to go and get them.'

Lily looked at him seriously. 'And then you come back to my place afterwards?'

Ben agreed just so he could go.

By the time he got back to Sheung Wan he felt almost feverish, made worse by the scorching weather outside. The drink thing was freaky, maybe he should go see a doctor. He tried not to think about it, thinking about it made him sicker. He cranked up the AC, threw up into the toilet, and then fell into a deep sleep in his room.

Lily hurried back to the lab after the lecture had finished. She knocked on the door of one of the smaller labs which undergraduates weren't normally privy to, and walked in. The post-doc looked up at her. He was standing by a microscope, with Ben's Coke bottle next to it. 'I was just about to call you,' he said.

Ben's phone rang waking him up.

'Ben! Ben! I've been calling you!' It was Lily, she sounded panicked.

'Uh, have you? I just woke up so maybe I didn't hear it.'

'Is Cassidy there?'

'Uh, I don't know, I haven't seen him, I just woke up.'

'I'm in a taxi, I'm coming to your flat. I want you to leave the flat Ben, right now.'

'Why? What's wrong? Is this about that murder story again?'

'I will explain to you later, but leave now, right now.'

'All right, all right,' he said, because she sounded so frantic.

'Okay,' she sounded relieved. 'I'm nearly there, I'll meet you downstairs.'

As she put the phone down Lily saw the antiques shops up ahead. 'Driver, stop!'

It was starting to get dark. He still felt queasy but much better than he did earlier on. He got up and gathered his books, packed some clothes and stuffed them into his rucksack. He went out to the living room to put his shoes on, reached for the front door then stopped.

Cassidy's room door was open.

Ben looked around. Nobody there. He peeked in. The room was small, just big enough for a bed and a wardrobe and that was it. Ben looked around again, then went in. There wasn't much to see, even the bed only had a thin pillow. He shivered, and looked up. The AC in the room was blasting away.

He didn't know what he was looking for, maybe some sign that Cassidy was or was not a murderer. He opened the wardrobe to look inside. Unremarkably it contained clothes. He noticed under the bed was a large drawer and pulled on it. It rolled open. He jumped back.

'What the f—?'

It was Cassidy, asleep on his back in the bed-length drawer.

Ben's phone rang.

Cassidy's eyes flew open, they were bloodshot.

'Ah, Ben.'

Ben backed out of the room, with horror seeing Cassidy rise out of his drawer. He ran to the door, but Cassidy stopped him.

'You can't go now Ben, you've seen too much.'

Ben tried to break free, but it was like he was wrestling with a demon. He howled and kicked Cassidy in the chest as hard as he could, but he didn't budge. Cassidy grinned like the Cheshire Cat, revealing a set of fangs.

A banshee cry reverberated through the flat. The grin on Cassidy's face slipped as a long blade skewered his head. He let go.

Ben stumbled back.

'Lily?'

The blade was yanked out and Lily stood back, holding the sword in front of her. Through tunnel vision Ben just about managed to work out it was the magician's sword from the antique shop.

Cassidy turned around to face her, and bared his teeth. He lunged.

Lily lashed out. With a hum the sword sliced cleanly through the air. Cassidy's head fell on the floor and rolled to the other side of the living room.

'Lily?' Ben was on the floor, pale and sweating, and staring at her. He was clutching his chest, he felt like he was having a cardiac arrest.

'Ben?' She kicked Cassidy's legs out of the way and ran over to him. 'Are you okay?' she repeated several times as she tried to check him over.

'Lily, I don't feel good, I feel like I'm going to die. . . .' He was breathing like he was having an asthma attack.

'It's okay Ben, Cassidy is dead now,' she hoped that would calm him down, then saying words in Putonghua which Ben didn't understand but were supposed to soothe him.

It seemed to work, as she watched his breathing gradually slowed down.

And then the expression in his eyes changed.

'Ben?' A look of realisation and horror passed over Lily's face. Slowly she stood up and moved back.

Ben continued staring at her as he stood up as well. His face was getting paler and paler, his eyes more and more bloodshot.

Then he bared his teeth.

'No, Ben, no!' A sob hit her throat.

She lifted the sword.

Appetite for Destruction
Vaughan Rapatahana

'FUCK YOU, FUCK YOU!' he screamed at the Technicolor computer screen flashing in front of him. 'I hate you, I'll kill you, I hate you. Tonight it is my turn!'

Wu Ka-kay was addicted to online games, so much so that his entire sleep-wake pattern had become completely inverted. He now slept all day, while often savagely chewing his fingernails as he stared jagged-eyed at his bright screen all and every night.

He ate very little else, so nourished was he by his obsession.

He had even set his electronic alarm clock to wake him at six-thirty every evening, so he would be able to prepare for that night's impending session of *Thrall of Duty*.

Ka-kay now wore a full array of army fatigues 24/7 and rarely showered. Forget about teeth-cleaning.

His hair had grown so long and so rapidly, despite his lack of healthy diet, that falling lank black locks now lay in heaps all over the unswept floors of his tiny Housing Department apartment in Tin Shui Wai, just across the bay from Shenzhen. The hair mingled untidily with the detritus of candy bar wrappers from the diminishing stock his estranged mother had sent him, and on which he also occasionally gnawed.

Ka-kay never noticed the floor flotsam, such was his obsession with trying to be the master of this, the most popular war game in southern China.

'Fuck you!' he screamed again at the screen, as his forces took yet another huge hit from his prime opposition. It was run by his nemesis, Sai Man-oh, a part-time clerk at the Education and Manpower Bureau in Wan Chai, dealing in denying travel claims during the day, but dealing out death nightly. Sai Man-oh flawlessly flayed all and any opposition; indeed he remained unbeaten. On the rankings of *Thrall of Duty* exponents, he was always number one. While Sai Man-oh never once said anything as he played online, he did break out in song when he was winning.

Wu Ka-kay could vanquish all other gamers, but not Sai Man-oh. Always runner up, Ka-kay was in a permanent fury.

Days passed, then weeks, with the bags around Ka-kay's eyes now resembling a raccoon's. His mobile phone never worked, for he never left his cramped apartment to go and top it up. No one rang and he would have been too preoccupied to answer even if they had. He certainly had no desire to ring anyone, for he had long since given up any pretence of going to work, looking for employment, responding to the earlier massed text messages from debt collectors, or scanning the voluminous pile of creditors' letters becoming mixed in a sort of thick paper mulch underneath the front door, a door he had not opened for a considerable time. He had also long since ignored the knocks from, presumably, the selfsame debt collectors. Besides, these rappings had diminished in importance for him. Only one thing mattered: becoming number one.

He played on, the hairs of his thin wispy beard rasping at the corners of his mouth as he crunched down on the keyboard while he dealt with any enemy trying to negate him first. His fingertips now no longer hurt, transformed into extensions of this very keyboard, where they spent much of their lives now, when they were not being gnawed at by him.

His only focus was the annihilation of as many troopers thrown at him every night as he could; sometimes he also offered a satanic smile when he destroyed the tanks and armoured vehicles thrust against him. Ka-kay only paused when he wiped out a careless colonel or a general – but these occasions were disappointingly few and far between. Yet he never once could even bruise Commander Dr Shroud, the supreme leader of the main opposition, the Alliance Front, despite his many months of trying. Ka-kay knew who Dr Shroud was: Sai

Man-oh's night-time persona, supreme at his craft. What delight Man-oh took in repelling Ka-kay's massed attacks and how casually he proclaimed his prowess for all the other gamers to see afterwards.

Wu Ka-kay despised Dr Shroud. He detested the depiction of the master leader on-screen – the shiny bald pate, the horn-rimmed spectacles, and especially the practised sneer. The latter's walking stick was like some kind of magic wand of destruction. Never coming close to thrashing this elusive leader made Ka-kay wilder. Yes, his fingers were by now skilled executioners, faster than sound, and his eyes had developed some sense of extra sensory perception too. Yes, he seemed to be able to kill at will – online anyway. Everything and everyone, except this bastard Dr Shroud. Ka-kay could almost hear him laughing, wherever he may have been lurking right then.

'Aaah!' he screamed as his front-line troops lost another swathe of good men, 'I will kill you! I will kill you! Your time is now.'

Weeks crawled by. Ka-kay had somehow remodelled his entire biophysical system so as not to require nutrients and vitamins and his few toilet stops had dwindled to a sudden flushed flurry every few hours. The amount of liquids he sipped on would fit into a small sized cup and was usually a concoction of stale tap water and a modicum of the tong lai cha that remained from the enormous stock he had bought several months ago, when he had last functioned as some sort of rational human being. His entire emotional range – never very extensive to begin with – had subsided to a few fleeting feelings of fear whenever the enemy, Dr Shroud, was about to kill his forces. But more and more of late they had become volcanoes of intense rage, as his desire to kill his screen enemy merged inextricably with all the long-suppressed rages and hates and desires for revenge of his entire thirty-six years of existence.

For Ka-kay, his magnetisation to screen massacre sublimated his own inner vortex of unexpressed emotion. Abandoned by both his parents; brought up by a matriarchal maven – his paternal grandmother; leaving school at twelve; a battering ram procession of inane and underpaid jobs; his chronic inability to 'find' a girlfriend; this instinctive predilection toward online gamesmanship mastery. He could not even succeed there, always being beaten by Dr Shroud.

Ka-kay almost believed Shroud was an actual flesh and blood entity, completely dissociated now from the adept clerk with the magic fingers, named Sai Man-oh.

'Aaaaaaargh,' was about Ka-kay's verbal limit now. He spoke to no one, no one spoke to him. Ka-kay may have heard some loud rapping at his front door on occasion, but if so, he had also dismissed the sounds as stemming from the screen. 'Aaaaaaaargh,' he sputtered again.

Meanwhile Sai Man-oh sang lustily every time he won. Right then he was yelling at the top of his voice, for anyone to hear:

> *'If you got a hunger for what you see*
> *You'll take it eventually*
> *You can have anything you want*
> *But you better not take it from me.'*

Three years ago, although it only seemed like one, Ka-kay had bought a snub-nosed 0.38 revolver online. Back when he was a working entity out in the 'real' world. He had purchased it in a paranoid fit after suffering several run-ins with credit card debt collectors. Even then, everyone had seemed to be against him.

Now he stuffed its cold compressed bulk deep into the waistband of his camouflage pants. Twitching, he twisted the trigger mechanism in a sort of proxy masturbatory spasm, especially when the kills racked up and the enemy backed down. He had ammunition for it somewhere too, but that was not a concern right then, as somewhere outside in the early morning air a solitary screaming siren was chasing an errant motorbike joy rider. He didn't even register this screeching sibilance.

'Kill, kill, kill,' groaned his mind.

Ka-kay no longer worried about paying for his internet connection, as the squat apartments were serviced by the regular free service endemic to the SAR. Hong Kong made it easy for web junkies and war game addicts to caress their craft. As for his utility bills and rent, there had been so many waivers of late for the vast swelter of Combined Social Security Assistance recipients like him, that it never once crossed his besotted forebrain that some day soon someone more determined than tired collectors of stale debts would come bashing on the front door to collect the stacks of money that he did owe.

The front door was warped at the bottom by the mountain of demand mail. Ka-kay was never going to make even a cursory attempt to put it right. He was no Mr Fixit even when he was a fully working mechanism himself. The taps leaked. He had not used the washing machine for so long it probably had turned up its own toes and died a natural death. The worn-out microwave wasn't much different: it hadn't been fired up for many months now.

There was also something else Wu Ka-kay didn't know about: himself. At least himself during the daylight hours, when he presumed – if he ever thought about it – that he was abundantly snoring in his unmade bed.

In fact, for the last frantic month or so now, Ka-kay had been pacing around his cage during the day, clasping the snub-nosed revolver and in infrequent spasms, aiming it at the walls. Once or twice of late, he had uplifted the damp dank curtains night-shading the windows everywhere and pointed the gun outside, way down onto the ground twenty-three floors below. His eyes, completely accustomed to flashing lights and cartoon figures, hallucinated enemies there.

All the time, however, he was asleep.

The sleeping Ka-kay had no inkling that he was also a sleep-walking Ka-kay, a hypnagogic menace: a further rift in an already riven individual. In all, he was like the Russian doll that he had once seen in a Stanley market, years before. A layer of onion skin personalities, connected only by a definite desire to vanquish, and vanquish violently; for even when he was sleeping he snored angrily, sharply, savagely.

Awake or asleep, the synapses in his overwrought brain were like pinballs lusting for the major strike, the final appeasing jackpot, whereby his own misshapen and murky life would be lit up in a vast lightshow of meaning and ultimate sense.

'Kill, kill, kill,' his brain muttered as mantra, 'Kill, kill, kill. Tonight I am top. Tonight I am top.'

Sai Man-oh, on the other hand, slept soundly after dismissing all on-screen opposition well into the early hours, before travelling into work every day to dismiss a few more claimants for travel subsidies. He – once or twice at least – smiled to himself about that idiot in Tin Shui Wai who could never beat him online. When was he going to wake up and see that Dr Shroud was invincible?

Man-oh picked up another juicy bone to chew on, a leftover from last night's meal and wiped out a few hundred more of Ka-kay's men.

The time for resolution had to come; it always does. A resolution for Wu Ka-kay's deranged night shift and demented days. Debts for his rent and utilities – despite what he may have once thought – were now due. The government subsidies only stretched so far.

The knocking on the door had recently redoubled during daytime hours, as Ka-kay slept or snooze-wandered, almost always with the snub-nosed revolver proffered in front of him like a warm handshake. More lethal now he had located those bullets during one of his several nightmares. He had loaded the gun, a subconscious riposte to the rapping.

The recent banging and the calling out of his name by the building's security staff had had no effect, for although he was stealthing around inside, Ka-kay was oblivious. At night he was fixated on wiping out the bad guys; during so-called waking hours he was on the same mission, hallucinating murderous thoughts as he wandered.

'Fuck you, you bastard, fuck you.'

The more the slamming outside, the more Ka-kay seemed impelled to hunt down Dr Shroud once and for all and to deal nefarious things to him and his cronies; those troops dressed in the annoying black and white uniforms, the pawns Wu Ka-kay extinguished as easily as a light bulb most nights. Not that there were too many live light bulbs still illuminating his poky apartment anyway.

The loud winds and rapid rains had started quite early the evening before this latest sequence of heavy door knocking, and the screams and screeches of both were intensifying. In his fixation on his game, he was oblivious to the gathering gloom. The night wore on, wet and bedraggled like a stray cat, and as hungry for attention. If Ka-kay had been bothered to cast aside a curtain he may have noted that the darkness outside was ominous and pitch-black, a variety not normally seen in over-illuminated Hong Kong. Indeed the lights of Shenzhen just across the nearby harbour were particularly visible through the sheets of squall and the gleeful gusts.

But he sensed nothing, only raged further as he saw that bastard Dr Shroud order fresh commands to his assembled troopers, all dressed in the same uniform clothes, all clasping their weapons. Ka-kay leaned even closer to the monitor, his own eyes now pulling him into the gory scene in front of him: dozens of dead, heaped en masse, massacred by him.

'Kill, kill, kill.' But Dr Shroud refused to die. Their war battled on.

Hours passed. Morning crept in under cover of its cousin night; not that Ka-kay had sensed the slightly quieter, more well-lit ambience outside. Yet sheets of dismal rain were still rippling under dark clouds, saturnine through the chinks in the curtains.

Sitting sulkily, beaten again, Ka-kay had yet to collapse onto his thin mattress. Such excitement. And then such disappointment, such despair.

He had had Dr Shroud, had almost been able to squeeze the life out of him, but his trembling fingers had pressed down one microsecond too soon. The chance at violent nirvana had been lost. 'I will kill you . . . Aaaaaaaaaargh.'

It was Ka-kay's worst night ever.

Sai Man-oh, all the time singing, had merely been teasing him, playing with him and stretching their screen time presence into the day, when the door war also would soon begin. Snoozing in his Kennedy Town flat after their long session, Sai Man-oh was dreaming contentedly about travelling to Macau to see Guns N' Roses. His father would pay, his father had money; his government job paid well.

Finally, at about ten a.m., Wu Ka-kay did crash onto his thin bed and fumble into sleep, just a few minutes before even more concerted bashing began on the battered door. Yet again, he was unaware of the disturbance outside and the accompanying loud calls of 'Mr Wu, are you there, please?' from the Housing Department area boss and a couple of his cronies from the Social Welfare Division.

The sound of the key in the lock some time later bypassed him too, as he began to sleep stalk in an untidy arc around his small bedroom. A wild waft of wind whistled just beyond the building, drowning out the other noises. The security guard had been asked to use the master key to enter the premises. The powers-that-be finally wanted to see what lay behind the closed door and why no one had paid a bill in months, nor responded to repeated calls from welfare workers.

The security guard snapped the door chain and shoved open the reluctant door.

The departmental visitors and the security woman, herself also smartly dressed in a freshly ironed white shirt and neatly pressed black trousers and clutching a walkie-talkie that looked like a portable detonator, all almost tripped headlong over the pile of yellowing papers and letters on the tiled floor. But they regained some sort of composure as they drew themselves together and glanced around the sparse living room, redeemed solely by the large and vibrant computer screen which never died. As they entered, they sighted nothing living anywhere, nor heard anything but the wind outside.

And then came the weird, wild scream from the single bedroom, a scream followed by a skinny apparition. Ghastly Wu Ka-kay – for it was one of his selves – came at them, bedraggled, raving, incomprehensible, deluded and wild, clutching a gun, the weapon pointed. Awful and dreadful, his hair attacked them in thick waves of dandruff and associated scurf, his body odour marching ahead. His shielded, semi-occluded eyes were menacing and he was spitting, frothing, from his mouth. He was incoherent, a curious mixture of yell and yodel. One gun-bearing arm was raised in their direction and the other was clenched across his own chest, twisting his army fatigues into a tight clump.

'Aaaaaaaaaargh!' was his noise, 'aaaaaaaargh!' Ka-kay just had to be rid of Dr Shroud and his henchmen and women who now were right there in front of him: there would be no more nights like last night.

It had to be Shroud, for Ka-kay would know his bald dome and his clever little snide smile anywhere. More, Shroud was bent over a walking stick, his killing device par excellence. The two suited troopers with him were lesser versions of Shroud, given that one of them had hair and the other was scribbling on what must have been a master strategic set of plans. Ka-kay, his somnambulist eyes scarcely open, levelled his arm and pointed the revolver at Dr Shroud.

The coiffured CSSA official punched Wu Ka-kay flush on his stubbly chin. The latter flinched and then flailed, falling onto the hard floor, where he lay spilled like a limp jelly. His gun rebounded off the computer table legs, no longer dangerous.

Mr Sai Ho-soy, the bald and bespectacled middle-aged man who walked with a full frontal limp, the leader of this team of mid-range bureaucrats, Ka-kay's 'Dr Shroud', spoke. 'Another one? How could no one know of this man's behaviour, or indeed of his very existence? No one seems to even miss him. . . .'

His crew muttered in assent. Indeed, some very strange creatures lurked in the Hong Kong SAR.

The security woman was dismissed and the door was scraped closed behind her.

The other three drew out their chopsticks and choppers. A sudden whiplash of wind serenaded them.

'I certainly am hungry,' trilled the minion with the clipboard, drooling. The hirsute CSSA official was already dragging the comatose Wu Ka-kay into the shambolic kitchen, a large carving knife in his other hand, while 'Dr Shroud' was sitting on the cramped sofa, anticipating the scrawny feast coming their way. He swiped a gnarled hand over his shiny bald top and licked his lips with relish and stated in a rather matter of fact manner, 'Remember to save some for my son.'

The gas cooker was still functioning.

The Tangle

Marc J Magnee

WHEN HE SET OUT an hour earlier the sun was hot on his back, but he liked it hot. The clouds, what few there were, were high and white and promising nothing that would spoil the long walk he had planned.

There are different ways to walk from where the rail line ends if you want to reach Sai Kung, a picturesque and popular seaside spot in the New Territories. You could go up and over the mountain, not an alpine trek but a long enough hike. You could even walk alongside the road if you were brave enough and didn't mind being buffeted by passing trucks and buses, engulfed in their trailed miasma of fumes.

Robert chooses a different, longer, route, one suitable for a man in no hurry, with nobody awaiting his return. He walks along the road and dips into each village he happens across to sample the individual atmosphere each one offers. At the beginning it was a simple matter to walk in off the road, along the flat, towards the water. As the road begins to steepen, to narrow and wind into the greener and more hilly and wild areas, each village takes a little more purpose to visit.

On these walks Robert insists that no watch, no phone, nothing modern be brought. What is an escape if the world continues to impose itself at every turn? No, this is hiking in the old tradition. The way it must be. Just you and the road ahead.

This village, a collection of old, three-storey houses, hidden from the road by thick stands of protecting trees and steep, vine-covered ground, is Hung Sha, or Red Sand. Who could resist the intrigue a place of that name carries?

The Tangle

Stopping to look over the houses far below, to the water beyond and to catch his breath from the struggle up the hill, Robert drinks some water from his canteen. He returns it to his backpack and walks down the narrow access road into the village.

Barely twenty steps into the village the air cools from the umbrellas of trees that reach over the path. More than that, the light is less intense, weaker, as if a veil has been drawn over the sunshine, unseen but there nonetheless. Robert's smile fades away like the light. Everything feels closer. The open spaces between houses seem narrowed, as if they are drawing together, for comfort or to crowd, a solid face against the interloper.

For the first time he notices water, reddish-brown, running in narrow, branching rivulets beside the path, like the colour of dried blood, or paint. *Rust from old pipes,* he thinks, *these old places, falling apart.*

The sun on a warm, Hong Kong day can heat the brain, inflame the mind, produce thoughts that in cooler times would not occur. He pinches his eyes together with his fingers, drinks a little more water, and moves on.

On a longer trek the trick, Robert has found, is to walk slowly, take short steps, look around and don't rush. It gives a man a chance to take it all in, even to muse on life in a way the daily grind has no patience for.

Since Vanessa went away less than six months ago everything has felt flat. He misses her but when he takes time to be honest with himself, he is relieved too. His life was difficult with his wife around but there are parts of her he wishes he still had. Her smile and her crazy laugh that made you laugh along with her. You couldn't help it. The way her voice went soft when a day had gone badly, soft and feminine the way a woman should be. So many things come to mind when he thinks of her, then he remembers how cruel she could be, how she would sometimes belittle his triumphs in front of their friends. That he would not miss. With her gone his life has changed so much.

As Robert walks along the narrow streets and paths that lead through the village the silence grows. How can silence grow? It grows slowly, so slowly that you don't know the world has hushed, drawn away, until there is none of it to be felt. Robert can feel that drawing away now. There is no swoosh of traffic on the road above, hidden now by walls of trees and closed, silent houses. No dogs bark as he passes as so many have in other villages along his walk. Even the leaves make no sound. The trees' branches stand unmoving with no breeze to disturb their patient waiting.

Robert tells himself to move, go faster and get out of this place, but his legs will not hasten. The torpor all around has enveloped him.

Ahead, down towards the water, a tangle of vines and bushes line an even more narrow path, barely wide enough for one to walk, and nowhere to pass should another happen along. And it comes to him, something he had not noticed. He has not seen another soul walking, cleaning, sitting on a balcony, or even the sound of a cough or a clearing of a throat behind a closed door.

He stops for a brief moment to listen. Nothing. No human sounds, no animals or insects. The incessant frogs, a constant feature of villages all along the shoreline, are mute. All he can hear is a faint lapping of water on an unseen shore – nothing else. He begins his slow walking again. He wants to stop longer and rest for a moment but no, his body keeps moving of its own accord.

Some few metres along an odour finds his nostrils, not unpleasant, not especially, just weeds and grasses decaying into the marshy ground all about. After living in the highrise jungle there is something comforting about natural things, even if it is the decay of weeds.

More footfalls, slow, so slow, with the feeling that the day may never end. Despite what must have been an hour's walking the sun still stands at the same aspect it held when Robert first turned into the village. It was losing light though. As one feels it on a misty day when rain clouds threaten, that feeling of the world being held in cotton wool, the shrouding of sound and light into the smallest space and you, at the centre of it, cocooned and apart from everything. Robert is feeling that now.

The thickest of the tangle lay just ahead.

What was that? A rustle of branches? The sound was sharp against the cloying silence though it was barely above a whisper. A leg, no, an ankle, the barest glimpse of an ankle, naked and vanishing into the tangle. But who? No other soul has he seen all this lengthening morning. Morning? Afternoon? Evening? In this fading light what time could it be? He feels it will soon be night.

He glances behind. He has passed a bend in the path and all he can see, behind and before him, are trees, and tangles of vines and bushes to either side.

Three footfalls, then four. The subtle decay smell rises. It becomes foul, a stench like meat left out and forgotten on a warm day. His feet stop.

On his left is an opening, more of a rip in the tangled bush, like a path made by animals that travel by night. Inside, with the fading light, nothing can be seen. The tear, a metre high and wide like the bower of some large bird, draws in all around, with the same pull that has been drawing him to this place. Grasses bend toward the tear as do the small brambles on all sides. Within the space of a few breaths Robert stands, then kneels, at the threshold. He does not know why but he is powerless to resist.

He begins to crawl.

Passing over the threshold, all light departs. Turning his head around he sees nothing . . . all he feels is the drawing-forward. Beneath his hands and knees the ground is soft and spongy and a little sticky. His hands feel the slow binding that honey makes between fingers when spilled.

Sounds are close and subdued. All around, even above, is the sound of many things moving. Nothing is walking, only squirming. It reminds him of worms, not one but many, hundreds perhaps. There is a touch, sticky but without purpose, a blind reaching bump by something small but emphatic, pressing forward.

Robert's mind is spinning, trying to find something that makes sense. It finds nothing. There is nothing here that conforms to any notion of anything real in the world. And the stench. His stomach heaves though no desire can turn his wish to vomit into reality. His guts roil at every wave of fetid air that issues from all about him. He tries to scream when the hundredth something bumps and squirms against his legs and hands, but no sound will come.

And all the time he crawls onwards, towards what?

Minutes pass like hours, without relief. Or are they really hours? Every muscle aches. His eyes sting from the putrefaction all about. Somewhere along the way he has lost his boots and socks. He feels things he would rather not between his toes.

More hours pass.

He sheds his final remnant of clothing in the blurring, endless agony of the crawling, when, he does not know. And yet he continues, naked, invaded at every opening and soaked in every pore.

It would have been impossible to imagine however many hours ago his ordeal began, but he has become accustomed to the horror of his journey. As things squirm into him, into everything exposed, he has become numb to it. As his hands and knees and toes suppurate blood and whatever else into the uneven ground, he no longer resists.

He has stopped thinking or caring. He only crawls, forward and forward and forward, without end. His eyes stare and see nothing in the blackness.

Then a pinprick. The finest needle of light penetrates the black. Robert neither speeds up nor slows. He simply crawls.

In a minute or an hour or a day, Robert perceives, somewhere in his mind, laid waste by agony and incomprehension, a growing of the light. While it should be blinding in the stygian gloom, its slow growth gradually reveals whatever hell this tunnel is.

If Robert were capable of feeling anything now it would be abject horror. The worm creatures are in reality grotesque and deformed pieces of human anatomy. Fingers, eyes, legs, penises, ears, and every other piece of corrupted flesh and offal writhe and heave forward, craving the light. And Robert surges forward with them.

As the light grows still nearer, the human remnants recede a little at a time until Robert, such as he is, torn and past maddened, sheds the horrific cargo from his body, inside and out.

When he reaches the end of the tunnel his hands find no purchase in the sudden drop away and he tumbles out and downward into a marsh of thick mud and tangled reeds. For a moment he is blinded, then the muddy water sloughs the mess away.

Darkness has not fully fallen or it may be the middle of the day. What light there is has a distant, remote, diffuse air that gives nothing away of time, if time resides here at all. A mist, thick and heavy holds all the world at bay.

Senses Robert's mind had turned off to numb him to the tangle's terrors come back in a slow, pitiless and relentless, wave. Sound fades in, slowly rising from a whisper to a shout to a keening scream. On his knees he slams his hands over his ears to deaden the din but it does no good. Hands or no, the assault penetrates deep inside his mind.

The distant croaking of frogs. Mosquitoes buzzing all about him. They land, begin to drink of him then leave buzzing louder at the first taste of his soured, tainted blood. The sound of the gentlest of waves lapping at the shore. All of these sounds are amplified beyond pain.

And as quickly as they rose, they fall away once more.

The distant frogs are now truly distant. The mosquitoes, having learned of the poison of this target, buzz at a safe distance. All is near to silence, peaceful.

Small waves touching the shore mere metres away come in stronger, little by little. And then a new sound, the sound of wood creaking. It is the creaking of something big, not a rowboat or an abandoned crate, something large enough to fill the air with its presence, solid and very, very old.

Robert's heart hammers as the creaking grows to a shriek of tortured timbers struggling to stay together. And then it arrives. A ship, its cracked and warped timbers, devoid of paint, rushes hard into the shore, grating and terrifying.

It all ceases.

All sound falls away. Robert is fixed to the spot where he kneels in his nakedness now aware of all around him but unable to move unbidden.

His chin tilts, or rather is tilted, upwards.

Another drawn-out creaking comes followed by a loud crash, sand and water flying, stinging his torn flesh where it touches. A gangplank has been dropped at the side of the ship. Then silence.

A figure, disjointed in its movement and covered in the torn remnants of a garment or bandages, shambles, dragging its nearly useless limbs down the gangplank, stopping metres from where Robert still kneels.

A voice, as spectral and harsh as a claw dragged down a steel door, speaks.

'Say it.'

Robert's mind emerges from the last traces of its cocoon.

'Say what?' says Robert, his voice restored, faint, tinged with fear, rasping from dryness.

'Say it.'

'What, say what?'

'What you did.'

'I didn't do anything. I was just walking,' Robert pleads.

'What you did before.'

Robert's mind clears by minute degrees, by the second. He scours his thoughts to fathom what the voice means. And then he knows.

'To Vanessa you mean?' he asks.

'Va—ne—ssssa.'

'I didn't do anything. She left me and took Katie with her. She went overs—'

'NO!'

'But she did, she. . . ?'

'NO! WHAT DID YOU DO?' the spectre roars.

Vines extend from the marsh and attach themselves to Robert's ankles and rise to entangle his wrists.

'Say it,' the spectre says in a whispered hiss.

'I did nothing. You can't make me say. . . .'

The vines tighten and pull Robert's legs and arms apart. The pain intensifies torn tendon by torn tendon.

'Stop, I did nothing. She left me.'

'SAY IT!'

The vines tighten still further and Robert begins to scream. Then he shouts, 'Okay, okay, I did it.'

'Did what?'

The vines tighten yet further.

'I killed her. I killed Vanessa! Let me go. Please!'

'We know what you did,' the spectre says.

'Then why are you doing all th—'

'You need to ask? And what about Katie?'

'I did nothing to Katie. She ran away and I couldn't find her.'

'Correct. We have Katie.'

'You have—'

'Yes. She sleeps. She knows nothing.'

'Can I see her?'

'NO!' the spectre roars, 'She is not for you anymore. She sleeps for now.'

Robert cries.

'Your tears are an insult. STOP!'

'What will happen to me?' Robert asks, sniffing.

The spectre says nothing. The vines stop their pulling and hold Robert as he is.

A light breeze rises. The tattered robes of the spectre fill. From beneath the robes arms bring forth a tangled pile of blood-soaked rags. The pile is placed on the ground a metre from Robert.

He studies them and sees what they really are, the pieces of Vanessa's body, the pieces he threw from his boat into the sea off Sai Kung months ago.

'Enough!' He had struck her with his car's jack in their garage at home when she dared to question him, again, on a decision he had made. His rage burned, white-hot. 'How dare she? What sort of wife was she?' He cut her up with a wood saw.

Katie saw the attack and ran, disappearing before he could catch her. He had not seen her since nor had he heard anything of her. No police had come for him so Robert assumed she had met a bad end somewhere. 'Two birds with one stone,' he thought back then with a smile. 'That solves everything.' It was then, with his newly-found freedom, that he began his walking. 'Bitch can't stop me now.'

Vanessa's torn and battered face lies amidst the tangle of flesh. One eye is open, beyond seeing, the other is closed and blackened.

Robert cries out, 'What are you? How can this be poss—'

'We have always been here Robert, in these waters and on these shores. You were summoned.'

'But how, this is imposs—'

'It is not impossible for we are here. Why do you think this village has this name?'

'I don't kn—'

'Nothing is by accident, Robert. What evil taints our waters shall never go unpunished. You did not kill Vanessa, not really, you only brought her here to us. And she is here to greet you now.'

Vanessa's voice wafts on the breeze.

'People like you bring only pain to the world. It is only fair that the pain of the world should be visited upon the creature you are. I had faith in you. You were the one great love I could hold when the darkness came. And you betrayed my love. I never imagined you *were* the darkness? Never forget, you did this. You did this to me and you did this to you.'

'Vanessa, please. I didn't mean to—'

'Yes, Robert, you did.'

The vines holding Robert's arms and legs resume their pulling. As they tug and tear at his body, wrapping around him still more and more, he screams, long and loud. Nobody hears. The village has never heard, down the years. An arm comes off his torso first, then a leg, as piece by piece he is torn into shreds.

The life held in the body of Robert floats as a mist above the ground, then descends toward the remains of the meat and bones that were once Vanessa.

Drifting to the gangplank, the spectre enters the ship and the rotting hulk pulls back from the shore leaving no trace. No grain of sand is disturbed.

Robert's pieces are one by one pulled toward the tangle and at last, slither inside to merge with the rest of the dismembered bodies of the murderous and evil.

Even as Robert's flesh and bones and eyes and fingers and all the rest mingle with their peers, the mist of his life floats down into Vanessa's carcass, stitching her together, little by little, as slow as the sighs of the long dying, over the hours of darkness.

As dawn is poised to arrive the final touches are made to Vanessa's body. The mist that has hung in the air for all those hours now falls as rain. It is a salty rain, for the mist is distilled from the tears shed by the many who have lost loved ones to undeserved deaths. The tears of this multitude gives salt to the ocean and at last the evil finds its dissolution.

In the chill of the half hour before sunrise Vanessa stands, clad in moonlight. She walks across the temporary isthmus to the island that low tide has created and there, standing in the lee of a thicket of trees, is the spectre and Katie, who appears to be sleeping, yet stands perfectly still, frozen in place.

The spectre tears off its tattered robe and holds it out to Vanessa. But the spectre's body is not a body at all. It is nothing, a void. Even as she looks back to the filthy and torn robe hanging in the air it has transformed into a pastel-dappled, diaphanous shift, light as a feather. She slips it on over her head. Her feet are now clad in braided, T-strap sandals.

Vanessa bows her head to the spectre as its vague shape fades more and more until it can no longer be seen. Only a thin voice, barely there at all, whispers, 'Love her and always remember.'

Katie awakens as the first rays of the morning sun touch her face. She turns to her mother. 'Mum, why are we here so early?'

'You fell asleep sweetheart but it's lucky you slept. What a day we are going to have.'

Katie smiles and so does Vanessa. The girl has no memory of that evening, of her mother's death or her father's presence in her life.

Five years after her return to life Vanessa goes back to Hung Sha Village. It is a sunny Tuesday, a little overcast. Katie has thrived and has just begun secondary school. Vanessa has seen her safely to the school gate and has come down here for a final time.

She is wearing the same dress she wore on her return, now her favourite. It never wears or ages. It breathes life at every touch.

Winding down the hill into Hung Sha, a village filled with colour, sound and light, Vanessa finds the narrow path where the tangle begins. Only she, and the few others like her whom she has met over the years, know where the entrance is. She finds it and sits on a fallen branch. The entrance is illuminated by a ray of light from the sun.

As she gazes into the entrance she sees what she has come for. Among the writhing, heaving viscera within the tangle there is a fragment of Robert's face, a piece of cheek and an eye. She would know it anywhere, the way it stares.

'Hello Robert. It's been a while.' Her voice is light, airy. 'I'm doing so well without you. Katie too. She doesn't remember you at all, you know.'

Vanessa looks for recognition in his eye. There is a flash, gone in an instant.

'Robert, I have wondered sometimes, in quiet moments, would you have killed her too that night? I think you would have, you know, the man you were.'

She stands, stretching her arms above her head, glances back and breathes a long breath out. Her body relaxes.

'Enjoy the centuries remembering why you're here, Robert. That's it for us, Robert. I shan't return. Goodbye.'

Vanessa's dress tosses in the breeze as she strolls along the narrow path leading away from the tangle. The sun bathes her face in light.

The faint sound of light traffic filters through the trees up the hill.

An old, keen-eyed woman pauses from sweeping the path outside her house and tips a little nod to Vanessa. They share a brief smile and each go back to their lives.

A stair creaks . . .

A Smoke-long Description of a Monster
Kate Hawkins

I AM TO DESCRIBE A MONSTER, a worryingly, frightful creature, scarier and more real than any other tale you will read between these pages. There have been many prophecies on its impending approach. Some choose to believe and try ever so hard to slow its arrival. Others let their suspicions be sidelined and continue on their way, living their life as they always have, never realising that inevitably they are calling it, drawing it, encouraging it. Slowly at the start, but hastened by the greedy desires of others, the build up to the creature appearing in all its insidious nature happens far quicker than anyone anticipates.

As you read this short ('a smoke long') story, it is watching you. At first you may not notice where it hides but as the monster grows it can't help but be seen. People will mourn the life they wished they could have had. A life without the miserable sorrow inflicted upon them by the dreaded agony of a vast giant. Once it arrives there is no escaping. It visits our cities, and it swims in our rivers and seas, it makes homes underground and flies through the breeze. And here in Hong Kong it shows itself in all its force.

If you walk through Causeway Bay, be ever so careful. For you will not wish to witness the breathless terror on an expectant mother. Her face gasping from the clutches of our miserable beast. Can you hear her suffer? Or did you see the old lady in Sham Shui Po, sitting in the gutter, clouded in a black perfume? She wrestles with all her strength against an ominous perpetrator. Or have you met children who are clasped at the throat by an invisible but ever so present pressure. Children confined to an inside world because the warnings suggest that something dangerous is near. Can you not feel it around you?

This danger seeps into the most pure surroundings, as it knows no other pursuit than the dismal decay of life.

There are those who believe in magic. I never have. They think that some potent antidote, some alarming contraption, will capture this festering horror, but it is too large, too everywhere. It permeates every crevice. It taints the virginal wonderment of our breath and infects the moral images of how life should be. But we created it.

Some claim that it comes from elsewhere. Part of it does, though we create it here too. We help it breathe, as it suffocates us. This is the devastation of our dilemma. Year upon year we encourage the monster to grow.

Hong Kong with its millions of people rushing through streets and alleyways, MTR lines and markets, are blissfully ignoring the magnitude of its presence. The omens, though, were appearing long before its take-over. What worries me is that we've come to accept a dangerous life devoid of protection. No one is safe.

I realise the peculiar description of my prose may lead one to be dismayed. But I ask you this. How many other gothic stories can claim seven million dead a year?

P O L L U T I O N.

City of Light
Luke Reid

D OCTOR KWAN STOOD ON the little footpath behind the ugly, light blue hospital building. He pressed his hand heavily against the wall, absently tapping it with his forefinger and drew hard on his cigarette. Number eight for the day – a new record for nine a.m. Although he was young, a tiny bald spot was emerging at the top of his head and reflected the blue of the building.

The nurse, Jenny? June? Genie? Anyway, she stood patiently waiting for him to answer her question, a look of poorly disguised distaste on her face as he tapped and sucked, tapped and sucked. Gaining no insight from the tangle of bushes he was staring at beside the path, he crushed out the cigarette against the wall and sighed away as much as exhaled the last lungful of smoke. He stood up properly, pulled his glasses off and cleaned them against his shirt.

Still not meeting her eye, he made a choice and answered in a boyish voice, 'Put him back under. Speak to Doctor Hayes and ask her opinion on dexmedetomidine before you do though. He hasn't improved much so far.'

'Thank you doctor.' Her clipped English and short, sharp steps stayed in the thick air long after she had departed, and still Doctor Kwan stood there, pondering. The muggy air at least felt sort of pollution-free in this little pocket of solitude. The hospital backed onto a messy chunk of Hong Kong that had long ago become lost between towering blocks of apartments and stores. It was a fenced-in and jungle-strewn concrete trail that kept its own time, winding its secret path through the permanent shadow between monoliths.

The boy would hate this place, Kwan thought as he wiped beads of sweat from his top lip.

The boy had been admitted two days earlier, screaming. Really screaming, about the dark. All the lights in and around his room had to be kept on at all hours or he would somehow fight his way across oceans of sedation and burn through the surface of unconsciousness shrieking fresh lungfuls of terror.

Kwan's career had really only just begun, but he had never seen or heard of anything like it. But it was yesterday, when the police informed them who the boy was, that he had started smoking again.

This boy, who looked for all the world like a twelve-year-old, was identified as Eugene Lam. He had gone missing sixteen years beforehand around the Sheung Wan MTR. Vanished without a trace. He was twelve at the time.

Doctor Kwan shivered to expel the thoughts. The heat and humidity were no match for the icy tendrils that licked at his skin. Looking back momentarily at the hospital doors, he pulled out a fresh cigarette. Stopped. Then put it back in the pack and reached for his phone instead.

Gary To tapped away carefully at the tiny keys on his ridiculous new BlackBerry phone, frowning in concentration, when a stack of papers slapped onto his desk, shocking him.

He suppressed the urge to blurt out seven very satisfying words and instead lowered his phone and droned at the article-covered wall in front of him.

'Good morning, Amy. Thank you for terrifying me. How may I help you?'

'How did you know it was me?' came the response behind him.

'Well, firstly,' Gary swivelled in his chair, looking over his glasses at the new addition to their team, 'I'm a wizard.'

'Ha ha. Very funny.'

'And secondly, you're the only person that says hello by exploding with enthusiasm for their work. Now, what's this?' He jerked his thumb at the papers on his desk.

She burst into a frothing soliloquy about some ancient missing-persons case.

Already accustomed to her zeal, Gary lent half his attention to her story while the other half admired the shape of her face. More than twice her age, he managed to keep more lurid thoughts to a bare minimum, but it was hard to ignore how pretty Amy Cheung was. She had a round face, dark almond eyes and a little button nose that shaved years off her already diminutive age. The long black hair that she wore across her face in a deep swoosh of fringe always somehow stayed intact, irrespective of how excited or animated she became.

In contrast, Gary's hair had begun to disappear from the front altogether. His trendy horn-rimmed glasses and fancy shirts did little these days to hide his fifty-six years.

As the latest addition to a team that had been together for over a decade, Amy was an electric dynamo, simultaneously jolting new life into the news crew while also forcing the three men that made it up to face just how old they had become.

She stopped speaking, snapping Gary's attention back to the present. His eyes shot up to hers.

'Did you hear what I just said?'

'Well, I. . . .'

'Ugh!' she rolled her eyes and shoved past him to snatch up the papers. It didn't bother her as much as she thought it would, the way they sometimes looked at her. She'd been apprehensive upon joining them, one girl with three men, but Gary and his team were harmless, and they did good work. It sometimes felt like having three dads. Well, two dads and one creepy older brother. . . .

Amy ignored him and waved a printed news article in front of Gary's face, slapping it excitedly. 'This kid – Eugene Lam – has just popped back up after like sixteen years off the grid. He vanished with a bunch of his friends, right?' Her Canadian twang got worse the more excited she became, reminding Gary of the voiceover girl from the Fox channel. 'But now he's back. No explanation, nothing. And get this.' Amy walloped him hard in the chest with the back of her hand. *She's strong,* Gary noted. 'He. Hasn't. Aged. A. Day!'

A wheel turned slowly in Gary's head. Not an industrial cog-covered hub, more of a bamboo water wheel. It lazily drifted around behind his blank expression until finally clicking into place and he sat up with a gasp.

'Wh— Huh? What?' He snatched the papers out of her hands, an article about the missing boy dated 1999, a police report from the same year and a medical report dated yesterday. Male, Chinese, aged ten to thirteen years. There was a snapshot, obviously taken with a phone. The colour was terrible, but it was almost certainly the same boy.

The hairs at the back of his neck stood up. So did he.

'How did you get this?'

'Don't worry. Nothing bad.' Amy smiled and Gary's eyes narrowed, the jaded newsman awakening. 'Nothing bad! Don't worry!' she repeated. 'I'm sort of . . . dating one of the guys that works at the hospital. A doctor. He thought I'd be interested. And he was right! Right? Riiight?'

Her enthusiasm was infectious. And Gary had to admit that this seemed a lot more solid than the flights of fancy and tenuous connections that she'd placed at their feet since joining six months ago. Chasing stories was Amy's job, but chasing ghosts was her passion. The others lived with it because they needed her, but now it looked as if she may have actually found something.

He scratched his head, still looking at the medical report. This was a long way from their usual arena of LegCo-member chasing and dry political analysis. At length, he finally dropped his arms. 'Fine. Okay, follow it up.'

'Yesss!' She pumped her fist like a sports star while her perfectly-swooshed hair remained perfectly intact, and then threw a soft punch onto Gary's shoulder. 'You won't regret it, Gary! Call up the crew; I bet we can get cameras in there tonight!' She raced across the room, snatching up her purse and was gone.

'The Crew' consisted of Carson Woo, an old friend of Gary's and possibly the laziest writer in the whole of Hong Kong, and Can Ai the cameraman, a strange but dependable sort who had been with them for the last nine years. The A-Team they were not, but they had produced solid freelance news, both print and film, for a long time. Gary reached for the BlackBerry again, frowning.

It had taken Amy a good twenty minutes on the phone to get Carson down to the hospital, in front of which he at last stepped out of a taxi. His mop of thin black hair hung limp down over his eyes and his polo shirt bulged over a protruding belly. He was already beginning to sweat in the sticky morning air.

He squinted about and spied Amy leaning against the access ramp talking to a young doctor. She twirled her hair around a finger as she spoke and laughed excessively. *Spare me,* he thought. Not in the mood to be chasing ghouls and goblins today, and desperate for air-conditioning, he strode over and barged straight in between the two flirty youngsters.

'Amy, I'm here. Let's do this.'

'Oh, hi Carson.' She looked at him, a flicker of annoyance passing over her face before she plastered one of her patented too-cute smiles over it. Turning the smile on the doctor and placing a hand delicately on his forearm, she whispered. 'Thanks, Stephen. Sorry – Doctor Kwan.' She laughed, 'Carson and I have got this. He's a total professional.' She added, 'Call me,' in a low voice then shot a wink at Carson, who rolled his eyes.

The doctor, a bespectacled baby with a fresh bald spot, blushed pink and toddled off, entirely pleased with himself.

'Ugh. Way to barge in, Woo.' Amy said, turning to him once they were alone, but she was still smiling.

Carson had been in a foul mood brought on by, in order: Being woken up by a car horn at seven a.m.; realising he could at last no longer fit into his favourite pants; and finally getting harassed for twenty solid minutes by someone, that he was beginning to realise, it was not physically possible to stay annoyed with.

He wobbled his bubble face side-to-side, hiked his 'fat pants' up over his expanding midriff and sighed, giving up on being grumpy. 'Sorry Amy. Look, let's just do this, all right? You know ghost stories aren't really my thing.'

'No, this is the real deal, you'll see.' Together they entered the hospital and began to walk as if they belonged there while Amy relayed the entire story to Carson for the second time.

They soon found Eugene Lam, but realised quickly that he was heavily sedated. Carson kept a lookout, while Amy snapped a shot of his medical charts and began to gently shake his arm, explaining, 'Just in case he's only asleep, gosh.'

'He's not going to wake up, Amy. Let's come back later,' Carson hissed from the door.

'Fffo.'

'Wait. He's saying something.' Amy pressed 'record' on her phone and gently shook his arm again. 'Eugene,' she said softly, 'Eugene Lam?'

The boy clenched his fists suddenly and began to speak quietly. 'Four times four. Four for the dark. Four for the light. Four four for for four four for for. . . .' He trailed off.

'This is wrong. We need to get out of—'

'Shh!' Amy cut Carson off.

'Four . . . four for the day, four for the night.' Eugene Lam's voice became clearer and he began to speak more loudly. 'It's too late to go dark. Too too late. Too late.'

'Wha. . . ? I don't get what he's—'

Amy let out a squeal as the boy sat straight up, grabbing her by the wrist as his eyes shot open. His pupils were dilated and black. He stared into Amy's eyes and began to yell. 'Leave the lights on, don't turn them off. It's too late to go dark. Don't turn them off. Don't!' He yelled the last word. Amy wrenched her hand away and he lowered back down to the bed, closed his eyes and began to fade again. 'Four times four. Four for the dark. Four for the light. Four four for for four four for for. . . .' until he was no longer speaking.

Too shocked to notice the feet pounding down the hall, Carson and Amy turned as a gruff-looking nurse appeared at the doorway.

'Who are you?'

Amy stammered, rubbing her wrist. 'We're just. . . .'

She looked at the phone in Amy's hand and Carson's notepad.

'Get out! Get! Out! Or I'll call security.'

They beat a hasty retreat, curses following them up the hallway.

Later, sitting in an empty pub, both on their second drinks, Carson and Amy had Gary – the decision maker – on speakerphone.

'No way, Gary. This kid was not faking. Something is seriously up. I mean, he was yelling about light and dark. And the number four?'

'Death.' Carson said, staring into his drink.

'I'm still not happy at all with what you did,' said Gary, ignoring Carson, 'but I have to admit, that footage you sent over is . . . unique.' He paused.

The pair looked over their drinks at each other.

'Okay?' Carson prompted.

Gary sighed. 'All right, look, this is getting weird, but. . . .' He sighed again. 'It turns out that there's apparently something going wrong with the lights around Sheung Wan station.'

'What do you mean?' Amy asked, nervously excited, her heart rate creeping up.

'They're starting to fail. To brown out or fade or something like that.' Carson and Amy exchanged another glance. 'Given the where and the what, there's obviously something kooky going on.'

This is it, Amy thought. She was close to a real story. A story of the unknown. A real break!

'We should go down there,' she heard herself say.

'We?' Carson responded. 'After the hospital? And you know what they say about the "phantom platform" or whatever they call it.'

'You afraid, Woo?' teased Amy.

'A little, yeah,' he said with a nervous laugh, before taking another swig of his beer.

'We'll all go,' said Gary. 'Look, I'm sure there's an explanation for this. Besides we need a proper cameraman so I'll get Can down there. I'll bring food, he never stops bloody eating.'

'Fine.' Carson finished his drink and pointed at Amy's half-full glass. She shook her head and he slid out of the booth to go to the bar.

'Sounds good, Gary. See you guys there tonight. And thanks,' said Amy.

'Thank me if this is actually a real story.'

After midnight, just before the MTR station was due to close, Carson, Can and Amy met at the convenience store on the corner. Can swanned down the street toward them, a tall, wiry figure in a grey T-shirt and jeans carrying his bulky camera in a sports bag. He was one of those guys that looked young at a distance, but when he got closer the wrinkles around his eyes and his greying hair were revealed.

He looked Amy up and down in that creepy way he always did as he passed them, and without saying a word went into the store to buy himself a snack.

When he was done they sneaked onto the so-called 'dead' platform. They had no idea whether this was really where Eugene Lam had gone missing, but it was as good a place to start as any.

Amy's heart was in her throat as they found an access door, Can expertly popped it open and they filed through.

'Just wait here,' Carson said at the end of the platform. 'There are probably still cameras here, so let's wait for Gary just in case.'

Amy nodded and leaned on the low barrier, looking down at where the tracks should have been, and the bricked-over tunnel entrance. Can opened a tube of chips and ate as he stood.

The platform was empty and still. With no advertising and walled-over tunnels with no tracks in them, it was like looking at an X-ray of a close friend. Backstage. Like peeling back a layer of normality.

After five minutes of nothing but listening to Can chew and Carson breathe heavily, Gary arrived carrying a bag of food containers.

'Took your time,' Carson said, squinting at the bag.

'We should have done this earlier, there was almost no one around and I had to circle back so I didn't get seen. Anyway, let's eat, I'm starving.' Gary pointed to a spot near the middle of the long platform and they began to make their way toward it.

'What have we got?' Can asked

'Ah, just crispy noodles with. . . .'

'Whoa.' Amy stopped walking.

'Hmm?' Carson turned back to her, followed by Gary and Can.

She stood still, pointing down the platform. They all turned back in time to see lights flicker out.

'The hell?' Gary muttered.

Another bank of lights blinked and died as they watched. Then another.

'Don't suppose anyone thought to bring a torch?' Carson ventured

'I've got a pocket one,' said Amy.

'I've got one,' Gary said, pulling a long silver torch out of his rucksack and handing it to Carson. He cleared his throat. 'They're just turning the lights off for the night. We should've known they'd do this.'

The lights in front of them went out. They all stood quietly, looking at one another.

Overhead, there was a flickering and then darkness.

Can and Gary found themselves standing in a cone of weak, yellowish light about three metres wide being cast down from the roof, and Amy stood in the beam of Carson's torchlight. 'Thanks Carson,' she said, squinting against the glare and stepping toward the lit-up area.

'No problem,' he replied from the darkness. 'It got really creepy in here, really fa— Ack!'

His voice cut off and the torchlight spun in the air, flashing spastically. It hit the ground and blinked out just as Carson let out a horrifying scream. There was a tearing noise, his scream shot up to a bloodcurdling pitch and stopped suddenly.

'Jesus Christ!'

'What the fuck . . . Carson! Carson!'

They yelled into the darkness, but no one left the light. Amy, pallid white, swung her tiny torch beam wildly into the murk, but there was nothing to see. 'What the hell was that? Carson!' The torchlight barely penetrated the dark. 'Oh my God. Ooh my God. Oh my God. Oh my God.'

Gary put his hand on her shoulder. 'Amy. Come on. Come on. Let's just . . . let's just relax for a minute. Just listen.' They stood in silence, straining their hearing for a full minute, just the sound of their laboured breathing filling the air. 'Goddammit . . . Carson! Carson? You'd better not be screwing around!'

Silence.

Can flicked on the flash of his camera and shone it into the black, but there was nothing other than platform. 'He's gone.' He looked around at Gary and Amy. 'He's gone.'

They looked at one another, huddled in the pool of light. Amy shaking, Can's eyes wide. Only Gary seemed to be at least half coping.

'Hello?' he called into the gloom. 'If there's someone out there, this isn't funny!'

Silence echoed back.

'What the hell is this, Amy?' Can turned to her with a sneer, shining the camera's beam into her face.

'I . . . hey, turn that off.' She shielded her eyes from the glare. 'I don't know. None of us knew.'

'Knew what?' He took a step forward.

'Hey!' Gary yelled, putting his hand on the thin man's chest. Can struggled to get by him, knocking Gary's glasses off and they skidded away into the shadow. 'Take it easy, Can! This isn't anyone's fault.' Gary softened his tone but kept his hands on him, 'Look, we don't even know what's happening here. This could just be Carson screwing around.' Amy was on the edge of the circle of light, trying to put Gary in between her and Can as he glared at her. 'Hey. Can. Look at me.'

Can met Gary's eyes.

'Dude.'

He stared back for an uncomfortable length of time, but finally he sighed, dropping his shoulders. 'Okay, okay. Sorry, Amy. God, it's just. . . .' He gestured out to the dark. 'I mean, what the hell was that?' He turned away from them, lowered his camera to the ground and sat down cross-legged, sighing again.

Gary looked down at him for a moment, before turning to Amy and giving her a reassuring nod. 'Okay,' he mimed.

He reached down and patted Can on the shoulder. 'It's okay, buddy. We'll figure this out.'

He said the same thing to Amy, adding 'Here. Can I borrow that?'

Amy handed him the small torch reluctantly.

'I'm going to see if Carson is there.'

'No!' Amy burst out, almost grabbing his wrist. 'Don't.'

'I'll be fine. Look, take care of the noodles, all right,' he said, smiling.

'You don't know what's out there.'

'I know Carson is. What if he's injured? We can't just sit here and do nothing. I'll just have a quick poke. And I need my glasses anyway.' Now she did grab his wrist. 'I'll be two seconds.' Still smiling, he pried her hand off, patted it and flicked on the torch.

Can was looking around in silence as Gary slid into the inky darkness, the little beam of light illuminating a tiny spot in front of him.

The spot vanished for a second, but popped back on again. Amy's heart leapt. 'Gary?'

'All good.' She heard him whack the side of the torch. 'Crappy little thing.'

It went out again.

'Gary?'

There was no answer.

'Gary!' Can bellowed, shocking Amy. Still no response.

They exchanged a worried glance, and Can stood up. As he took a breath to yell out again, a massive spray of hot red liquid hit them. Amy screamed.

She screamed and screamed until a shadow began to appear on the floor.

It moved slowly towards them. It oozed, a slow viscous pool. They tried to move away, but it crept through the circle of light, a rich red. Inch by inch, encroaching on them. It moved like molasses, dark and moist, occupying the floor, until they were at last forced to step, gagging, into it.

Through her sobbing, Amy heard a voice.

'What?' she called out in a wavering voice.

'What?' Can responded thickly to her.

'W— I heard someone.' Balancing on her toes, she wiped her eyes and called out again. 'Hello?'

Four times four.

'Four times four.' She whipped her head around. 'Can, did you hear that? Four times four?'

'What the fuck are you talking about?' he hissed back, stepping up and down on the spot.

Then they both froze. A sound came from the dark. It was a sliding noise. A slow, hissing as of something being dragged.

Someone.

They didn't move at all, neither of them even breathed, as the noise moved toward them. It came closer and closer until it sounded as if it were inside the circle. Can began to cry silently, his fists clenched at his sides.

It was beside them now. Shhhhhhh. Shhhhhh. It continued past them, just outside the pool of light, invisible in the dark.

The sliding began moving away from them. It faded so slowly, retreating further into the dark until they were once again left in silence.

The floor was a sticky mass of blood. They were trapped in an unmoving blob of light, an island in an ocean of blackness. But at long last exhaustion took sway. Can managed to wipe away some of the blood with his bag and Amy huddled on top of it, hugging her legs, and fainted.

She awoke groggy and sat up with a yelp as she remembered where she was.

The light overhead was still casting its yellow glare down on them and she uttered a quiet prayer of thanks.

Can awoke with a groan, also having succumbed to fatigue. His side was covered in blood. Amy stood quickly, brushing her skin in a panic, but stopped, letting out a small gasp.

Directly across from them, not ten metres away, was a vending machine, softly lit in the dark.

Can saw it too. 'What the...?' he whispered to himself. And he eyed it hungrily.

'Don't. Don't go there.'

They both looked down at the plastic bag full of old noodles, covered in blood, and Can kicked it into the darkness. 'We're going to starve here if we can't get out. How long has it been?'

'I don't know.'

'We need to get over there.'

'No,' Amy whispered. 'No, Can. Please, you can't.'

He licked his lips and shifted his weight. 'I've got an idea.'

'No,' she pleaded.

Ignoring her, he grabbed the camera and lifted it over his head so the lamp was shining down over him. He smiled at her and went to step out of the light.

'No, Can! Don't!' Amy grabbed his shirt.

'Get off!' He bashed her hand out of the way, lifting the camera again. 'We'll starve!' and he walked quickly to the vending machine under his own tiny cone of bright white light.

The platform was silent as he crossed. Amy held her breath.

After five agonising seconds, he entered the small, soft halo of yellow light coming from the machine with a victorious smile on his face and, turning, gave her a thumbs-up. She felt weak from hunger, but didn't want him to risk the journey again. *Just stay there. Please.*

He put the camera down, careful not to leave the fuzzy haze of light he was in, and fished his wallet from his pocket. She could only see his back as he held it to the machine and punched a button. DOOP. Amy jumped at the noise – the card reader was deafening in the inky vacuum of the platform – but her mouth still watered when she heard the candy bar hit the dispenser.

Can didn't even turn around. Amy could hear him tear the packaging open and scoff it, his shoulders hunched over. DOOP. Another candy bar hit the dispenser. Doubled over, he devoured it too. Then a third. By the fourth he was on his knees in front of the machine.

He ate and ate and ate. Amy was calling out to him, but he couldn't or wouldn't hear her. He kept eating, faster and faster. The front of the machine had chocolate and blood smeared all over it where he repeatedly mashed the buttons.

'Can!'

He stopped. Hunched over his fists.

'Can?' Amy repeated much more softly into the renewed silence.

She could see his shoulders rising and falling as he breathed, still on his knees bent over the pile of chocolate wrappers and mess.

Slowly, he began to turn his head. His body barely moved as his head twisted, just rising and falling with his heavy breath. It twisted and twisted until Amy thought it would break.

'Can?' she cried out, tears streaming down her face.

Finally, his body began to shift as well and in the murky light his grin became visible. A terrible rictus in a mess of bloody chocolate. His whole face, and the fists he held up to it, was smeared with chunks of the candy he was gorging. His eyes were dilated completely black.

Amy covered her mouth and stifled a whimper. Her legs buckled. *No no no no.*

The dead eyes bored across the blackness separating them. *Yessss,* they said.

A voice issued from inside Can's face. 'It's too late. Too late to go dark. We need more.' The grin widened, almost breaking his face in two. Slowly he raised the fists filled with chocolate bars and began once more to lick and chew as it oozed everywhere.

Her crying was uncontrollable. 'Can. Please. Please don't go. Please.' Amy's heart thundered in her chest. She couldn't bear to meet those eyes again.

She sobbed into her hands and rocked back and forth on the floor.

'Amy.'

The voice iced down her spine. She squeezed her eyes shut as hard as she could and sobbed again, rocking harder.

'Amy.'

She jumped up with a scream. That voice was *right* in her ear.

She screamed again, slapping her hand across her mouth. Can was standing now, right at the edge of his little pool of light, staring across the darkness at her. Chocolate chunks oozed and dripped from his fists. She breathed hard in and out through her nose, forcing the screams back down.

He spoke.

'A man can't live on candy alone.'

He stared at her, motionless. Amy, unable to move in the middle of her pool of light, held both hands clamped over her mouth and stared back through sheets of tears unable to look away. Her breaths came ragged and hard.

'You can't turn it off.' Can continued in that ghastly voice, 'A man needs . . . more.'

'No.' Amy whimpered.

He stepped forward to cross the distance between them, leaving the haze of light from the vending machine behind him and the darkness swallowed him.

A scrape, a wet cracking noise and a sudden gust of wind. Can screamed for less than a second before a much louder cracking noise silenced him. Amy, pressing her hands hard over her ears, wailed, screaming and crying, but could not block out the long hungry tearing noises coming from the depths of the darkness.

At length the noises stopped and the silence returned, filled only with Amy's quiet sobs under her cone of light. The vending machine began to dim. And still crying silently, she watched as it blinked several times like a fluorescent and was swallowed by the blackness.

The platform was a fathomless, formless space. An abyss of hungry, malevolent dark. And she alone in a pinprick of light was the only thing keeping it at bay.

Four times four, said the voice in her head.

What's in a Name?

Joy Al-Sofi

A SEETHING DARKNESS CROUCHES *at the end of a narrow hallway. Nearer the entrance is a door with a bulb that's never switched off. Its feeble glow, as insubstantial as stretched moonlight, battles against the blackness that surges beyond; this tiny overhead light ends as if sliced by a knife. The air is charged with menace; walls, floor and ceiling ripple with barely-contained creatures seeking to emerge. Shrieks and incoherent whispers assail the imagination which supplies the command, 'Go back, go back, GO BACK!'*

Cross the threshold, silence reigns. Ominous afternoon shadows steal over the buckling floor, surging up the walls to snuff out every trace of light. Flat 35-F is empty and waiting.

Pearl Matthews was damaged but didn't know it. To some she was irresistible. But not to her boyfriend of several years who had found it far too easy to leave her for a job back in the UK. He hadn't asked, or replied to her suggestion, that maybe she could come with. The isolated village house had become a mausoleum of unhappy memories. She was looking for a new place to live. Step by step her search brought her closer to the thirty-fifth floor of the cloud-scouring Cormorant Towers in the aged industrial area of To Kwa Wan where after looking at many flats she didn't expect much, but as soon as the lift doors opened, it felt just right. They showed her 35-C and she took it.

Moving in kept her busy and just trying to find everything in the jumble of unlabelled containers was exhausting. For several nights, she slept all the way through till morning feeling more refreshed than in a long time. Her co-workers at the language centre complimented her, asking had she done something different, maybe to her hair.

The second week, she had a frustrating day at work, sending her thoughts into a well-worn groove of trying to undo the past. She awoke in a sheen of sweat, her heart pounding. Subliminal, soft but steady, the air thrummed like hovering wings above her bed. Terrified, she lay unable to move. Her eyes on the bedside clock. It told her the time, 3.00 a.m., 5 April, 2014, 3:01, 3:02, but not what was happening. Finally her entire body jerked and the sounds, the spell, or whatever it was, vanished. She bounded up from the bed but stopped not knowing where she was going. Her knees turned rubber and down to the floor she went where she sat trying to sort out what had just happened. Of course, it was only a powerful and vivid dream; one that had seemed real. Or maybe some kind of fugue or paralysis on awaking; she'd read about that, a medical condition. It could be treated.

Her attempt at making sense of what she'd just experienced wasn't enough to keep her from tumbling into the familiar closed loop of seeking the one path that could have changed everything. She kept blaming herself for not doing the impossible, wearing her need for atonement like an internal hair-shirt that never stopped chafing.

The next few days were busy and she slept well. A new, male teacher started at the centre. She admitted on the phone to her mom that she had waggled her eyebrows after he'd walked past and that when Phil asked her to coffee a few days later, she'd hesitated, to not look too eager before saying yes.

Coffee was followed by another date and then a dinner with dessert at her flat. Late in the night, Phil got up and wandered from room to room. Something about being there, the place, put him on edge. He didn't know. Had to get out. He was sorry. What about his place next time? He'd call. Pearl was incensed and insulted but in the end felt relieved to have discovered early on. They stayed friendly but distant.

She was feeling on edge herself when the same happened with Roger and Greg. Now she'd met someone else, would it be the same?

He'd asked to share her table. Pearl looked up from her book and saw a tall, sandy-haired guy with a shy smile. She said yes. They chatted about the things people chat about when they meet. Exchanged contact info, invited each other to Twitter and Facebook.

At work, a favourite student, Ling, arrived late, very quiet, with her head turned away, buttons missing and fresh bruises showing. Pearl summoned up her long set-aside social-work training, and carefully elicited what had happened. Ling's mother had come into the little girl's bedroom smashing and breaking all of her toys. It wasn't only the toys that had been attacked. Pearl felt swamped by long-ago memories of Julie.

Her boss said it would probably be fine, keep a close eye out and anyway there wasn't much they could do. Pearl nodded but vowed this time would be different; what happened to Julie would never happen again, not on her watch.

Lesson plans couldn't keep her attention that night. Outside her flat, buildings were lit up all around except to the left where an unremitting blackness provided a perfect backdrop to project Ling's dark hair and Julie's blond, while dark bruised eyes became blue ones. Pearl had followed protocol at every step, but official procedures had not been enough. She hadn't saved Julie. She entered that long-ago day again, looking for that one step that would have made all the difference.

From within the darkness a fury raged. No mere amplification of her own distraught condition, this was hatred and these feelings weren't coming from her. Hairs rose on the back of her neck as the rage jumped the gap and came straight at her; she threw herself to the floor and lay as if bludgeoned. Luminous shapes formed and dissolved; susurrations, nearly below the range of hearing, filled the room; then piercing the night was the wail of a baby.

Her thoughts disorganised, she clutched the desk to pull herself up and yanked the curtains closed, ending the visions and sounds. A searing pain exploded behind her eyes in a burst of dazzling lights. She ran out, knocking the computer to the floor, scattering her plans.

Pain, thoughts and images tumbled over one another. She'd sensed an agony far more powerful than her own turmoil. Where she sought exoneration, the other sought vengeance. Curled up in bed, fearful of what the long night ahead might bring, how much she needed someone in her life. She had prided herself on her strength but she could feel it slipping away like sand through a child's grasp. Unable to think, she stayed in a rigid ball. Sleep was long in coming.

When she woke, filaments of dreams clung to her mind like cobwebs. She had a day to face but she hesitated when she went to her study to retrieve her work. She was trembling, had she really seen, felt . . . that? The plans lay in a jumbled pile, not strewn about the floor as she was sure they'd been. Through a crack in the curtain, she saw a neighbouring flat that she hadn't noticed before. A row of recessed windows overlooked a large balcony and deep shadows from the railings fashioned a prison of black bars against the windows. The space between the two flats shimmered and flexed.

Pearl gathered up her papers. She felt so alone. There was no one to talk to about what she'd experienced and felt. Michael: she'd call him after work, see how he was doing and see could they meet up later in the week.

When she got to work, she tuned out everyone, barely focusing on her students. A co-worker, Flora, stopped her as they were leaving and Pearl felt compelled to say something. She mentioned strange noises. Flora laughed. If Pearl wanted noisy neighbours, she should come to her place. 'You wouldn't believe it. They get into it all times of the day or night.' Pearl, smiled and nodded. Flora had no idea.

She was disappointed to reach Michael's voicemail, hoped she didn't sound as spooked as she felt. Whenever she looked towards the other flat, nothing, but when she looked away, something. Pulsations, low insistent, indecipherable, angry. Was she having hallucinations? No, that was unacceptable.

She left all the lights on that night and fell asleep immediately. If she'd had any dreams, they were gone when she awoke to disappointment. No message from Michael. Was he going to end up like Phil and the others?

Pearl was relieved to see Ah Lai was the security guard and receptionist the next morning. She knew a smattering of English and Pearl sometimes gave her some *gratis* English tutoring.

'Joh san!'

'Joh san. Miss Mafu. Today, you early.'

'Yes, well, I. . . .' Pearl revised what she'd say while Ah Lai spoke Cantonese to an interrupting co-worker.

Ah Lai turned back, 'Sorry.'

'It's about the flat across from me. But not the hall, across from my study window. . . .' She stopped at the confusion clouding Ah Lai's face. 'Sorry, I'm not being clear.'

'What name, what number?'

'Oh, I don't know. I can see the windows and balcony from the small bedroom window. Can you tell which one it is?'

'Not sure. You have some problem?'

'No, well, yes. Oh, it's just I . . . something on their balcony made me wonder, you know?'

'Clothes drying not allowed on balcony.'

'Clothes? No, no. Ah. I can't explain. Never mind.' There were only a couple of possibilities. 'I'll get the number. We'll talk again.'

'Okay. Bye-bye.'

She would go and see when she got home, get the number, meet them and find out about those lights and sounds. The strong haze of day made it all seem less important, especially when Michael called and they made plans for Sunday dinner. She made no mention of anything else. It was too odd.

It was nearly ten p.m. before she set out; a bit late for a visit to an unknown and bizarre neighbour. She couldn't think of what to say. She'd just check the number and if she heard anyone, play it by ear.

She turned into the hall she crossed when going to the lifts. After a right turn at the end, she could see a poorly-lit doorway down on the left. Beyond it, nothing. The flat she was looking for lay in total darkness. With her stomach churning, she stepped into the corridor.

Above 35-E, a light jutted, gleaming faintly on a sturdy metal gate; its dim bulb illuminated jagged Chinese characters pasted on both sides of the entrance; fierce door gods and generals with upraised swords glared back at her.

Willing herself to move past the lone outpost of light she took a single step and her feet refused. The temperature plummeted. Condensation plumed from her mouth like dragon's breath. Chilled air crept across her toes then seized her legs in an icy grip. Within the walls something slithered. The darkness seemed to lunge at her. Plaintive whispers grew into shrieks of terror. 'Go away,' 'No, no, no!' 'Help!' And finally, faintly, she thought – no, she couldn't have – 'Pearl!'

She fled, slamming her door and throwing the latch. Cries resounded in her ears as tendrils of blackness oozed under the door and streaked her vision. She leaned against the wall, fighting off panic, telling herself that she couldn't have heard her name, promising to get a metal door. Denying. She'd get door gods too, lots of them.

It took a long while for her breathing to ease so she could move away from the door. She wasn't proud of running away but at least now she knew which flat it was. She would talk to Ah Lai again. With shaking hands, she pressed her mother's number in Los Angeles but hung up on the voicemail. She wanted to call Michael but it was too late. She didn't know him well enough. But just thinking of him made her feel better.

Ah Lai was not behind the desk in the morning. But it all felt better in the daylight. Pearl vowed she'd go back all the way and knock on the door of 35-F. No stopping this time.

The windows of 35-F remained dark and quiet. Maybe it was empty; a spec flat bought for investment might account for that black hole at the end of her floor, but not for the flickerings, or the darkness, or the icy cold, or the whispers, and not for the way it had made her feel. The terms of her lease didn't seem to have an exception for what she'd experienced. There was no way to leave that wouldn't cost more money than she could afford. She got a strong metal door instead and hoped that would be the end of it.

By Saturday, Ah Lai was back at Tower 2.

'Ah Lai.'

'Joh san, good morning. Miss Mafu. You okay?'

Did she look that bad? She'd have to get some more make-up. 'I'm okay, thanks. Say, what do you know about the people in 35-F?'

'Oh, not sure. What you mean?' Ah Lai's words were normal but the look on her face was anything but.

Pearl bent over the counter, 'Ah Lai. Something's not right about that flat.'

'Not understand what you mean. I don't know people in that flat. No people in that flat.'

'Wait, you don't know the people in that flat or that there aren't any people there?'

'Yes.'

'Ah, Jesus,' Pearl swore under her breath. She'd had conversations like this before with her students.

'I mean, is the flat occupied now? Are there people living in it?'

'Can't say, need to check.' Ah Lai leaned closer, '35-F long-time big problem. Very trouble. Even feng shui master couldn't fix.'

Pearl didn't know what to think but was relieved to know it wasn't just her who had a problem with 35-F.

'See you tonight.'

'Tonight.'

That evening, Ah Lai told her that 35-F was currently empty but couldn't say for how long.

Pearl wondered how the people could have left so fast. But surely that meant the problems were over.

When she talked to her mother she tried to sound upbeat. She told her about this new man she was going to dinner with the following day. Her mother kept asking what was wrong.

The next morning was Sunday, her day off. Pearl went through the motions of breakfast. She wasn't ready to face the day, or think about anything. By her third cup of coffee however, she remembered Michael was coming to take her to dinner.

Through the window she could see something was different at the other flat – an ordinary wicker chair stood on the formerly empty balcony, its back to Pearl. She couldn't quite make out what was resting on it through the chair's slats. Something was moving on it, probably just shadows or a gust of wind fluttering a left-open book. A chair was solid and real. Seeing it pleased her. Somebody, with normal things had moved in, most likely a family.

The next time she saw it, the chair was facing Pearl's flat. She smiled at the large, almost life-sized doll sitting in the chair, its black hair flung into streamers by the strong wind. It was a family, with children. She'd like to see the child who'd placed the doll there.

She could bake cookies for the new tenants but her kitchen was the size of a bathtub and anyway most Chinese she'd met were not big on American-style sweets. Of course, she didn't know if they were Chinese, but odds were. And children usually liked cookies; it would be an excuse for a visit.

A few minutes later, she noticed the chair was now sideways to her vision, directly facing the harbour. The doll, its stiff legs straight ahead, was sitting very near the edge of the chair as if enjoying the view. Without warning, the doll fell back, its legs pointing to the sky. A short while later, the doll was sitting up again.

While Pearl watched, nothing happened. She'd look away and its position was changed like someone was teasing her. She determined to watch and see whomever it was but minutes passed and nothing happened. And then the doll sat up, twitching and jerking. No one else, only the doll, and it moved like a living thing, rocking back and forth gathering speed until it was a blur of black, whipping the wind.

Pearl shuddered. The wind, it had to have been. But she knew there were those who would tell her she had a ghost for a neighbour. Pearl thought it likely a child or someone playing tricks with strings, manipulating the doll like a puppet. But remembering how it looked made her skin crawl and she remembered her grandma saying something about someone walking on your grave. Best to forget she had seen it. Better she hadn't seen it at all.

It was time to get ready for her dinner date but a haggard face stared back at her from the mirror. She hoped she had enough blush and concealer to fix the dark circles under her eyes and the wan cheeks. She wanted to look good for Michael.

Twilight rendered the doll invisible by the time Michael arrived; the only emanations she sensed were good ones coming from him. The dinner was nice too. The rest of the night was even better and Michael stayed snuggled close to her until morning and she felt a curse had been lifted.

They made breakfast and the coffee lasted until almost mid-morning when Michael kissed her a long good bye.

Dark clouds sent ominous weather warnings. Heavy rains were approaching. Before long a sheet of water cut her off from the outside world. After the black rainstorm passed, bunched-up clouds, flushed pink and purple, scurried toward distant hills, rumbling reminders they'd be back.

The chair was still there but something made Pearl grab her binoculars. Both chair and doll had survived the storm. The doll's clothes were streaked with dirt and torn into wind-blown tatters. Its hair was matted against its dented and deformed head. The once-charming face was now bruised and scratched, its features battered.

The doll was standing on the seat, leaning forward almost as if grasping the rails and scrutinising the street below. Pearl's hand rose to stifle a scream as the doll lurched forward and plunged off the balcony disappearing into deep shadows. As it fell, she heard a piercing cry. Waves of goose bumps racked her body. Her blood felt as if it were ice. Down went the binoculars as she stumbled against the desk, knocking papers and books to the floor. She reached for her phone but it slipped from her fingers.

She fumbled for it under the dislodged papers and pressed 9, 1. Oh! She stopped at her American miscue. She needed 999. Then laughed, teetering on the edge of hysteria. 911, 999? Was she really calling the police to report a fallen doll? And yet it had looked so like a real child that had just hurtled itself off the balcony. She knew it was crazy. The emergency services would think *she* was crazy.

What she'd seen kept replaying in her head. She couldn't stop shaking. Nothing serious had happened but it had felt violent and horrifying. She knew it would be impossible to convey how it had seemed to her. She had witnessed a doll . . . she didn't have the right words to explain, not what, not why. A doll. Absurd.

She should go over and explain what happened to the doll. As if someone who left an item outside in a heavy rainstorm wouldn't know why it went missing. She looked at the row of blank windows. It could wait till morning.

Michael. She needed to say hello, just hear his voice. What she'd seen made her feel sick inside but she couldn't tell him. He was too new in her life.

By the next day, the idea of reporting it or visiting 35-F had lost all its appeal. What would she say? The chair was still there. They must have fastened it down and if the doll had been important, it would have been too. She'd seen a doll get blown off a balcony in a storm. Big deal. It wasn't like they could just go down and fetch it back up. No benefit to them in knowing, or she in telling.

Work kept her busy. She talked with Michael throughout the week, they'd see each other on Saturday night, turning her thoughts toward the future, away from the balcony.

A couple days following the storm, Ah Lai was back behind the counter.

'Good evening.'

'Good evening, Ah Lai. Look, I've been thinking, uh, wondering. . . .' Pearl took a deep breath, 'I mean I want to speak to the people in 35-F. Could you maybe call them for me?'

'Where?'

'35-F. I want to talk to them but maybe they don't speak English.'

'Sorry Mrs Mafu. 35-F? Nobody there. Move out already.'

'Oh, but . . . that's so fast?' She'd heard nothing of anyone moving out. 'Never mind. Thanks anyway.'

Gone. She wouldn't have to go down that dark corridor or explain why she thought she needed to talk to people she didn't know, about something they probably had no interest in. Back in her flat, Pearl scrutinised her dark neighbour. It was true, the chair was gone, the balcony deserted. She wondered when they'd taken it away and how she'd missed the commotion that moving meant.

The next night, Ah Lai waved Pearl over. 'Good evening, Miss Mafu.'

'Hi, Ah Lai. Say, is it time for an English lesson?'

'Maybe, few minutes. This week so much trouble.'

'Trouble?' Pearl had never given a thought to Ah Lai's having troubles of her own.

'Have you heard what happen outside in street?'

'In the street? When? No, no. I don't know what happened. Tell me.'

'From window. Somebody died.'

'What! You mean fell out of a window, someone here? That's terrible.'

'No fall. Police come ask about lady live Tower 5. Walk outside. Something fall, she die.'

'Wait, wait.' The doll plunging from the balcony flashed through her mind. 'You mean, something fell on a woman walking by? Was killed right here? Oh no! That's awful. What day?'

'Yes, so nice lady too. Before use to live Tower 2. I remember she . . . ah. . . .'

'What's the matter? You look . . . I don't know, but. . . .' Pearl's voice dropped to almost a whisper.

'Where you ask me last night.' Now Ah Lai was whispering too. 'She live there.'

'What? Last night? I uh . . . oh . . . in 35-F. . . ? Used to live 35-F?' Ah Lai nodded.

'Here newspaper. You see picture is our building. You keep.'

Pearl took the newspaper to one of the lobby sofas where she looked at the pictures in the Chinese-language article. She questioned what it meant that a woman who once lived in 35-F had been killed walking outside by something that fell from an unknown location. But she was sure it had come from this very building, from 35-F, exactly the same place this woman had once lived. Pearl could hear the theme music from the *Twilight Zone*.

She worked through it step by step: the lady still lived in the complex so had every reason to be walking by. Nothing spooky in that.

And even if it was on that same day, it didn't mean the doll from the balcony was what killed her. For heaven's sake, how likely was that? It was a big storm. A doll? Not a chance. But maybe that was why the people in 35-F had moved out so fast. Or had they been arrested? Even if it was the doll, how could anyone know where it had come from? And besides, no one could aim a doll in a storm and expect it to kill someone. Impossible. What was she thinking? Lots of stuff blows from everywhere. But that doll sure hadn't looked like it just fell. It looked like it was taking deliberate aim. Who exactly would she tell *that* to?

She went to bed wanting Michael who was safe and strong and she needed that, to press against him, feel his warm skin and lock her fingers into the hairs on his chest, to have him enfold her, kiss and soothe her with a calm explanation, letting rationality ease her fears. She wished Michael was there. Just the idea of Michael felt comforting.

Pearl's job kept her busy. Ling showed no more troubling signs. Ah Lai never talked about 35-F again. Michael and Pearl got closer and closer and a few months later, he moved in.

Pearl told Michael all about what had happened on her first assignment as a new MSW and the little girl, Julie, whose own mother had killed her. They agreed if they had a daughter, they'd name her Julie as a tribute. She'd have the middle name Ariana, after Michael's mother. It felt like the atonement she had been seeking.

Not long after, a couple got off the lift on the thirty-fifth floor with them. Turned out they had leased 35-F. Interests in common led to visits between the two flats. The corridor was now lit and brightly painted.

At the end of 2015, Pearl and Michael moved back to the USA for the birth of their daughter. Pearl has not told anyone what she saw that day. 'Thought she'd seen,' Michael would doubtless say and laugh, in a nice way but she wasn't ready to let go. She'd tell him one day. Just not yet.

2 February, 2016 – Hong Kong Coroner Rules
Anna May Lee On-mei, 46, killed by unidentified falling object, 10 August, 2014. Neither the object nor the location it came from was ever identified. Witnesses reported a blur that

disintegrated after nearly decapitating the victim whose husband and teenage son received lesser injuries.

The family's history is a tragic one. Four years earlier, their daughter, 2, Julie Lee Ju-lei, was abducted and is still missing. Two years before that, another daughter, Ariana Lee Hei-on, fell from the balcony. Multiple injuries, burns and broken bones in various stages of healing were found on the child's body. There were no reports of abuse and it was not considered relevant to the child's death. The mother's death was ruled an accident just like the child's.

28 October, 2017 – Grisly Discovery
Bones confirmed to be the missing Lee child discovered in the thirty-fifth floor flat in To Kwa Wan occupied by the Lee family at the time they reported the abduction. The police have opened a murder investigation.

Appendix – Dates of Chinese festivals relating to the dead
Ching Ming – 5 April, 2014
Hungry Ghosts – 10 August, 2014
Cheung Yueng – 28 October, 2017

Soho

Anjali Mittal

AMY WAS WOKEN BY HER ALARM CLOCK. She reached out in the dark and turned it off. She felt gentle kisses on her bare arm and a warm breath on her neck. 'Not now Simon,' she murmured and rolled away from him. 'Ow,' she screamed as he pulled her hair back, grabbed her arm and squeezed her neck. His fingers held her in place and she pushed with all her might to free herself. She choked and jumped up as she tried to pull away from him. She wiped the tears off her face and looked around in disbelief. Simon was not in the bed. In fact he was not even in the room. His nightclothes were neatly folded on the armchair and she was alone.

Had it been a dream? Hand on neck she walked into the living room. She saw him reading the paper with his mug of coffee. How could she think that he would hurt her? She smiled and went to kiss him good morning. When she emerged from the shower later there were signs of bruising on her neck and her head hurt where her hair had been pulled. *How strange.* Not being able to make any sense of it, she thought it best not to discuss it with Simon.

A few weeks passed and the bruises faded as did the memory of it.

Amy thought fondly about their wedding in a small country chapel in the heart of Surrey. When she fell in love with the young Chinese man from Hong Kong, she did not think twice about abandoning her family and home to move to his country. Her family had moved from Hong Kong to England two generations ago and now here she was, back in the same city, helping Simon run his family restaurant in Soho. Amy had put her law career on hold for a while for this and it took six months to turn the dingy place into something more modern and classy.

One day Amy decided to set the table for them after the customers had left, in their apartment above the restaurant. She wanted it to be a romantic evening. The rose petals in the crystal vase released their fragrance under the flickering light of the candle. She turned on the music, selecting *Lady in Red,* filled the glasses with wine and placed the first course out. She went to fetch Simon from the bar. He was sitting on a fluorescent purple bar stool, where they had sat side by side and clinked glasses to celebrate the success of the opening night of the restaurant which had been featured in the *South China Morning Post* and *Time Out.*

'Come on darling,' she said. 'I have a surprise for you.'

As they walked towards the candlelit table Amy stopped in her tracks. The wine glasses had toppled onto the table cloth leaving large blood-red stains on the pristine white fabric.

'How did that happen?' exclaimed Amy. She looked around. There was nobody else in the apartment, not even pets.

'Never mind,' said Simon, affectionately squeezing her shoulders. 'I'll mop it up.'

'But the music and the candle?' whispered Amy. 'It's all gone. I'd set it up.'

'I'm sure you had,' said Simon, grinning as he poured out some more wine. 'Perhaps the place is haunted.'

Amy ate her meal in silence.

The following day it was an hour before the staff were due to arrive at six. Amy cleaned the wine glasses until they shone. Simon said they needed more ice.

'I'll go to Wellcome around the corner,' he said. 'I won't be long. Why don't you get the wine from the cellar?'

Amy grinned and leaned over to kiss him. 'Okay, darling.' She wrapped her cardigan around her as she watched him walk out down the steep slope to the shops. She felt a chill even though the sun had been shining moments ago. A layer of mist rose from the ground and then stopped. It made her shiver. She stood and watched it for a while, this light grey sheen of mist, hanging in the pitch dark background. She anticipated thunder and lightning, although it had not been forecasted, and when it did not come she turned away from the window and headed to the cellar. She opened the door and fumbled for the light switch. She walked down the stone steps. She knelt to pull out bottles of Cabernet Sauvignon and Merlot and wiped off the dust that had settled on them. She lost track of time and soon it was quarter to six; she stood up and dusted her knees. She heard footsteps above her.

'Simon, is that you?'

Nobody replied. A door slammed.

'Anybody there?' she shouted, climbing up the stone steps balancing the bottles in the bag she had brought down for that purpose.

The naked bulb above her started to flicker. She looked at it and quickened her pace. A tinkle of glass smashing resonated in the cellar and it went dark. In a panic she reached out for the wall and ran up the steps feeling her way up to the blade of light shining through the open door. Her heart was racing. When she was almost there the door shut. Amy screamed and let go of the bag.

Thud, thud, thud and then smash. The light bulb flickered back to life, illuminating the green canvas bag swimming in a dark red pool of wine and shards of glass. Amy was about to push the wooden door when it swung open on its own. She ran towards the bar and shouted.

'Simon, Simon, is anybody there?'

She sat on a bar stool to steady her breathing. A few moments later she heard the key in the door and Simon walked in. She threw herself off the stool and ran into his arms, knocking the bags he was carrying onto the floor.

'What's the matter?' he said. 'You look like you've seen a ghost.'

'Somebody was there, I swear.'

'Nobody else is here,' he said with a smile. 'How can they be? They don't have a key.'

As he was consoling her, the doorbell rang and Simon let his mother in. Amy explained again and took them to the cellar door. Simon's mother flew into a rage at the mess.

'You stupid girl,' she said, jabbing her finger into Amy's shoulder. 'Don't you know how expensive that wine is?'

Amy gasped. Tears stung her eyes at her mother-in-law's rapid-fire Cantonese, much of which she could not understand. 'Look at me when I am talking to you,' she shouted in English. Amy looked up and to her horror saw her mother-in law's eyes turn blood red.

'Now, now Mother,' Simon said as he embraced her. 'Calm down. It's only wine. Amy, I think you need to go upstairs. You've done enough damage for one day. There's no need for you to be here. Mother, let's go and tend to the customers.'

They made their way to the restaurant. Amy was dumbstruck. *Had that actually happened?* She had heard of wicked mother-in-law stories but this was beyond that. Could she have imagined it all? She got into bed, took some tablets and pulled the duvet over her head. She would wake up in the morning and hopefully it would all be fine.

The next morning she could not move as Simon was curled around her and held her close. He was in deep sleep. If she shifted she would wake him. She looked at him. Perhaps it had all been a bad dream. The sun streamed through the gap between the curtains and let in the light which shone directly on Simon's face. He stirred. Taking the opportunity Amy wriggled out from his grasp and went for a shower. She enjoyed the water beating down on her face and stood in the cubicle for a few minutes longer than usual, washing away her fears. Wrapped in a towel, she emerged and opened her wardrobe to choose a light summer dress. As she pulled open the wooden door a creature as large as a puppy ran out.

She screamed. She stared at the rat that sat defiantly in the corner of the room and then scurried away.

'What is it now?' said Simon, rubbing his eyes.

'A rat,' said Amy. 'A huge big rat came out of the wardrobe.'

'Not again,' he sighed.

'No, look,' said Amy, pointing at the cupboard. 'There may be more in there.'

Simon pulled open the mahogany door. Amy let out a yelp. Almost all of her dresses had been chewed. They were destroyed. The phone rang and Simon explained the damaged dresses to his mother. Amy edged her way towards him for comfort but he looked at her coldly and said, 'Mother said that this was bound to happen. It's your punishment for destroying the wine last night.'

Amy felt dizzy. Why was Simon, the love of her life, acting this way? This could not be happening. 'Simon, what are you saying?' she said, hugging him tight. 'You don't mean that. It's me, Amy. You know I would never do anything to hurt our business.'

'My business,' he corrected her as he got out of her clasp and pushed her aside. 'It's *my* family business. And you should remember that.'

The next few weeks became unbearable. Mother and son tormented her each day. She worked all hours serving the customers. She did not mind the work; it was her time for normality, meeting interesting people. They complimented the style of the place and the food, a great boost for Amy. She met Cynthia, Robert and Suzie, who had all returned after their degree courses in England. Now back in the city they were looking for jobs and often came to the bar. Robert and Suzie were a couple and often slipped away leaving Cynthia behind. Being the same age, Amy and Cynthia got on well.

But when the staff left at the end of the day, things went downhill. She once heard the piano come to life and when she went to investigate she saw the keys rising and descending on their own. The rubbish bins outside clanged uncontrollably and when she looked she saw them bashing against each other in mid-air. Doors opened on their own, and sometimes when she hid under her duvet she would hear footsteps approaching her, getting louder and louder. Fear now engulfed every pore and inhabited her body with such intensity that she prayed like she had never prayed before and slept with a cross under her pillow. She faced each day with dread.

One evening she heard sounds coming from the parlour below. Simon was asleep beside her. They had just locked up for the night. She tiptoed downstairs and looked through the door. The tall lamp in the corner of the room was on, illuminating the two armchairs by the ornamental gas fireplace. A fire had been lit. She edged her way to the wall by the door and peered in. Just above the sound of crackling wood, she heard whispering.

'She will become one of us soon,' said a female voice. 'Don't worry.'

Amy tried to get a better look. Her mother-in-law was comfortably sunk into the leather sofa, red wine in one hand, a cigarette in the other. When she saw the occupant of the second chair her jaw dropped.

'She has to, otherwise I will make her,' laughed Simon. His eyes were like two large red marbles popping out of their sockets just like his mother's had been, flashing like the stop lights at a railway crossing, on and off.

But she had just left Simon in bed! She tiptoed back upstairs and made her way into the bedroom. She heard the snoring before she saw him. Simon was asleep where she'd left him. She put her hand across her mouth to muffle a scream. She needed help.

She decided to confide in her good friend Cynthia. Cynthia was a Hong Kong girl and would know what to do. She told Amy about a lady in Mong Kok. Mrs Lee was an astrologer and an expert in paranormal activity. On her day off, Amy told Simon that she was going to church. She took the MTR with Cynthia then battled their way through the crowds. Climbing the narrow broken stairs Cynthia pushed aside a beaded curtain and they entered a dingy room with not much but a round table and a few rickety chairs in it.

Cynthia rang the little golden bell that was by a jug of water and they seated themselves around the table. Mrs Lee entered, gasped and then shrieked, pointing at Amy, and ranted in Cantonese.

'What is she saying Cynthia? I don't understand.'

Cynthia waved her hands up and down. 'Let me listen.'

Mrs Lee finally stopped and sank into the chair opposite them, her energy depleted and her pale face further withdrawn.

'She says there is evil around you,' said Cynthia. 'You must get away. That is what she keeps repeating.'

Mrs Lee asked for Amy's address. When Cynthia gave it to her she shook her head and muttered something under her breath. She brought out a slipper and a feather and beat them on the table. She then held onto Amy's hand and mumbled for a long time, her eyes oscillating up and down. Finally when she let go she spoke to Cynthia. Cynthia put some money into Mrs Lee's palm and then pulled Amy out of the room.

'What, what is it?' Amy asked. 'Tell me.'

'You are in grave danger,' replied Cynthia, hanging onto the banister of the stairs. 'Your husband's family are geong-si. They are like zombies; corpses that hop around and kill living beings to absorb their yang energy. You must get out.'

Amy started trembling. She sat on the cold concrete step leading to the bustling street. Cynthia sat beside her and held her. 'It's all right. I'll help you.'

They walked back towards the MTR in silence. Then Cynthia pointed to Langham Place where they found a Starbucks and sat down with a coffee.

'We must have a plan,' said Cynthia. 'Mrs Lee said that as long as you get out of the country and are oceans apart, they cannot harm you anymore. You must get back to your family in England. I am leaving in a week. We could go together.'

'A week is a long time,' sobbed Amy.

'I know,' said Cynthia, 'but you need time to escape without arousing suspicion.'

Amy did not feel any better, but Cynthia was right. That evening, as she walked through the door, her body was flung across the room and she hung there, glued to the wall, halfway up. She heard cackling. Tears streamed down her face as she tried to unpin herself from the brick panel. Simon entered the room and came towards her, his eyes demonic red. He pulled her down so that her feet touched the cold floor and brought his face closer to hers. The red eyeballs exploded and large drops of blood oozed down his face. Amy screamed and closed her eyes. Then silence. Slowly she opened them. She had screamed. Why hadn't anyone heard her? His mouth was open and his face came closer to hers. He had a wicked smile. Amy shut her eyes again and stopped breathing. She was in Simon's grasp. She tried to squirm her way out but he held her tight.

'Trying to play hard to get, are you?' he whispered through her hair. Before she could answer he put his lips on hers and kissed her till she could breathe no more. His hands wandered up her skirt and she was unable to move. The doorbell rang. Simon grunted, looked towards the door and reluctantly let go of her. Amy ran upstairs. She put her passport, her wallet and a few precious belongings in her handbag and locked it away. She knew that they would not let her leave just then. She would have to choose the right moment.

The next few nights there was knocking on doors, the blender turning itself on in the kitchen, groaning from the empty bathroom. Simon turned from his normal self to the monster with bulging red eyes more often than ever and when his mother visited, Amy felt physically ill not knowing what they would do next. She knew now that geong-si were relentless and deadly. The day her mother-in-law spat at her she knew she had to escape. She had overheard mother and son talking about a 'brew' that evening that would rejuvenate them. Amy kept her handbag under the till behind the ice buckets. She served the customers, hoping this would be the last time. She had just poured out the second glass of wine to a well-groomed man when she saw Simon walk towards the dining room. The silver ice buckets clanged as she clumsily reached for the handles of her handbag. With it in hand she raced out of the bar, running down a steep hill, balancing on the uneven concrete steps that led to the main road. When she was convinced that she had blended into the crowd, she stuck her hand out to hail down a red taxi.

'Airport please,' she gasped.

For a good ten minutes she kept glancing back, to see if anyone was following her. The radio was on full blast in Cantonese, but she was not about to complain. At least she was on time. She texted Cynthia – *40 minutes*. Then she sighed and sank into the old smelly seat of the taxi and took comfort in the fact that she was safe. The tall buildings grew smaller, like her deep rooted troubles as she left the city behind. They went past the shipping containers loading and unloading goods. She felt no melancholy leaving. The sooner she got away, the better. The taxi driver looked at her through the mirror, smirking with a look of desire she had seen only too often in some unsavoury customers who came to the bar. Amy looked away and when she did he started singing loudly. She was uncomfortable but if she got out now, where in the world would she find another taxi? Gritting her teeth she mumbled a prayer and kept her head down and her eyes on her phone.

The screen on her iPhone flashed. *We know where you are!* Amy jumped. The message was anonymous. She dived into her handbag and produced a 500-dollar note and waved it to the driver. 'Faster please, faster,' she said.

The driver grabbed the money and winked at her and then put his foot down. Amy clutched her bag ready to dive out as soon as they arrived at the airport. She glanced at her phone from time to time in case there was another message.

She focused on thinking happy thoughts. That had been her mantra all her life. If ever a negative thought came to your mind, replace it with a happy one. She pictured the apple tree in her parents' garden, and collecting the apples that had fallen to bake a pie. She imagined her mother coming to the patio with lemonade and snacks just in time for when her father arrived from work. The picnic mat under the shade of the birch trees that swayed in the gentle breeze with Roxy, her puppy, jumping on and off it. The sound of laughter as her sisters pulled the gift her father had brought home and fought over it. All the time she imagined these happy thoughts her eyes were shut tight and a slight smile crept over her face.

When she opened her eyes she gasped. Everything around her had turned grey. The water, the lights on the building, the once colourful bollards of the toll station, everything. Grey, lifeless, and without a soul around. She panicked. Her phone buzzed and she fumbled to look at the message. *You cannot get away.*

The taxi driver was paying at the toll station. Amy tried to open her window and when it did not budge she shouted for the driver's attention. He ignored her.

'Help, help,' she screamed, at the lady in the toll booth, both her hands on the window glass trying to claw it down.

Soho

Nobody heard her and nobody paid attention. She leaned forward and pushed her palm on the taxi driver's shoulders. She looked at the mirror, the one he had been glaring at her throughout the journey to get a glimpse of his face, to get his attention. There was no reflection in the mirror. The mirror was a dark shade of grey like a murky pool of ink, swaying from side to side. The car was moving at speed. Amy tried to open the door. She had to escape. She was locked in. She pushed and she scratched at the glass and she screamed and she cried but the car sped on. She saw a sign that told her she was one kilometre from the airport. Five more minutes she told herself and I will be with Cynthia.

Then the car stopped. It stopped in the middle of nowhere. The road was grey, as was the vegetation on the hills. The sea was menacing, rough and the waves rising up and down with the promise to destroy everything in their way. It doesn't matter thought Amy. All I need to do is get out. I will walk to the airport if I have to.

She could not get the doors to open. She yelled and cried to get the attention of the driver. Slowly he turned around. Amy's nails dug into the old worn out seat and she screamed. The lecherous face of the driver was the same but his eyes were red marbles. The driver flicked his hair and leaned towards Amy. He started to climb onto the back seat. Amy recoiled and tried to move away. He grabbed her with one arm and slid his other hand up her thigh and whispered.

'You're not going anywhere. You are one of us.' He lifted her skirt until her flat belly was exposed. Amy squirmed. She knew what was coming next as she felt the garlic smelling breath on her skin.

'Look,' he whispered again, playing with her hair. His wet lips touched hers. 'I'm not lying. You are geong-si. It is growing in you.'

Amy looked down as the foul taxi driver caressed her exposed midriff. Nothing could have prepared her for what she saw. There between his stubby fingers and dirty finger nails, on her milky pale flesh flashed two red lights. On and off, on and off.

The Alpha

Véronique K Jonassen

Sunday, Taikoo Shing District, two p.m.

Ana was standing by the living room window. Outside, grey clouds were hovering over the city, silently brushing the top of busy sky-scrapers. The pavement on the street below was still wet from the previous rain and joyful children were jumping around the field of puddles surrounding them from all sides. Taxis were honking, buses were racing: everything as usual on a summer day in Hong Kong.

Ana noticed a tiny raindrop dangling in the wind on the top edge of the window. She started to count. She had kept the habit of counting everything from childhood. It did not matter how sig-nificant it was: the steps she walked every morning from the subway station to the office, the seconds between lightning and thunder, or the number of beeps before the doors of an MTR carriage closed – exactly twenty, same for each station. Now, she counted how long it would take for this drop to capitulate, let the wind crush it and break it into pieces.

'Are you ready?' Sam's joyful voice echoed behind her. Ana smiled, keeping her eyes on the drop.

She was always amazed at how positive Sam could be. Far from their hometown in Paris, he was a rock to her, and she knew how lucky she was to have him. He had supported her when she was struggling to find a job in this unknown city at the other side of the planet. He never doubted her.

'Are you sure you want to go hiking?' she answered softly.

The clouds were becoming darker and were circling in the sky like predators before a hunt.

'It will be okay,' Sam's voice was confident. He put his hands on her shoulders and slid a strand of her long blond hair behind her ear.

The raindrop finally broke. *Seventeen seconds.* For a moment, Ana thought she heard it scream.

Sunday, Tai Tam Country Park, three-thirty p.m.
Ana was breathing heavily as she counted the steps in her head. They had reached the 347th and last step of the staircase linking the city to the entrance of the Tai Tam Country Park. They were now exactly halfway to the top of the mountain and one hour and fifty minutes away from their final destination on the other side of the island.

Sam and Ana had both fallen in love with this hike. The open areas along the side of the trail could offer unobstructed, breath-taking views over the city, the Victoria Harbour, all the way to the nine mountains of Kowloon and the outlying islands. Today, however, the clouds made a lid covering the city and a thick fog was rising, so Ana and Sam couldn't see much.

A raindrop hit Ana's forehead. The clouds had taken a deep, dark-blue tint, resembling a pack of panthers preparing for attack. The wind, which had been gentle for the past hour, strengthened, prompting Ana and Sam to increase their pace. A sharp bolt of lightning broke the sky in two, instantly followed by roaring thunder. Ana jumped. Sam swiftly took her hand and led her back down the trail. 'Hurry!' He dragged her along the path.

The panthers showed their claws, the clouds opened the tap and the rain poured on Ana and Sam's heads.

They raced downhill back to the entrance of the park, but the trail was unrecognisable. The path had narrowed and knobby fingers of branches reached over their heads, scratching their faces and arms like barbed wire. Ana had the strange thought that they must look like Hansel and Gretel lost in the woods. The clouds were approaching and spread slowly on the trail. In a few minutes, the rain had created streams of water over the ground.

Blinded by the rain, Ana did not see the tree root sticking out of the earth. She tripped on it and lost her balance. Her hand slipped out of Sam's grip and she fell heavily in the mud. She tried to get back on her feet, but the ground was too slippery. Sam went to her, grabbed her arms firmly and was about to pull her back up when Ana caught sight of something behind the trees to the right of the trail.

'Wait!' she exclaimed. Sam looked at her, surprised. Her clothes were covered in dirt and mud was stuck in her hair and on her face.

Ana looked more attentively between the trees and saw a small glittering object about three metres from the trail. It was shining enough to be visible in the rain and the dark.

'Let's go!' Sam pulled her back to her feet. Ana could barely hear him above the downpour. She knew they should run back home but she was too intrigued by this shiny object.

'Look!' She pointed to the trees. 'Behind the bushes!'

'I don't see anything,' Sam looked at her, disconcerted.

Both shivered at an unexpected gust of wind. Ana headed for the bushes, crossed over dead branches and squeezed between the trees. The wet tree leaves stuck in her hair. Thunder roared like a raging tiger.

'What are you doing?' Sam shouted, with panic mounting in his voice.

Ana staggered on the uneven ground. When she reached a taller tree a few metres away from the trail, she saw a small key swinging on a low branch. It was attached to a red key chain, shaped in the form of three capital italic letters, *TKP*.

'What's going on?' Sam caught up with her, confused.

Ana looked at Sam and froze, astonished. Right next to him, behind the tree and hidden from the trail, was a shelter.

'Nice!' Sam exclaimed when he turned his head and saw the shelter. 'How did you see that from so far away?' he asked, laughing and hurrying to take cover.

The shelter was small, made out of black wood, only four poles and a roof, but spacious enough to protect them from the rain. There was a bench to sit on and a small shrine in the corner with an incense holder in front of it.

Ana and Sam rested on the bench. The rain was pouring. Sam took off his backpack and pulled out a water bottle and sandwiches.

Relieved to be protected from the storm, Ana forgot about the key. She drank, grabbed a sandwich and both ate eagerly. As Ana enjoyed her food, she didn't notice that she hit the branch behind her holding the glittering key. It was invisible now in the shadow of the shelter. The key moved with a tremor and slowly slid down along the branch and fell into Ana's open bag.

When the rain finally died down, Ana and Sam left their refuge. Night had fallen. They hiked the rest of the trail in the dark, helped only by the light of their phones. They got home exhausted, scratched all over and covered in mud, at nearly midnight.

Monday, MTR Island line, eight a.m.
The familiar beeps of the MTR doors closing sounded like sweet music in Ana's ears. The train compartment was busy. Passengers in office clothes were doing their best to ignore each other, hiding behind their books and their phones. Standing in the middle of the compartment, Ana was struggling to keep her sleepy eyes open, still recovering from the exhausting hike the previous day.

Between two stations, the train suddenly braked and people bumped into each other. An elegant older woman with long grey hair in a ponytail fell into Ana, pulling her out of her daydreams. Ana gently helped her up. The older woman smiled and her surprisingly bright and lively brown eyes looked intensely at Ana. Ana smiled back and wondered where she might have seen her before.

At North Point station, the train became crowded. A tall man, at least two heads taller than the other passengers, entered the carriage. He stood straight about two metres away from Ana, and faced the other side of the compartment. When the train started again, he slowly turned around facing her. An icy electric current spread down Ana's spine. The face of the man was . . . melting. Large pieces of skin and flesh were sliding off his cheeks and hanging on the side of his neck. Ana could see the bone of his left jaw and his back teeth sticking out. His forehead was rotten, with large black holes above his eyebrows and scars deep enough to put a finger in. The remainder of his dark hair was dusty with pieces of earth in them as if he had crawled out of a grave.

The man's eyes met hers and she instantly jerked, praying he did not see her.

No one else seemed to have noticed him. The other passengers were calm and kept staring at their phones. Ana closed her eyes and tried to slow down her heart. This couldn't be real. Maybe lack of sleep was the reason and she was hallucinating.

The train slowed. They were reaching Fortress Hill station. Ana raised her head. The tall man was still looking at her with his protruding eyeballs. The train stopped. Stunned, Ana looked at passengers moving in and out of the carriage as usual. The tall man began to move slowly towards her. Ana was about to scream when someone grabbed her arm firmly. It was the grey-haired lady. An impressively strong grip for such a slender old woman. Ana was standing still, petrified, when the woman put her mouth to Ana's ear.

'He knows you can see him,' she whispered. The beeps indicating the doors were about to close started their ditty. Ana automatically began to count them in her head. The man was approaching. *Four beeps.* The older woman looked at Ana. Her eyes, previously brown, turned bright blue. *Eight beeps.*

'Run!' She shouted.

The other passengers jumped with surprise. *Twelve beeps.*

A second to react and then an adrenaline rush. Ana shoved the passengers in front of her just as the tall man reached out towards her. *Sixteen beeps.* She squeezed through the tight crowd and jumped out of the train as the doors closed behind her. *Twenty beeps.*

Monday, Causeway Bay District, Pure Yoga, five-fifteen p.m.
Still frightened from her morning commute, Ana took the tram to the yoga centre. It was before rush hour and she was happy that it wasn't too crowded.

The yoga centre was small, but newly renovated and luminous, exuding a sense of cosiness from the gold-brown wooden floor and the colourful sofas in the lobby. Ana felt instantly at ease. The place was empty, apart from the staff behind the counter.

The two yoga studios were located along a single corridor extending from the lobby to the changing room. Ana went to the back of the second studio, lay down her mat and sat down. Crossing her legs, she put her hands on her knees and closed her eyes. She had to relax.

She breathed deeply through her mouth and focused on the air filling her lungs. She could hear the voice of a teacher in the next room and then a second person entering the studio. She opened her eyes. A young woman from the changing room wearing a bright yellow top and blue pants crossed the studio and sat down at the very front of the room, facing Ana. Ana had not been to this studio for a while, maybe this was a new teacher.

The woman took a sip of water, then pulled up her beautiful black hair into a bun, which showed off her long and thin neck. Her hands were slim, her body lithe. Her skin was beautifully pale. She smiled when she noticed that Ana was looking at her. Ana felt her shoulders soften. She had made the right decision coming here. She looked at herself in the mirror: she looked tired and worried. A deep wrinkle had formed between her eyebrows. Definitely she would need more sleep.

Out of the corner of her eye, Ana saw in the mirror the reflection of the new teacher who was still working on her hair. Ana blanched. The image in the mirror was nothing like the beautiful woman sitting in front of her. The eyes were bright red, with deep dark circles underlining them. While her skin was still shimmering white, blood drooled from the corners of her mouth and down her jaw, neck and chest. Her bright yellow top was covered with red spots. She passed her tongue over her mouth and Ana saw two very long white canines.

Ana had the feeling that the ground was shaking. She stood up quickly and hurried out of the studio keeping her eyes to the ground while the teacher calmly watched her leave.

Ana ran to the changing room and rushed into an empty toilet to throw up. The walls around her were shrinking, but Ana forbade herself to faint. She had to get out of there as fast as possible. *What was happening today?* She stumbled on the way to her locker. She was alone in the changing room, which scared her even more. Where were the other club members? Wasn't the class about to start? She grabbed her gym bag, her hands shaking.

A few seconds later, Ana carefully opened the door to check the corridor was empty and left the changing room. The sound of her pumping heart seemed to be filling the space. On her way to the lobby, she stiffened when she heard muted voices coming from the studio she had just left. A man and a woman were arguing. Ana panicked when she realised she had to walk past the studio to reach the elevators.

The voices stopped. Ana tiptoed carefully down the corridor. She could feel drops of sweat rolling down her back. When she reached the door of the studio, the voices rose again. It was the same deep voice she had heard from the neighbouring studio. The door was slightly open and Ana could see the woman with the yellow top moving her arms nervously in front of a man in his forties. The man had tanned skin and what looked like waves of black and dark grey threads floated around him, circling his chest and arms like snakes. Ana's throat tightened.

In her hurry, she didn't notice her bag was open, or that the key was sticking out of it.

'I saw it! I'm telling you!' The woman was waving her arms if front of her. Her face seemed normal now that Ana could see it directly.

The man shook his head. 'Are you sure?' His tone was so deep it reverberated around the entire room.

'She has the key!' The woman's face was red with rage and a vein was showing on her forehead.

'Impossible!' The man paused, but he sounded worried.

The woman jabbed her finger towards him.

'I don't know how, but I'm telling you she has it. It was the key!'

Ana leaned against the wall. Her hands were wet with sweat. She had to leave this place as fast as possible, but her legs were paralysed and she did not dare walk past the door. Ana tightened her grip on her gym bag, debating what to do, when she noticed something below her shimmering in the dim light of the corridor. The key she had found in the forest was sticking out of the front pocket. Ana stopped breathing.

'And she saw me! She's a threat! To us all!' shouted the woman.

Terrified, Ana peeked through the opening in the door. Her mouth became dry.

The man was pacing the wooden floor with heavy steps and pinching his fingers to his chin. The black threads around his arms were sliding up and down, circling his wrists and elbows two centimetres from his skin. He stopped abruptly.

'She shouldn't be able to see us, even with the key,' said the man. 'There must be something else.' His voice was even deeper than before. He paused.

'Maybe she's a witch . . . or . . . maybe she's an Alpha.'

The woman shrieked. Her whole body shivered.

'We killed the last Alpha more than fifty years ago!'

The man cleared his throat. 'Whatever she is, we need the key back. We've worked too hard to live quietly in this city. Invisibility is all we have.'

The woman clapped her hands in excitement. Ana was feeling dizzy.

'So for now, we need the key,' the man added. 'Without it, she's harmless.'

The woman stamped her foot.

'*Do not kill her,* you hear me?' the man's voice was so deep it sent waves around the room that made the walls tremble.

A ding as the elevator arrived.

Ana awoke from her trance. She had to get out of here. This was a standard elevator: eight seconds until the doors closed. She was about twenty metres away. If she ran fast, she could make it.

She grabbed her bag tight and sprinted down the corridor. At the same moment, the woman opened the door of the studio. Ana raced past. *Two seconds.* The woman gave chase and with incredible speed jumped in the air and tackled Ana to the floor. *Four seconds.* In the fall, the key flew out of the bag and landed right in front of Ana's hands. As a reflex, Ana grabbed it. The woman rushed at Ana's bag that had fallen at her feet. *Six seconds.* While she was searching through the bag, Ana crawled the last few metres of the corridor. In a desperate gesture, she extended her hand towards the elevator. *Eight seconds.* The doors closed, hit Ana's hand and re-opened.

While Ana pulled herself into the elevator, she heard the heavy, measured steps of the man down the corridor. Her lower lip was bleeding heavily, blood dripping onto the floor. She must have cut it in the fall. The woman was ripping Ana's bag into pieces and then stopped, her nostrils flaring. With her eyes shining red and locked on Ana's face, she jumped towards Ana, her open mouth showing those oversized canines. Ana clenched her hands and closed her eyes, waiting for the inevitable. Suddenly, the key trembled, and a dazzle spread through Ana's fingers. The vibration became so huge that Ana struggled to hold it and opened her fist. A ray of light projected out of the key and hit the woman in the air, throwing her back down the corridor. She hit the wall before falling at the man's feet.

Ana was in shock. The woman was lying on the floor, motionless. Ana looked at the man standing in front of her. She crawled to the back of the elevator, fearing another attack. Instead, he slowly tilted his head forward, in what looked like a bow.

The elevator doors closed.

Monday, Taikoo Shing, five-forty p.m.
When the doors reopened on the ground floor, Ana rushed out of the elevator and ran out into the street. Times Square area was crowded and she felt disoriented for a moment as she got pushed from all sides by pedestrians. She needed to leave the area as fast as possible. She crossed the street and headed north, walking fast and looking behind her regularly, praying that the two monsters were not following her. When she reached Hennessy Road, she jumped into a tram.

She found an empty seat and took a breath. Her heart was pounding in her chest and her forehead was covered with sweat. She looked around. The tram was busy with passengers bringing back groceries from the nearby market.

Ana realised she was still holding the key in her hand. She could still feel the heat from the light piercing through her fingers. That key had saved her life. She discreetly opened her hand to look at it. She had clenched her fist so hard that it had left a mark and she could read the letter 'P' from the keychain engraved in her palm. Ana observed the keychain carefully. 'TKP'. What could that mean?

The tram shook and stopped. A few people got in. A young man sitting in front of Ana stood up and gave his seat to an older woman that Ana could only see from behind. Long and thick grey hair in a ponytail. The key suddenly lit up. Ana was startled and dropped the key which hit the floor. She quickly picked it up.

'Hi Ana,' said the older woman in front of her. She slowly turned around to face her.

Ana froze as she recognised the woman from the MTR that morning.

'How do you know my name?' she asked with a shaky voice. The tram had started and Ana felt like a mouse caught in a trap as she realised she couldn't get out of it and run away.

'I see you have the key,' the older woman added, ignoring Ana's question and looking at her hand. 'You have to take great care of it.' Her lively brown eyes smiled at Ana who was staying on guard.

'Don't be afraid of me,' she added softly. 'I am here to help you.'

'Who are you?'

'I have known you since you were a child, Ana.' Her narrow shoulders moved up and down as she was speaking. 'But you couldn't see me before. And I couldn't approach you before you were awake.'

'What do you mean?' Ana asked, confused.

The key vibrated softly and sent sparks of light around. Ana hastily closed her fist.

'See, the key is moving. It's celebrating,' the older woman laughed. 'It waited for you for a long time. We all did.'

Ana felt dizzy. 'I don't understand.'

'That's why I am here, to guide you.' Ana felt as if she had lost all strength to fight. She had no choice but to trust this woman.

'You are an Alpha, Ana. It means you have the ability to see.'

Ana, bewildered, looked at the older woman's golden brown eyes.

'There are many magical and some also evil creatures,' she continued. 'They are invisible to the human eye, but not to Alphas. Only you can see beyond the spell.'

'You can see them too, are you an Alpha?' Ana asked carefully.

'I was, a long time ago,' the woman's voice took a sad tone. 'Now my role is different.'

The tram slowed and stopped. Both remained silent as passengers exited.

'Why are those creatures attacking me?' Ana asked nervously as the tram started.

'You are a threat because you have the power to destroy them.'

'I don't have any power!' Ana replied astonished.

'You don't know it yet,' the older woman smiled. 'With the help of the key, you can do more than any other Alpha before you.'

'There are others like me?'

The face of the older woman became dark. 'A long time ago, there were many like you. But the creatures killed them all. At least we thought.' She looked at Ana intensely. 'I don't know how the key found you, or what brought you to wake up, but you are our only hope.'

The train was reaching the last station.

'What is TKP?' Ana asked urgently.

The woman stood up. 'I will tell you everything you want to know. But for now you need to rest.'

She exited the tram, Ana following her.

'Go home,' the woman said with a confident voice. 'I will make sure they don't find where you live. You will be safe.'

Ana watched the woman walk down the street and disappear at a corner. Without realising it, the tram had brought her right in front of her apartment. She looked up at the window and saw the living room light was on, indicating that Sam was back from work. Ana was relieved, but she couldn't tell him what happened, at least not now.

She took a deep breath, put the key in her trouser pocket, and walked home.

Look Twice Down Ladder Street

Peter Humphreys

D ARKNESS CLOSES IN *and the bright lights of the party recede into nothingness. A routine walk home. All downhill from here. The blank faces of nocturnal apartment blocks. Souls of discretion. Getting steeper. Two streetlights out of action. Occasional pools of orange light letting roaches perform tap-dances. One step at a time. She tries to be alone with her thoughts. You're being watched. Nonsense. Pull yourself together. This is Hong Kong. Man up. But the dizzy feeling returns. She stops for a breather. A fog coming in off the harbour. Reclaiming the city. She sees the exposed roots of a stone wall tree fused to the brickwork like arthritic fingers. She reaches for them. They recede. No good. Must get home. She ups her pace. A cough. Not far behind her. A cough? Fuck off? Not welcome here? The alcohol toys with her emotions. She starts to run. She falls. The end.*

Inspector Robert Chan dropped to his haunches, exhausted, having picked up an unexpected amount of speed on his descent down Ladder Street. Hollywood Road was lined with police cars. Small groups of officers in sky-blue, short-sleeved shirts loitered beside them. Chan's reputation as a laid-back 'uncle' meant one or two faces felt free to express amusement at his condition.

'Kids,' he muttered. 'I'd like to see them do it any quicker.'

Chan hauled himself up and scanned Hollywood Road through the drizzle. This was the side of Sheung Wan that the rich were drawn to: smart antique shops with signs requesting 'No Photo' and 'Ring bell for entry' beside Visa logos and long-winded testimonies to the authenticity of imported Chinese artefacts. The cars parked beside the police vehicles were Jaguars and Porsches, though Bentleys and Ferraris were not uncommon here.

One level below, down another steep stone staircase, were the market stalls and junk shops of Lascar Row, each boasting their own set of profitable keepsakes; these designed for the scores of frugal backpackers who explored the area around Ladder Street like giant grazing tortoises. Here there was Chairman Mao memorabilia, opium pipes, and photos of the old, slightly-less-crowded Hong Kong. Maybe even find a bargain antique of the future – a cracked Bakelite telephone or finger-worn adding machine.

Clunk-click. Clunk-click.

Chan returned to the body. A photographer was circling the woman like a demented crab, taking shots from every conceivable angle. Pausing from his work, he leaned across to tug the victim's skirt over tanned thighs, as if to preserve some modesty. For goodness sake! When a woman dyes her hair that colour, vanilla ice cream, and wears an outfit made almost entirely of gauze, it's not because she feels ashamed of her body. At least not in any superficial way.

'Do not touch her again,' he instructed the youthful snapper, who nodded without looking up.

He could understand the fascination. While the discovery of a body relieved of its soul, sad and broken on a Hong Kong street, was an almost daily occurrence for his squad, a white female body such as this was rare indeed. So where were the mourners? One level up an old man was fishing drinks cans from a rubbish bin with his chicken-bone arms. He paused to cough impressively and the noise merged with Chan's ringtone: Stravinsky's *Adoration of the Earth*.

'Chan speaking.'

'Accident?'

It was his boss, Superintendent Kenneth Wong.

'Sorry?'

'The press want to know.'

'The press?' Chan tried to stay patient. 'Since when did we worry about the press?'

'We have to prove we have nothing to hide. Before they uncover it. It's the new openness.'

'You'll have to give me a bit longer, sir. Forensics aren't even here yet.'

'Call me as soon as you know anything.'

Would there be as much fuss if he were investigating the death of a Filipina helper who'd fallen while cleaning her employer's outside windows? Or a construction worker who'd tumbled from his bamboo scaffolding, midway through a thankless task?

'What do you mean,' Mimi asked, '"she looked like that kind of girl"?'

They were sat in the cramped living room of their two-bed apartment on Flower Market Street, across the water from where the body of Carole Dixon had been identified late that afternoon.

'You know – the big hair, the tall shoes, the tiny outfit.'

'And underneath all that, did she still look like that kind of girl? I suppose you went to the morgue to give her a final once over?'

'Mimi. . . .' Chan pleaded.

All he wanted was to be left in peace to eat his noodles and watch TV. It had been a long day, much of it taken up with the unfortunate Miss Dixon. When a boyfriend had been located, he'd been rude and aggressive, and exceptionally unhelpful concerning the victim's final movements. A party, they'd been at a party. And by all accounts he'd gone home with someone else. What a life they led up there in Soho!

Just as Mimi calmed down, and seconds before his noodles became irreversibly congealed, the house phone shrilled. There was no question of ignoring it. If it wasn't police business it might be one of their daughters calling from England, whatever the time difference.

'He's right here,' said Mimi.

Chan swallowed a last edible noodle. It was the new pathologist, Wai.

'You're sure?'

'Yes,' Wai repeated. 'Broken neck. No other marks on her body. No signs of struggle.'

'A clean break.'

'Should I call Superintendent Wong?'

Chan looked at his watch.

'It's late. Why not let him sweat on it tonight – call him first thing in the morning?'

'Okay. Will do.'

'Goodnight then.'

Mimi looked at him long and hard.

'What?'

'You'd better start being nicer to that boss of yours.'

'Or what?'

'Manners cost nothing – isn't that what you're always telling me?'

'If manners cost nothing, that man would still avoid placing them in his shopping basket.'

'Like Kenneth Wong does his own shopping!'

A fortnight later Chan was in Wong's office studying a lengthy article in the *South China Morning Post*. It had been prompted by the verdict of accidental death delivered on the Carole Dixon case the day before. Although the findings of the coroner, assisted by Wai's good work, were straightforward, it hadn't kept the story off the front page.

'Escalators,' said the superintendent.

'Excuse me?'

Chan was finding it hard to remove his eyes from the smiling blond girl. Sometimes in syndicated photographs victims appeared to know their time was up. More often they seemed to be without a care in the world.

'Planning Department are requesting permission to install escalators on Ladder Street. About time I'd say.'

'You don't think the history of the area warrants preservation?'

'Do you have any idea, Chan, what our ancestors had to do in that near-vertical neighbourhood – back in the old days?'

'A bit of shifting?'

'Up and down they went, heaving ungrateful foreigners from pillar to post on cushioned chairs. Why should we keep the stones where they spilled blood?'

'To remind us that somebody is always carrying someone else around in this world?'

He didn't care what Mimi said – he found it impossible to be anything more than civil to this man.

'Your daughters both study in England, don't they?'

'Correct.'

'Well . . . don't let them forget their roots.'

'I won't. Now if you'll excuse me. . . .'

Case closed. With any luck he wouldn't see his boss again until the New Year's banquet.

Falling. Falling. A beautiful starry night. She hadn't noticed before. Twisting in flight she thought she saw a pair of eyes. Watching her. From the heavens or the Earth? The Earth. Here on Earth. Falling back down to earth. Where it all began. Where everything must end.

The thick, blue-grey smoke of a hundred incense sticks poured out of the red and green glazed chimneys of Man Mo Temple on Hollywood Road. Inside, beside a shrine to the god of literature, worshippers lit stick after stick in order to gain a blessing upon their great, un-published novel, or on the masterpieces penned by their grandchildren to snag stars for their high school diplomas. Outside the temple, a small but curious crowd had gathered.

'Back, please,' Chan urged, as he passed through the police cordon.

The latest fatality appeared to have tumbled down the same section of Ladder Street but hadn't rolled as far forward as Carole. Hence they found themselves at an intersection with the inoffensive-looking Square Street. The photographer nodded; he was done. Chan stooped and gently pulled back a sheet, pattered with oversized daisies, which had been placed over the victim's upper body.

He had been expecting a second expired gweilo, but this woman, while around the same age as Carole, was not so far from home. Her eyes were closed, her frown fixed, but that couldn't hide her soft facial features. Spears of long, freshly-snipped hair protruded 360 degrees about her fractured skull. Chan checked himself before reluctantly concluding that, like Carole, she was beautiful.

'What do you think?' he asked, sensing Constable Ho's minty breath at his shoulder.

'Highways Department maintenance,' Ho concluded. 'Someone's for the high jump.'

'This isn't about the Highways Department. There's nothing wrong with Ladder Street. I ran down it after we found Miss Dixon.'

'You . . .' Ho looked up to where wide, roughly-hewn steps were shaded by unkempt foliage, 'ran all the way down?'

'From Caine Road. What of it? Stare at me like that for much longer and I'll make you do the same.'

Chan looked at the victim's shoes. Like Carole, she'd been wearing heels, but not a type likely to cause anyone but a drunken incompetent to fall.

'And your thoughts, Ling?'

'A handsome woman, expensively dressed,' Constable Ling replied.

'Well said.' Chan was impressed with her ability to objectify the corpse, a skill he'd struggled with for years.

'What do you want us to do, sir?' an officer enquired from the foot of Square Street.

'Keep this street sealed off to the top. I want forensics to study exactly where this unfortunate person fell to and from.'

'Yes, sir.'

'Come on then.'

The two constables followed Chan up the shallow gradient of Square Street. Sprinkled with graffiti and patrolled by stroppy cats, it seemed a world away from Hollywood Road. Most of the shops were shuttered up; Chan would ask his officers to seek witnesses from the pastel and grey residential blocks later. About to turn back, Chan noticed a brown paper bag outside one of the shops. They went over.

'A McDonald's meal,' Ho announced.

'Thank you Constable, I'm familiar with the brand. I'm just wondering why anyone would leave an uneaten takeaway meal outside a shut-up shop.'

'Maybe they thought better of it?' Ling suggested.

'Hmm.'

They left the abandoned food and found Wai completing his initial examination.

'Anything you can tell me immediately, Wai?'

Wai removed his facemask and latex gloves. He had longish hair that he kept scrupulously clean.

'Nothing. Just impact marks on her knees. And then her skull – crushed.'

'Could she have been attacked before falling?'

'It's possible. But to me it looks like one impact, to the side of the head, on landing.'

'And no sign she was pushed?'

'If she was already off-balance, it wouldn't have taken much.'

Another drinker? Just as Chan was beginning to convince himself that the residents of this district must live in a permanent state of inebriation, he spotted a perfectly sober face in the crowd below them. The face was topped with a buttery fringe. The eyes were swimming-pool blue. Chan recognised Carole's boyfriend, Billy Des Faux.

'Mr Des Faux? Billy Des Faux? I'd like a word please.'

The handsome figure cannonballed away from the circus of activity. The street was clogged but that didn't matter to the escape artist; Chan saw Des Faux sully his white jeans sliding across the bonnet of a taxi before racing past a 7-Eleven towards the myriad alleyways of Soho.

'After him,' Chan ordered Ho and Ling, then called HQ and discreetly requested backup.

Robert Chan sighed. In front of him was an old-fashioned cardboard file marked 'Yeung, Eva (Miss)'. Across the table from him sat the brooding presence of their one-and-only suspect for the murder, or manslaughter, of two young Hong Kong women. And what had they done to deserve such a fate? As far as Chan could tell, the women had been guilty only of holding this Frenchman in bafflingly high regard.

'And when am I allowed my next cigarette?' Des Faux snapped, before reverting to the defensive position he'd maintained all day – all knees and elbows.

'When you've finished answering my questions,' Chan replied.

'It is ridiculous that I cannot smoke here, on Death Row.'

Chan maintained his professional poise, if only to set an example to Constable Ho.

'This isn't Death Row. We haven't had a death in custody since the British left. Now please tell me everything you know.'

'I tell you at the time,' Des Faux huffed. 'Carole was a bit of fun. Nothing more. We saw each other every second weekend. It was no more than a. . . .'

'Fling?'

The businessman glowered.

'Tell us more about Eva Yeung.'

'I met Eva at one of her gallery launches. New Chinese artists? Something like that. What can I say? The champagne was flowing. She was all over me.'

Chan swallowed his distaste.

'And did Carole and Eva know about one another?'

'Maybe. How would I know?'

'There was never a conversation? Raised voices? Arguments?'

Billy Des Faux sighed, rubbing imaginary ash from the thigh of his shiny designer suit.

'Why trouble yourself, Inspector? I've told you I have an alibi in each case.'

The grey plastic phone sounded on the desk beside Chan. The ring pattern meant it was an internal call. No need to answer. It would be Superintendent Wong.

'Stay here,' Chan told Ho, 'and for God's sake don't ask him about the birds and the bees.'

'So, Robert, any progress?'

'Nothing new.'

Wong fumbled with his electronic cigarette.

'But you think he did it?'

'Ling interviewed his alibi, Ms Xu. They're either very well-rehearsed or Des Faux is telling the truth about being with her both nights.'

Wong sucked on his toy smoke.

'Yes, I took advantage of looking in on that one. Looks like a prostitute.'

'Ms Xu *is* a prostitute, sir. Although rather a high-class one, if you wish to make that distinction.'

Wong looked up sharply.

'Dismiss her testimony and we're home and dry. You know what these hookers are like. Drink. Drugs. Her word will never stand up in court.'

'With respect,' Chan tried to look sincere, 'the days of ignoring people in court because of their vices are long gone.'

'Oh really?'

Chan was surprised by Wong's bitterness.

'Trouble from above?' he ventured.

'Bastard-load of trouble,' Wong wiped a tissue over his face, then used it to spread muck around his incongruously fashionable glasses. 'Our friends in Beijing want the Frenchman found guilty and every-thing back to normal as soon as possible. Meanwhile the British are threatening to send in their own police if we don't sort out this mess.'

'Can they do that?'

'Six weeks ago a British citizen died. For a month we assured them it was an accident, now all of a sudden we turn round and say, 'Sorry chaps – might be murder.' What do you expect them to do?'

'Perhaps I can rephrase that,' Chan stood up. 'What do you expect *me* to do, with no evidence and a man downstairs who makes love with such stamina that we can rule him out for a total of twenty-four hours from two apparent crime scenes?'

'Something, anything,' Wong begged, but Chan made no promises before leaving the office.

'Just here, thank you,' Chan told his driver and hopped out near the Orgasmic Burger Shack, a hundred yards from Man Mo Temple.

While calm and leafy compared to his crowded corner of the territory, this area was sprouting newness by the day. Delis were clogged with European flesh while whitewashed art galleries enticed the unsuspecting with their alluring emptiness. Chan stuck to the script, asking the questions he needed to.

'Eva Yeung? Sure, I knew her. A tough woman, demanding, but she wasn't stuck up like some of the others.'

'Eva was *molto simpatico,*' an Italian art dealer told him, dabbing at his eyes with a spotted handkerchief.

'Thanks for your time.'

Unable to elicit a bad word about Eva, Chan returned to Ladder Street in search of that elusive loose step. He sweated uselessly up and down once more, wondering how many European lady-killers his daughters had already met. Only when he paused for breath did he realise he was being watched.

'Hello?'

The tiny figure wore a vest and shorts as grey as the stone bench on which he perched.

'I didn't see you there,' said Chan, approaching steadily, 'though I recognise you now.'

The old man had a dark, crispy forehead, covered with liver spots and no more than a few overlong strands of white hair to protect his sunburnt scalp. His facial features were small and delicate. Almond eyes peered out intently. A black cat skipped in front of him.

'Inspector Robert Chan, police.'

'I am . . . I am. . . .' he stuttered, dragging his legs up to his chest.

'Yes?'

'The Recycler,' said the man, in a scratchy, high-pitched voice.

Chan looked down to where Ladder Street met Square Street. A metal pushcart was piled high with neatly folded cardboard. He sat down beside the Recycler. Insects twitched in the trees above them.

'You saw them, didn't you?' Chan said, in English. 'I bet you saw both of them fall down here.'

The Recycler's eyes widened. They were red-rimmed but almost golden at their core. He stood up and started rambling in tongues, jabbing a finger through the air between them. Then he descended with stiffened panic towards his cart. Something stopped Chan from following. What good would come of hauling that desperate, shambling ghost into the station?

'Sorry to disturb you,' Chan called after him.

On the way to his ride Chan glanced down Square Street. This time, instead of a takeaway meal, he saw a mocked-up carton of cigarettes beside the same makeshift shrine. The shutters now up, the shop revealed itself to be a funeral directors. Long, cigar-shaped coffins were piled up inside, finished with a caramel coating – like cinema popcorn. Reluctantly, he recalled what an estate agent had whispered to him earlier that afternoon. Rents on Square Street were supernaturally low because oldies, like him, insisted it led to no less than the Gates of Hell. Lucky he wasn't superstitious.

When Constable Ling was told to hurry to a fire in a Sheung Wan backstreet, she considered making her excuses. What more could it be than a smouldering rubbish bin or faulty gas pipe? Arriving at the scene, she couldn't have been more surprised.

'Is he dead?' she asked one of the fire crew.

'No, but he had a good go. Covered himself with lighter fluid. If he'd been wearing more than rags he'd be finished.'

The Recycler was being helped to his feet, a blanket placed around his upper body. Smoke rose from his shoulders. He yelped with pain as he was helped towards the ambulance. Yet on seeing Ling he stopped and offered her a crooked smile.

'I did it,' he shouted. 'I did it!'

Ling was shocked.

'Did what?'

'Down they went. Plop-plop. Bang-bang. Crack-crack. Blondie and darkie. Double-dead. As dead as dead can be.'

He was speaking in riddles then lapsing into a dialect Ling couldn't understand. But despite his distress it was clear he knew something. As the ambulance door closed, Ling rang Chan.

'Inspector?'

'Ling?'

'We have another suspect.'

'I hear you're ready to confess?' said Chan, dismissing the bored officer from his bedside vigil.

The hospital was brightly lit but the Recycler's eyes were heavy, like an opium addict's.

'Share my noodles?'

The patient managed a weak smile. He was wearing striped pyjamas. Perhaps all this newfound luxury was making him sleepy.

'I know you killed those women. My colleague told me. My question is not *why* you did it – for we each have our reasons – but *how?*'

An ominous glow entered the Recycler's yellow-brown eyes.

'In your own time,' said Chan.

'I did it,' the Recycler hissed.

'Yes, I know. But how?'

'With my mind.'

'With your. . . ?'

The Recycler started to laugh.

'A powerful thing, the mind – even one as old as mine. Plop-plop. Bang-bang. Crack-crack. . . .'

'Yes, I know that part. Tell me one more thing. Who else was around when you caused these ladies to tumble to their deaths? You can't have been completely alone?'

'Yes, yes,' the killer snapped. 'The world sleeps long. These women never sleep and then . . . forever.'

The inspector frowned.

'And if I were to release you now?'

'Back to work. Back to work. Back to work.'

'I see,' Chan nodded, sensing his own meagre light bulb flickering into life.

Chan left the nephew's home on Lok Ku Road with his suspicions confirmed. The Recycler had lost his mind a week after being retired from the family business. Rather than report this to Wong immediately, he decided to visit the alleyway where Constable Ling had found their suspect. Avoiding the temptation offered by a minimalist gallery's icy air-conditioning, Chan chose to stoop under the snaggy awnings of a red and green market stall opposite. A bald, bare-chested man with round spectacles was hunched under a lamp, tapping a nail into a pair of cheap-looking office shoes.

'See the fire down here last week?'

'Missed the fire. Saw your lot. Almost lost my stock thanks to their hosepipes. Hope they're more accurate with their pistols.'

'Nice place you have here,' Chan told him, looking along rows of blocky, pea-coloured drawers, all of which could have done with a repaint.

'Man all right is he?'

'He'll live,' said Chan, 'poor chap. In any case, can I ask which stock you'd have been claiming on the insurance? No offence, but I've seen more promising. . . .'

Quick as a flash the cobbler opened a drawer, producing a pair of patent leather shoes in deep maroon. Chan was so taken aback that he laughed out loud.

'A salesman – I should have known it!'

He reconsidered the man. Middle-aged. Intelligent-looking. Good teeth. Incense burning where most would have had a lit Winston in a tinfoil ashtray.

'Best in all Hong Kong.'

'I'm sure.'

'Make you a pair, Inspector? Good price.'

Chan was about to walk away then stopped. The shoes had a beautiful, rich colouration, like a purpling sky on a clear summer's night. He thought of Mimi, bringing up the girls while he worked all hours. When had he last bought her something special?

'You make ladies' shoes too?'

'If you have the size.'

'I do.'

'A pair for each of us.'

'Perfect. May I recommend these suede half-heels for your wife?'

A canvas flap swished at the back of the stall and a heavy bag was dropped to the ground. Someone was returning from an errand, obscured by a floral curtain.

'Your own wife?'

'My business partner.' The salesman consulted his watch. 'Time to close up . . . Inspector?'

'Chan.'

'My name is Choi. See you next week when you come for the shoes.'

'We've got him this time, Chan!'

He shuddered at the memory of Wong's girlish excitement.

'We have?'

'Red-handed. Trying to leave for Paris. Must have thought we'd taken our eye off the ball. And you know the best thing?'

'He's completely innocent?'

'The media are here already, waiting for those clever-arse Brit detectives. Finally we have a result to show them – and the world!'

'Is that right?'

'Your work is done. Take a few days leave. You've earned it.'

'Almost there now, sir,' remarked Chan's driver.

'Yes, I can see.'

Half-a-dozen TV trucks were parked outside Departures. As Chan stepped out of the car he had to dodge a serious young man reporting to camera that a harder line must now be taken against foreigners who misused the privileges they were granted in Hong Kong. Chan slipped unnoticed past several more reporters before closing in on the police presence.

'Where is he?'

'You're not supposed to. . . .'

But Chan was too quick. His colleagues' eyes told him where they were keeping Des Faux – an unmarked room with a single officer posted outside, Constable Ho.

'I know he's in there, let me in.'

'Can't, sir.' Ho reddened. 'Super's orders. Case closed.'

'Been on the unarmed combat course yet?'

'No, Inspector.'

'Well I have. Stand aside please.'

Ho made the mistake of catching Chan's stare. He had done his best. Des Faux was sitting on a plastic chair smoking a cigarette.

'Up. Out,' Chan barked. 'That's right – you and the cigarette.'

'What?'

'I'm freeing you. You've wasted quite enough of our time.'

'I can leave for Paris?'

'You can go tomorrow night. First, I need a favour. Let's call it a honey trap, of sorts.'

Paris. We fell in love. Getting high on the Sacré Cœur steps at sundown. What a view. She descended into my catacombs. Didn't like what she found there. I would make it up to her. Go to Hong Kong. Make enough money for us to forget. My brother wrote me. She jumped. Or did I push her? From the Pont des Arts into the cool, dark waters of the Seine. Nothing can hurt me now. You who watch me, judge me. Fuck you. I will go home. Marry her sister.

Billy Des Faux lay motionless at the foot of Ladder Street, dead to the world, a snapped cigarette between bluish lips. A morning mist clung to the cold stone. Robert Chan teased up the collar of his overcoat and checked his watch. He signalled for the officers, some dressed as early-morning hawkers and street sweepers, to stay alert. Minutes later, when a stooped figure came scurrying up from Queen's Road, the welcoming committee flinched, but it was only the force's photographer, come to do his grisly business.

'Morning Inspector,' he mumbled, unzipping his bag.

'Morning. Blake isn't it?'

'That's right, Blake Fung.'

'Why so late, Blake?' Chan asked.

'What do you mean?' Fung was squatting by the body. 'I rushed here from. . . .'

'Because you weren't expecting this to happen?' Chan continued, 'Or because you were phoning your accomplice on the way?'

'Inspector, forgive me . . . I don't understand. . . .'

'We've no sheet to cover the body yet. You didn't think to bring one of the flowery curtains from the stall, as you did by way of a gift for the lovely Eva?'

Panicked, the youngster scanned his surroundings. Chan followed his eyes. There he was, lurking in the doorway of the funeral parlour.

'You can come out now, Mr Choi.'

Chan beckoned and Choi stood up, unfazed.

'Good morning, Inspector.'

The cobbler was holding a brown-paper parcel to his chest.

'Those for me?'

'Yes, I saw you were busy so I was waiting until. . . .'

'How considerate.'

'They might need some . . . adjustment.'

'I'm sure they'll be fine as they are.'

The mist was clearing. The cluster of street attendants was revealing itself as a phalanx of armed police officers. Ho indicated with his pistol that Choi should join the inspector, photographer and corpse.

'Just lay the package down here – slowly,' Chan indicated Des Faux's finely-tailored back.

'Wai, come and inspect these for me.'

The long-haired forensics man came forward and carefully tore the paper open, exposing two beautiful pairs of shoes. Mimi's were clean. Nothing but a few well-stitched pieces of patent leather formed into a surprisingly light, lilac summer shoe. Wai had more trouble with Chan's. The leather was excellent, black as night; but the heel seemed excessive – even for someone as mid-sized as his boss. He got out his penknife and prised open the base of one heel. Springs popped out at him. Wai recoiled. Chan stayed calm.

'Do you know what attracted Mr Des Faux here to both victims?'

Wong's limousine pulled up outside Man Mo Temple. Better late than never.

'Their grace and balance – Eva weaving her way through a packed gallery carrying two flutes of champagne, Carole dancing on a barroom table after twelve glasses of wine. Irresistible, no?'

Fung remained agitated. Choi was giving nothing away.

'It seemed incredible to me that either woman would have stumbled to their deaths. Yet neither did I believe that their lover had reason to kill them. Oscar Wilde told us "each man kills the thing he loves", yet it was clear Des Faux never loved these women enough to commit a crime of passion.'

'Inspector . . .' Wai was sitting on a step, cradling a dissected shoe, 'this is deadly.'

'In fact,' Chan continued, 'it took two minds, two motives to conspire in this plot against the young women of Sheung Wan. Mr Fung here, somewhat of a mechanical genius with springs and shutters, to engineer the shoes, and Mr Choi, artisan, to persuade the victims to buy them.'

Superintendent Wong had joined them, flustered.

'Two motives, Chan? I'd happily settle for one.'

'Ling?'

The young officer stepped forward, cleared her throat.

'The following recovered from Blake Fung's flat this morning: ninety-five photographs of Carole Dixon and Eva Yeung while alive, 563 photographs of them dead.'

'From the moment I saw Carole's body, I could see someone was rearranging the corpses – tugging at Carole's dress, sculpting Eva's hair. Playing with the bodies in a most despicable way. That was you, Mr Fung – a chronic introvert with no way of conversing with these women while alive, imposing his power in death.'

Fung looked down. Choi continued to meet Chan's gaze.

'Any comments, Mr Choi?'

'Congratulations, Inspector Chan. Your story is so neat and tidy, your loose ends wrapped up in a bow. The god of literature would be proud.'

'This is no time for compliments,' Chan insisted.

'Of my motivation I will say just this: there is only one way to change the minds of those ignorant of history and tradition, those who seek to stamp out our customs, those who ruin neighbourhoods like this with their superficial vision of the world. . . .'

'I also believe things move too fast,' said Chan. 'Fortunately my wife talks me out of homicide on a daily basis.'

Choi was duly cuffed. Ho completed his search of Fung, handing Chan a remote control handset that looked considerably simpler than the one for his home TV. Chan pressed the largest of three buttons and watched in amazement as the shoe in Wai's hands came to life, a metal rod emerging from the heel like the muscular tongue of a mollusc as it propels itself across the ocean floor. More than enough to sabotage the descent of any tipsy individual on the steep, stone stairways of Sheung Wan.

'Simple,' Chan remarked, 'and elegant.'

Choi closed his eyes. In his vision, the proposed escalators had already invaded his beloved district. Up and down the shallow, money-grabbing citizens went all day, merrily oblivious to their fate – for his friend, Fung, had found a way to simultaneously turn off the power and flatten the shiny stairways into metallic death slides; tipping the shoppers and partygoers down, down – into a hellish crush of ripped flesh and broken bones. He smiled. He was enjoying his fantasy immensely. Only upon opening his eyes did he recall that he was inside a police van being driven to the Wan Chai headquarters, through Hong Kong's original streets of sin.

Chan had dismissed the last of his officers. Only Wai remained, carefully bagging up the shoes and the remote.

'You can tell our budding actor to get up now. He's done his job admirably.'

Wai bent down next to Des Faux.

'Sir, I hate to tell you this. . . .'

'What?'

'It appears he's been dead for several hours.'

Chan buried his face in his hands.

'Do you want me to check his shoes?'

'Yes,' he managed, at last. 'Yes please.'

'Who knows,' Wai looked up with a schoolboy grin, 'maybe it was an accident this time?'

'Accident?' Chan looked to the heavens in despair. 'Didn't you hear? Tucked away on a Sheung Wan backstreet, where the devil knows your shoe size, lie the Gates of Hell.'

A casement sunders . . .

Never Look Back

Elizabeth Solomon

Kowloon – 31 May

Haya froze outside the bedroom door, nursing the mad hope that her children were alive. A pale pillar, paralysed by fear, Haya inhaled, held her breath and opened the door. Tiptoeing in, she listened for sounds of life over the hum of the air conditioner. Nothing. Cot deaths were a reality. What if the twins had passed in their sleep? What if. . . ? Sweat trickled down her jagged spine; it painted crusty semi-circles on the armpits of her ivory nightgown. She placed her palm above the nostrils of her first-born, her darling Adele. The girl's warm breath tingled on Haya's skin. Her son was drowning under a mound of blankets. She lifted the linen from around his head. Amos let out a sleepy groan. She stood between the two beds and squeezed the children's arms, as though the act of feeling their warm flesh would expel her demons. It worked. Just for a while, they were gone. Haya exhaled and floated out of the room.

4:40 a.m.: The green digits on the alarm clock glared at Haya, admonishing her. She should be asleep. Outside, dawn broke in red stains through the condensation on the fortieth-storey window. Inside, it was cold, a morgue, just the way she needed it. Anything to numb the pain. Haya crawled under the sheets and shut her eyes. Four years had passed, yet the throb was visceral. A vacuum. Her womb a desert; its flowers, her babies, ripped out of their placental earth. She could feel her imaginary twins, her perennial co-sleepers, Fear and Guilt, latch on to her sides, their buttermilk breath cloying on her limp breasts. Her real-life twins were fine. Yet, her mind kept slipping into darkness. Any attempt to sleep was futile. 'But, what if. . . ?' she thought. Her eyes shot wide open.

Haya moved on her pillows, hoping not to awaken her beloved Ezra. Her paranoia annoyed him. But there had been a time when Ezra had understood, when he had cared.

'Haya-*leh*,' he would whisper in her ear, 'It is just a bad dream. Everything is okay.'

Ezra's reassuring strokes would drag her back from her nightmares. His furious lovemaking would erase her fears for a few pleasurable moments. But his patience had run dry by the second year. As had his passion. Their relationship was like her body; once lush with a voluptuous sensuality, now a parched fata morgana, a mere mirage. Haya was nothing but a disruption to his sleep now; a thorn in his side, a rose he no longer craved. Also, he was often gone for work. Would he return from these far-away places he worked in – ruled by warlords, rife with disease? The fear was another plague with no cure. That often vacant side of the bed was another gulf Haya learnt to traverse alone. But today he was here, in bed with her.

Haya reached out to touch Ezra. He shifted in his sleep, turned towards her and threw an arm around her midriff. Hope rose in her heart, heat rose between her thighs. With closed eyes, he ran his fingers down the lacerations on her abdomen, her motherhood stripes. He tugged at the loose skin between her hips, distorting her belly button. Repelled, he turned away. Another silent rejection. His lack of desire was a jagged pill she had learnt to swallow. What could she do to make him want her again?

Haya pushed off the covers and began her morning ritual. She pulled back her dishevelled red hair into a ponytail and stared at herself in the bathroom mirror. A smattering of freckles, random constellations beside her nose, darkened her pale skin. Her cheeks, once rosy, hung like deflated balloons from her sharp cheekbones. Her eyes were metallic saucers, underlined by her dark circles. She looked away in disgust. Why would Ezra want her? Why would anybody?

She felt hot all over. She placed her palm on her forehead. Her body was blazing, and the back of her throat was itchy. There was no mistaking it. Fever. She was disappointed in her own body's betrayal. On the one day she had decided to take a break from her new life and return to her old. On the one day that she had lined up an indulgent day of shopping and a champagne lunch in Central. She was going back. Nothing was going to take away her freedom today. Nothing.

Haya rammed a double dose of painkillers down her throat.

Robinson Road – four years ago
Haya's life was split in two acts. There was the Sodom of her single life on Hong Kong Island. Act One. The move from her simple life in Park Slope, Brooklyn to Hong Kong for a lucrative job with its heady expat lifestyle. It had consumed her – all decadent desires fulfilled, every fantasy lived out, multiple material needs met. It had been a selfish existence, studded with sins. Lust soiled her sheets and mussed her make-up. Luxury items and designer dresses, gifts from her many banker-wanker lovers, overflowed from her closets. She could have anyone, so she had everyone. She was spoiled for choices, unlimited in her freedom. This was nothing like home. She was the good Jewish girl gone bad, addicted to the hedonism of her single life, yet feeling increasingly hollow.

Meeting Ezra had changed everything. He sat across from her, at that fateful dinner for young Jewish professionals her friend had dragged her to, looking at her with his puppy-dog eyes. He was different – clean cut and kosher. The kind of man one takes home to one's parents. He held the promise of filling her void, not her pockets. NGO management didn't come with the thrills and frills of the glitzy world of finance. A purer and fuller life was on offer. Act Two, Scene One.

'I'd like to see you again,' he said. She had agreed.

Conceiving the twins had sealed their fates. Haya gave up her executive PA job and her stiletto lifestyle. She deleted the names of her various lovers from her phone. She removed her mascara, and rubbed off the lipstick. She accepted Ezra's marriage proposal and followed him to the dark side, to Kowloon, a place she abhorred. It was too local, not sophisticated enough. But she took on her new role of housewife and aimed to play mother to perfection. She would look ahead, not back.

It had seemed like a good deal back then – Ezra delivered her from her sins, and she delivered Ezra's babies. Then came the twins, both sets of them. Her body gave birth to her twins; her paranoia bore their morbid doppelgängers.

Haya's old diary entry which arose amongst milky stains marked its beginning.

> First, I gave birth to Adele and Amos. Fear came next. Then,
> the fourth – Guilt. The doctors delivered twins. I delivered
> quadruplets. Fear and guilt, my creations, will follow me;
> they will haunt every waking and sleeping moment. My life as
> I know it, is over. This boggy mire of motherhood; I stand
> knee-high in its quicksand. I will try to be the best mother I
> can be – I will nurture, feed, coddle, teach, punish, and pray.
> But I am powerless. For when their time comes, I won't have
> a choice but to watch as my children enter life's battleground,
> only to be ripped apart by this cruel world. Life is fragile.
> Terrible things can happen at any time, without warning.
> Peace and sleep are mere. . . .

Haya's sentence stood incomplete. Like her. Exposed, a giant hole in her middle, made to stand on her own two feet too soon after her Caesarean section.

The scriptures claimed that women are born to be mothers. And good mothers, they say, sacrifice themselves for their children and husbands. But not her. Haya, like Lot's wife from the Book of Genesis, had chosen to turn and look back. She had looked back at the towers of her Sodom – Hong Kong Island. She longed for everything she had lost. She wanted to be wanted. She craved her singledom, the excess, and the sex. She had looked back, and for this flaw of her humanity,

she hated herself. And her punishment was apt. A single glance, a
sudden dart of pain. Lot's wife had had her swift legs rooted to the
ground, and her body made into crystalline salt. Haya's body was a
mess, her mind was a disaster; she was no good – neither as wife, nor
as mother. Inundated by hormones, maddened by insomnia, riddled
with guilt and crippled by anxieties, Haya was a living monument to
her fear, congealed in time and space, shackled at the edge of her
private Dead Sea.

She had sought help. Dr Doshi, her Indian paediatrician, peered
at her over tinted glasses through bushy salt-and-pepper eyebrows and
sighed, as though disappointed by her feminine display of weakness,
mucus, and tears.

'Fear is a liar,' he said as he scribbled a prescription for serotonin
inhibitors.

She swallowed his medicine, embraced his advice. She inhaled the
overly-sweet scent of jasmine that wafted up from the incense glowing
under his gilded goddesses.

'Remember,' he said in parting, 'The monsters are in your head, not
in your bed.'

Haya's twins were thriving, but she struggled with their doppelgängers. That pair, borne of her mind, stood hidden behind the
Espinoza family on birthdays, threatening to blow out the candles on
the cake of life whenever it suited their fancy. Life was the fragile spun
sugar that topped every new birthday cake-new fears, new guilt to slice
and partake of.

Would they ever pass?

Queen's Road – later on 31 May
Haya coughed. Apart from keeping her fever in check with more
medication, it had been an uneventful shopping day, almost enjoy-
able. Coming back to Central made her uncomfortable, yet she
couldn't keep away. Had she forgotten to discard that cheap cancer-
causing play-dough Amos's friend had given him? Had he found it,
ingested it? And her Adele, the dancer – she loved those somersaults.
Did she know that her spine could snap like a cracker if she wasn't

careful? Haya had asked her helper to be extra vigilant. In fact, she had spent hours listing the many worst-case scenarios and what-to-do-ifs to her childless nanny. Why wasn't she answering her call? Could the help be trusted to care as much as a mother did? Could anyone? What if. . . ?

The enjoyment was gone. Fear read off a long list of things that could go wrong, Guilt told her she could have been home to right all wrongs. Her worries were dead weights, dragging her to the murky bottom of the South China Sea. She had to break through the surface. Her fever was rising. She licked her lips. Her brain and body were parched, and she was giddy. The medicine wasn't working. She had to leave. Now.

The shopping basket clattered to the floor as Haya hurried out, ignoring the people around her. She scratched her arm. A nervous rash was working itself up her body. Pearly beads of sweat dotted her forehead. Once outside, she looked up. Clouds lined up like dark limousines, waiting to unload their grim passengers on the city. She raised her arm to flag down a blood-red cab. Red. Not her favourite colour. Too many unnameable associations. How could the Chinese consider it to be auspicious? Didn't they see the connection?

'*Goulung, m'goi sai,*' she directed the driver in her best six-toned Cantonese. She shut her eyes and leaned back on the black leather for the long ride across the tunnel.

'Flee for life,' commanded the twin voices in her head. 'Do not look behind, nor stop anywhere in this immoral plain. Dally not in sin and do not look behind. Or else be prepared to be consumed by flames,' they repeated, *ad nauseam*.

Haya stepped into the lift and wished she was alone. Her fingers trembled as they hovered over the numbers, then pulled back. Her distress rose with every floor. When the lift came to its final stop, the Indonesian helper, the last person out, gave her a confused look. Haya looked away. The shiny doors clanked shut. The soothing vibrations from the lift's engine massaged her. She stood in the metallic cage, frozen, in limbo. She waited. She hung between earth and sky, motionless. *What if . . . ?* She had to get home. She chose her floor and rushed out of the lift to her flat.

'Why didn't you answer the phone?' Haya demanded, as the helper opened the door. She rushed into the living room, but Amos and Adele were nowhere to be seen. Her helper was saying something, but Haya couldn't make out the words – they seemed muted, inaudible, underwater. Her temperature was peaking. She was losing her fluids, losing her sanity. She rushed into the children's bedroom. Everything in the room doubled in her vision. Except for her children.

Haya watched, incredulous, as the imaginary twins merged into her real-life duo. She blinked.

Amos and Adele looked up, puzzled.

'Mummy?' Two, not four voices asked in unison. For the first time.

Dizziness. Haya's world went dark.

Queen Elizabeth Hospital, Kowloon – 1 June

Haya woke up fighting the harsh glare of neon. She squinted against it. A sharp pain forced her eyes open. A nurse was kneading her collapsed veins, slapping and coaxing them to rise. She looked at her as Haya came to, smiled, and grunted something in Cantonese to the air. Victorious, she poked a hole in her arm. Dark liquid oozed from the tube into her flesh. A flash flood in the Judaean desert of her parched body. A euphoric high. Her mouth filled with the aftertaste of metal. A satiated gurgle inadvertently escaped her lips. Orgasmic. Next to her, an elderly woman moaned, as though responding, twitching in the last throes of death.

She looked up. A stern-looking man in a lab coat and face-mask was headed her way.

'Mrs Haya Espinoza?' He didn't wait for her to respond.

'Welcome back to life. Perfect timing, by the way. I need your signature here,' said her prince in white armour, as he handed her a clipboard, tapping his pen on a dotted line. He was impatient, as though he had better, more important things to do than to save lives.

'My name is Dr Chang.' His eyes crinkled around their corners. 'You have a rare blood condition which destroys red blood cells and depletes the supply of oxygen to the brain. Paranoia and hallucinations are common side-effects. This transfusion has saved your life. You are also dehydrated which will require a saline drip.' He checked his watch.

Haya signed the paperwork with her free hand.

'Visiting hours have begun. I'll send the nurse to get your family,' said Dr Chang, who then left.

Haya looked up at the bag of blood that hung above her head. COUNTRY OF ORIGIN: CHINA, read a bright label. This life-giving liquid had saved her. The Chinese were right. Red was an auspicious colour indeed. Haya turned and smiled as she saw Amos and Adele pushing through the ICU doors, running to her bed. Ezra was not far behind, his eyes ablaze with something new – a passion, a desire, a longing, for her. A new birth from her near-death experience. Tears of relief ran down her face. She tasted the salt. Salt. It was everywhere – in our tears, in our sweat, in the sea. There must be something sacred about it. And the tears had cleansed her. She could see. There was nothing to fear.

She would never look back. She wasn't going there anyway, not anymore.

The Bowen Run
Flora Qian

I T TOOK THE CAB ONLY TEN MINUTES to get to the Mid-Levels. Heather was half an hour early when she arrived at the meeting point of Bowen Road and Magazine Gap Road. It was a humid, warm spring morning and there were already a few runners passing her, carrying scents of cologne or deodorant. Most of them were in shorts with nicely built calf muscles – Heather watched the hairy arms of the guys in vests and the higher-than-usual ponytails of the girl runners swinging together at the beginning of the eight kilometre trail. They disappeared at the shady corner after a while. It was a pleasant sight in the early morning mist. She felt excitement climbing up from her stomach and she couldn't wait to run the trail for the first time with Marc, a veteran runner of Bowen Road on Saturday mornings.

Heather was standing before a child care home marking the start of the trail. 'Mother's Choice – pregnant girls' services support centre. . . .' she read the words on the pink sign in front of the building. There were a few other notices advertising an adoption service, and it made her think of Marc again. He had told her on their first date that he was an adopted child. 'Well, it has been a lot of information today,' he said over dinner at his favourite Thai restaurant. He had a very proud nose, Heather thought, straight and proud. His eyes turned from hazel to dark brown in the candle light.

'Did you ever meet your biological parents?'

'Only once,' his words always crisp. 'Met my dad once.' He didn't go further. And after a while he said, 'What happens before three years old somehow really affects one's outlook. Family is not something for me.'

Heather looked at him and listened. She liked to make analytical comments based on Freudian theory or other philosophies, but she found it hard to speak in front of Marc that night. Feeling awkward when he first greeted her with a hug and an attempt to kiss her cheek, Heather realised she was nervous and bowed her head. He was so much taller than her that standing up her face only came up to his chest. The kiss fell on her forehead.

He was so smooth at all this, she thought. And the same feeling crawled back while he was teasing the Thai waitress, making the service girl giggle a lot. Heather tried not to let this bother her. It was a chilly late-February night, and he put on his dark-grey suit jacket after finishing the main dishes. 'You have an amazing smile,' he said. 'It really warms my day. And I like that you don't have any make-up on, very natural.'

She was doing freelance translation jobs from home and didn't really need to dress up and powder herself.

'Want some dessert?' he asked.

She remembered she had brought something – soft-baked cookies. There were dark chocolate chips on top. The recipe had taken her some time to fumble through earlier in the day.

He looked amused. 'Are we supposed to have them here, in the restaurant?'

'Why not?' Heather laughed. So it is true what they say about Germans not being flexible with rules. She wasn't fond of stereotyping people in terms of ethnicity or profession, but there were certainly things in him that could be described as 'typical'.

The cookies tasted like a deep, sweet dream. Marc crumpled the paper carrier bag and left it on the table when they left. Kissing him near the Mid-Levels escalator, on his way back home, his tongue left a bitter-sweet chocolate flavour in her mouth. 'Coming to my place for some tea?' he whispered, holding her hand. His palm was warmer than hers. It had been a really cold week for a city like Hong Kong. He told her earlier that he had just bought a heater for the bedroom.

Heather shook her head a few times, as if shaking off a bad thought. 'Not too fast.' Later, she wasn't sure whether she actually voiced out this line in her head.

But Marc turned wary as well. 'I agree,' he said. 'When do I see you again? Meet on the weekend for coffee?'

Her feet had been icy cold that night when she lay in her own bed. Two blankets and still not quite enough. For the first time in her seven years in Hong Kong, she thought that a heater might be a good investment.

Heather called her parents in Shanghai while waiting at the start of Bowen Road. She didn't mind sharing her love life with them, but she had a hard time explaining to her dad in Chinese what 'out of my league' means.

When they heard that she had met a forty-five-year-old German senior banker, the first thing her parents asked was whether he was married or had kids.

'No, never married. No hidden wife or locked up girlfriend,' Heather joked. 'I investigated. You don't know how powerful the Internet is nowadays.'

She explained to them that Marc had first met her at an awards dinner where she emceed a year ago, while she was still working in the finance industry. It was an unusual occasion for her, wearing a black, off-one-shoulder gown and sparkling earrings, and all sophisticated and radiant with her good English and prepared script on stage. Her company was hosting the gala dinner and the boss, who always liked her language skills and poise in front of the camera, gave her the opportunity to be the spotlight of the night. A few men came over and exchanged business cards with her after the event, and Marc was one of them who wanted to talk to the 'most beautiful girl in the room' and sweep her off her feet. Like a sports race, she sometimes thought. Even the junior IT staff in her company who helped her set up the mic and podium were extremely gentle to her that night and asked her constantly if she wanted to eat something before the event. It was the dress, and the new red lip gloss, and the glamour of the whole money industry. Heather didn't remember much about Marc until he contacted her on LinkedIn many months later. She had been away from finance for half a year and was ready to go to graduate school in the US this fall.

'I don't really know what 'out of your league' means but I think my daughter should be confident enough to take any man she likes,' said Heather's dad over the phone. 'And he's fourteen years older than you isn't he? Not an ideal candidate I would say. . . .' That was a typical dad response. Although, over the years her dad had given her some great advice such as 'Look at a man's action instead of his words,' and 'Two people should be looking in the same direction instead of just looking at each other'. He asked Heather, 'Did you say anything to him about going to America?'

'Well, it's not confirmed yet is it? I'm still waiting for funding to come through from the school . . . but I did tell him there's a chance.'

'What did he say?'

'A bit disappointed? I don't know . . . he asked how many months we have . . . and said that it's hard to find someone who wants to settle in Hong Kong.'

'Hmmm. . . .'

'I have to go, Dad. Speak soon.' Heather hung up quickly as she saw Marc running over to her from the opposite side of Magazine Gap Road wearing sunglasses, a red top and shorts. She felt a bit guilty ending a conversation abruptly with her father but the excitement of seeing Marc took over.

They'd just started dating and she hadn't seen him for two weeks – he travelled for work constantly and ran his tenth marathon in Tokyo last weekend.

Heather had been confused that he didn't want to see her right away after he was back a few days ago, until he'd texted her early on Saturday morning, almost like an order. *I've been slack for the entire week and didn't do any exercise. Need to go for a run. Meet me there?*

It's okay to be a bit lazy after a marathon! she texted back.

Well, not me.

She changed into her sportswear and tied her hair up high. Ten kilometres was the longest she had done in the past but she also ran by herself every week.

Marc came close and kissed her lips. He held her waist close to him, almost bumping his body. 'Hot runner girl,' he said, admiring her tight vest top and running leggings. 'Let's go.'

After a kilometre, Heather found it hard to keep up with the marathon runner. She had her own pacing and usually 1K wouldn't exhaust her so much, but with her long-legged companion, she speeded up and was out of breath after a few turns. She stopped trying to talk and felt sweat building up on her chest.

'Are you okay?' Marc turned around and smiled. Effortlessly. She thought marathon running was just something executives in high finance liked to put on their CVs to show they were fit, tough, strong-minded and could work under pressure. And cigars, a lifestyle thing. And the girls, plural, she thought – if a man you are dating has both marathon medals and cigars, how could you be sure that they don't have the other conventional adventures? She felt jaded as she moved her arms, trying to catch his red figure a few metres in front. He was wearing the Tokyo marathon T-shirt, with some Japanese characters on his back and even a cartoon crab, which seemed to mock her speed.

'So far so good,' she forced a smile back. But he must have noticed she was slowing down.

'Shall I catch you on the way back? Keep your own speed darling.'

Heather was shocked. She hadn't thought he would abandon her in the middle of the trail and go on by himself. Although acknowledging it as a rational choice for runners with different paces, she felt her head spinning.

He studied her look, 'Catch you on the way back. Ciao for now!'

And soon he disappeared among the other runners ahead.

Heather wasn't a quitter and would never allow herself to walk a step no matter how slow she ran. But she almost felt like stopping on Bowen Road. A few teenage runners passed her, holding phones in their hands. She looked at the scenery around her – the hill on the right and the concrete jungle on the left – Hong Kong had an amazing mix of nature and city. A few steps further and the distant harbour lay shimmering in the morning light. Over the past few weeks, since getting her admission to graduate school and seeing Marc, she had begun to feel a special attachment to the city. She had spent most of her twenties here . . . and the city where you spend your youth is always the one you keep going back to, at least in your mind. She forgot where she read something like that. A few headhunters had found her public profile and tried to talk her into going back into asset management again. She didn't tell Marc she was going to those interviews.

'Are you clear about what you want the most?' her girlfriend Rachel asked one day while they were spending a music night together. She was doing the same thing as her, writing fiction while handling part-time jobs. 'I know that you've gone through a lot for this . . . six months preparation and now you're about to live your dreams. Giving up would be an awful pity.'

'I guess,' Heather said. Rachel made a joke about their choice in drinks, clothes and men, and she took a picture of Heather's champagne cocktail and ballerina shoes, and her own beer and sneakers. Sometimes Heather doubted whether she could be a real writer, and maybe there was something else that she wanted as much as her dream career. 'Don't they say that you have to deviate a bit to know what your real path is?'

'I don't know. You are so smitten now . . . show me his pictures. Are you sure you guys just started dating?' Rachel mocked her ruthlessly.

'If one has to make a mistake, it's best to make it as early as possible.' Heather thought of her reply that night while she was struggling forward on the trail. She read the markers along the way – 3.5 kilometres. She noticed there were quite a few people in red clothes that morning, and at last her marathon runner returned, brisk and high spirited.

They ran together for a while and this time she asked him to go first and wait for her back at the child care home. Thirty minutes later,

Heather finally reached the end with sweat all over her forehead and arms. Her top was soaked and Marc seemed to find it interesting. He stopped stretching his legs when he saw her and clapped while she ran to meet him. 'Well done, girl! You did 7K today, good work.'

'You sound like a trainer, or someone in the army.' Her toes were sore. Should have worn thicker socks.

'Well, I was in the army for two years, and apprenticed in the auto business when I was young. I knew what the real world was like before working for the banks, you know.'

He asked if she was keen for coffee at his place.

She thought about them not meeting for the past two weeks, the uncertainties and frustrations she had felt. Maybe it was time to find out. 'Coffee sounds good. Do you have something to eat as well?'

'Not really. My fridge is sad,' he said.

They were holding hands but Marc loosed them when they entered the building. Perhaps he didn't want the guards to see. He greeted the two Cantonese guards at the lobby.

'You are such a girl. . . .' he whispered into her ear.

She didn't understand what that exactly meant but they started kissing in the elevator, her arms around his neck and his hands underneath her sweat-soaked bra. Exercise is a strange thing – it does make you exhausted and full of energy at the same time, she thought.

'Jump in the shower with me?' He led her into his apartment. Glancing around, paintings, whisky and a cupboard of glasses, red candles on the dining table, motorcycle helmets, books, pizza delivery ads . . . no sign of another girl, yet.

He undressed himself and walked into the bathroom as if she had known him for a long time. Some music was playing in the living room, not those old songs she knew.

The water was hot enough to wash away the long run and the salt crystals on her skin. Her body now smelled of men's shampoo.

The curtain was not down; there was nothing in the way other than the view of the city down below. She wondered what would be the first impression of another woman on first coming to his place. She wondered whether there were many.

'Taste salty?' He smiled, watching her stand up.

'Not too bad,' Heather said. Bodies were fresh after a run.

'Sorry I didn't have my fruit this morning.' He had some quick wit under all circumstances. She remembered his habit of buying a mixed bag of fruit pack from an old lady for breakfast every morning.

'I feel nervous.' She looked into his eyes. 'It's been a while. . . .'

'Hmm . . . in that case maybe we shouldn't,' he said. Too much expectation on him? She had mixed feelings. Not that she was really planning to.

She asked him to hail a cab for her downstairs. He slipped into a T-shirt and sweatpants and came with her. When they walked past the guards, she was looking for traces of something on their faces but they showed nothing other than friendly smiles while he nodded. Heather felt she was a novice in a play.

She would have stayed if he hadn't told her after the shower that he'd been drinking with a friend the previous night. Two beers at first, and then a bottle of red, and some beers again, he said it with a breeze, 'Would have taken me less time on Bowen otherwise.' His hands traced the curve of her back. Heather didn't respond. She had waited for a few days after he was back and then texted him about how they hadn't seen each other for two weeks. He had said with a grumpy face emoticon that he had an appointment but he would do his best to see her soon.

'Was that a guy?' she asked quickly as if it was not important.

'No,' he laughed. 'A friend, she works for Cathay Pacific and was passing through town.' Heather didn't understand whether her profession was something worth mentioning.

'She was cabin crew?'

'Yup.'

'So you met a girl last night? Did you take her home?' As she said it, it sounded like a question that was not looking for an answer, one too stupid to ask.

'Come on, no. I have female friends.'

Doesn't need to explain, she thought. It was not too late to figure it out.

She checked her phone in the taxi, two missed calls from the headhunter and a message saying that the firm wanted her for a second-round interview. There was a Skype call from her best friend Chris as well – he lived in California and was excited about her coming to study in the US. He was a wheelchair-bound boy who was a year younger than her. 'Hey don't pick the James Bond looking guys,' he'd once joked, 'pick an ugly guy, would you?' Sometimes she thought that he spent too much time talking about nothing. Chris used to like sports back in high school.

Does a vulnerable body nurture a vulnerable heart? Heather wondered as the taxi made a turn. There was less greenery now as it went downhill quickly, making her stomach sink. What if your body is invincible, stout-hearted and goes a long way, at least for now, would that make you ignore the fact that human hearts are made gentle after all?

Home yet? Marc texted her a few minutes later.

Soon. No worries. He was heading to the tailor this afternoon for new suits. Someone special in town who knew his measurements. He had to cross the harbour to the 'dark side'. Heather knew that many people who live on Hong Kong Island barely visit Kowloon.

It was a good run, she texted back. *But I'm not up for any games. Maybe you are looking for a different type of girl to have fun with.* And maybe you are just not ready for what I'm about to offer, she thought, but that was not something to be uttered.

He replied after a while. *Totally understand you, Heather.*

So what do you think?

I don't know. Oh, my tailor passed away a few weeks ago and now his son has taken over. Strange situation.

I'm sorry.

She was indeed. Taking off her socks at home, she found a purple bruise on her toe, not sure when it got hurt. Maybe she didn't run enough and was easily injured. Maybe she was running at a pace that didn't give her enough time to look at the stunning scenery on either side of the trail. She thought about Marc being measured right now by the dead tailor's son and whether he was feeling the undercurrent of something. Her hair was still wet from the shower, and maybe so was his. She remembered them cuddling after the shower, and she sat up at one point after hearing the cabin girl story. He went away to bring her clothes from the dryer while she stared out of the window over the harbour. Ferries sailed from one end to another and she wondered whether small ships have a moment of discouragement when facing the vast ocean for the very first time.

To Kill a Da Siu Yan

CM John

A BUS ROARED BY, and for a split second nothing else could be heard. Diesel smoke filled the air, caustic, sickening. Then the staccato *bip, bip, bip, bip, bip* of the traffic light. Pedestrians from opposite directions tried to push away from each other like cells dividing in a Petri dish. This is the Canal Road Flyover in Causeway Bay, Hong Kong, and it is always crowded during daytime.

The da siu yan, the 'villain beater', sat here every day, hunched over, on her little red plastic kindergarten chair. People called her 'Grandma Wong', as though she was a member of their family, or perhaps in sympathy for her age. Her face was worn and tired. Time and nature had eroded away its surface, leaving canyons and loose skin on what was once smooth and lovely. There was sadness in her eyes, of disappointments, of dreams unfulfilled. And yet there was strength in her bearing, a raging against the dying of the light.

Sometimes people came to see her to take vengeance against whoever or whatever they felt had wronged them; unfaithful husbands, unfair bosses, or just bad luck. And she would beat the white villain paper which bore the name of the offender on an old brick with her ancient, eroded slipper. And she chanted as she beat;

> *'You have legs, but you can't walk!*
> *You have a tongue, but you can't talk!*
> *You have eyes, but you can't see!*
> *The Tiger's curse is there for thee!'*

The tools of her trade surrounded her; a crumpled red plastic sheet and more little chairs with smiling pictures of Doraemon and Hello Kitty seeming to approve of the dark work taking place. And there were incense sticks, statues of Sun Wu Kong, the Monkey King, and of Guanyin, the Merciful One, and oranges, mandarins and candles for good luck. In her hand, the da siu yan clutched her old, frayed slipper like a talisman protecting her against the Tiger's curse. Looking around and noticing that she was being observed, she placed a blank piece of villain paper on the brick and began to hit and chant again, just for show, like a fisherman dangling bait on a line. Her back was sore. Her hands ached. There was nothing else she could do to make money. Not anymore. She pleads to passers-by to 'Beat the villain who has wronged you', but they simply walk past, the vast majority anyway.

But tomorrow will be different. Tomorrow is the Waking of the Insects Festival when foul spirits awaken that must be appeased. And that means people, long queues of people. And money. And more da siu yan. Amateurs looking for easy pickings. The one day of the year. And after tomorrow, a holiday at home, with well-earned blissful rest.

Mr Wong looked at his sleeping wife, the well-known da siu yan who made such lousy money. He smiled to himself. Tomorrow the grumpy old bitch would begin dying. She believed that stuff she peddled, and it was going to be the death of her. His plan was so simple and so beautiful: offer her good money and then trick her into cursing herself with the vilest curses imaginable. It would scare her to death, while he played the caring husband. No one would ever suspect him. Then he could see Miss Lee any time he wanted. The mere thought of her made him tremble with anticipation. He couldn't wait to touch her again. Her skin was smooth and firm and she smelled so good. A smell that made him feel young again. Not like his wife. *Can't think of that now. Work to be done. Soon.*

He needed his wife's money. It was as simple as that. Her life insurance. She had been putting into it for years. A woman like Miss Lee had expensive tastes. But she was worth it. Every cent.

There was just one danger; his wife would recognise him when he went to see her. So he had purchased dark sunglasses, a wig and a hoodie and he would cover his mouth with a surgical mask. Lots of people that came to see her did the same thing, wanting anonymity when cursing someone. He just needed to make sure that he spoke differently. Not hard at all. He already felt nervous and restless. Only twenty-four hours till he saw his wife under the flyover.

It was noon during the Waking of the Insects Festival, and already Grandma Wong's hands were beginning to cramp from the constant slapping of the slipper on the brick. It was crowded. There was a long queue of people waiting to see her and other da siu yan. People stood, waving fans to keep cool, shifting their weight from one leg to the other. Each felt that every step closer to Grandma Wong was an achievement.

Looking out from under the flyover, Grandma Wong saw the light outside begin to darken. As the first typhoon of the year approached, there was heaviness in the air, a feeling of suffocation.

Twelve hours to go and then she could rest.

Time passed. Dark clouds began to gather, and the wind began to strengthen. Grandma Wong sighed. Some of the last queue joiners were leaving in fear of becoming drenched. For those who had invested more time waiting, this was not an option and the flyover loomed as a sanctuary.

The hours crawled by painfully. Seven hours to go.

There were only ten people still waiting in the queue. Grandma Wong's arms and shoulders no longer felt connected to her body. Her voice was little more than a hoarse whisper. But still the slipper rose and fell, and the chanting continued.

One hour.

The last client had just begun to approach when the thunder came, its sound reverberating under the concrete of the flyover. Lightning briefly lit up the sky to the south, revealing a hooded figure wearing sunglasses and a surgical mask. And then came the rain, sluice gates opened on a reservoir. Even Hong Kong's efficient storm drains could not cope with a downpour like this, pools of water collecting everywhere. The world had become alien. Gone were the people, the cars, the buses and the noise. Streams of water flowed down the deserted streets towards the lowest point, like the snakelike tentacles of a kraken searching for food in the dark icy depths of the sea. The stranger sat. The last client of the day.

Zero hour.

'Stranger, are you sure you want to do this?' asked Grandma Wong.
'Yes.'
'I charge one hundred dollars.'
'I will pay you $4,444.'
Four. The number of death. Four fours. Death in all directions. No escape. Grandma Wong's stomach began to clench, her heart beat faster.

'You must really hate this person to offer such a cursed number, stranger.'
'Yes. I want their death.'

Grandma Wong shuddered. She tightened her hand around the slipper.

'Why pay so much, stranger? Even the triads might charge less. . . .'
'So you do the ritual my way. Do you want the money or not?'
It's good money. There would be enough extra to survive for another couple of months. I have to take it.

'All right,' she replied.

Grandma Wong began the first part of the ritual. Fear dripped down beneath her shoulder blades.

'Stop!' the stranger commanded. 'No sacrifice to the divinities!' He took out a small hammer from his pocket and smashed the statues of Guanyin and Sun Wu Kong.

'Are you mad? No one attacks the Merciful One!'

'No mercy. No luck. Only death. Buy new statues.'

'This is perverse, stranger. The gods will be angry. . . .' said Grandma Wong.

'Give me the fulu, and the villain paper!' Grandma Wong gave both pieces of paper to the stranger. The stranger took the fulu and wrote 'Mr Chan' on it. Then he wrote 'Grandma Wong' on the villain paper. He brought out a small vial, removed its cork, and proceeded to pour the red contents onto the villain paper.

The cold dark feeling inside Grandma Wong began to take over. She felt a sense of being watched, observed and judged. Her hands trembled. 'What is on the paper, stranger?' she asked.

'Blood.'

Grandma Wong grunted. She had to see this through. The ritual could not be half-completed. Because it was the Waking of the Insects Festival, a piece of golden paper with a tiger on it would be smeared with pig's blood to appease the White Tiger. She picked up the paper effigy.

The stranger looked at her. 'No sacrifice to the Tiger!'

Confusion and fear etched itself on Grandma Wong's face. 'We must appease the Tiger! Who knows what will happen if we do not?'

A flash of lightning lit up the sky, reflecting in the stranger's dark glasses. 'If you want to be paid, do what you're told! And chant this while you beat.' He forced a piece of paper into her hand. Resigned, she began to beat and chant, the slipper rising and falling rhythmically.

> *'Death for the old,*
> *Life for the young,*
> *Flesh for the Tiger,*
> *From the da siu yan.*
> *Spirits will gather,*
> *Bones will crack,*
> *The Tiger will feed*
> *Upon your back.*
> *No escape, no respite,*
> *Your spirit fades into the night.'*

Thunder smashed across the night sky, as water flowed into the Flyover. *Gods,* thought Grandma Wong, *I need to finish this or I'll drown.* Water rose in ripples. The red plastic sheet began to shift and the oranges and mandarins began to roll away with the water.

Got to hurry now. Grandma Wong hit the villain paper with increased urgency, her arms and hands red-hot, agony. She chanted faster, her teeth a grimace against the pain, her eyes wide with fury and hatred against this stranger and the dark perversion that she carried out on his behalf. Terror drove her on. Faster and faster she hit, the slipper rising and smashing on to the paper like a gong being struck, her arms white-hot agony. She screamed and finally the paper broke.

'Ha!' screamed the stranger. 'It was your name on the paper. You will die!'

'What, this?' Grandma Wong said, as she plucked a red-coloured sheet from her sleeve and held it up. 'I thought you might try something like this, *husband.* I collected some of your semen from our bed, from when you slept with that little whore, and I put it here on this piece of paper with your name on it.'

Her husband appeared unperturbed beneath the sunglasses and surgeon's mask, but his tense posture betrayed his shock.

'Can you feel it, husband? The sense of being watched? The gods are angry. The question is, is it only your juices on the paper, or some from your little girlfriend as well?'

'You can't scare me, wife. You told me yourself that this was all bullshit.'

'Ah, you just never listen to me anymore. Stupid old man. What I said was, it's mostly bullshit, but not during the Waking of the Insects Festival. You really should pay more attention, husband.'

Grandma Wong's jaw dropped, and her eyes widened. Her husband snorted in disgust. 'I suppose you think this is funny, don't you? Well you're a great actress that's for sure.' And then he heard it: a deep, powerful growl, one that physically shook him and made the little hairs on the back of his neck stand on end. He turned around. An enormous white tiger, nine feet tall at the shoulder, fifteen feet from nose to tail. The expressionless black eyes of the tiger observed him, sliced through his bravado with intelligence and knowledge, a predator examining its prey. Mr Wong tried to move his legs, but he remained frozen in place, terror rooting him to the ground.

Almost casually the tiger raised a paw, turned it upside down and thrust three claws into Mr Wong's hoodie, lifted him clear from the ground. It smelled him and discovered his genitals. Then it tore them from his body, as if biting an apple. It tossed him to one side like a small child might dispose of a twig. Grandma Wong could only watch.

The tiger sniffed the ground, roared, shaking the flyover to its foundations. It bounded out into the storm, exhilarated, free at last to hunt. Through the torrential downpour it ran, a raw, wet, indistinct blur of motion.

Grandma Wong looked at her unconscious husband lying in the rising water under the flyover. Her station was destroyed, overturned chairs slowly floating away, fulu paper wet and unusable, incense sticks submerged in the inch-deep water. The water close to her husband was red now, he might bleed to death. She had not foreseen this, and she felt a sudden sadness. Yes, the bastard had cheated on her, and yes, he had tried to scare her to death, but watching the tiger bite off her husband's genitals and throw him aside on to the harsh bitumen of the flyover had shocked her. She stood up, and with a surge of strength, raised her tired, unresponsive, noodle-like arms and tore pieces from the red plastic sheet that marked her space. She bound them tightly over the wound with a thick cloth underneath to slow the bleeding. She put pressure on the area with her right hand. With her left, she took out her mobile phone and called an ambulance. With so much debris on the road and flooding, it would take some time.

Through the streets the white tiger ran, all but invisible in the torrents of the downpour. It reached a housing estate, much like any other, a square silo of concrete and glass. It smashed through glass and steel doors, shards of glass hurled through the air. A dozing security guard was jolted awake as a shadow passed before him. He saw the debris.

Just a lightning strike, the rest a dream. The tiger squeezed up a stairwell, body flattened down, following the scent towards Miss Lee.

Grandma Wong had never met Miss Lee. She had plenty of reasons to dislike her, the knowing defiler of her marriage bed. Still, she did not want Miss Lee's death on her conscience. The tiger would tear out her uterus; the ritual had authorised it, just like it had ripped away her husband's genitalia. Yet she had to make a choice. Finishing the ritual now might save Miss Lee. But ending the ritual would mean putting less pressure on her husband's wound, increasing the rate of blood loss, the chance of his death. But which to do? 'Well you bastard,' she said to the inert figure, 'You tried to kill me tonight. You and me need a lot of work, if we can be fixed at all. I need to think of myself first now. I don't want to be responsible for Miss Lee's death. It's you who brought all this down. Your life is in the hands of the gods. Let's see what they decide to do with you.'

Miss Lee was sitting in her living room watching a weather reporter gesture on television. A thud on the metallic security grill in front of her door. She walked up to the door and looked through the spyhole. She thrust her head backwards. Her mouth dropped open. Inch by inch she slowly strained her neck forward to the spyhole once more. Another thud, louder this time. Her heart pounded. *The Tiger is just a children's story. . . .* Panicked, she bolted for her bedroom, shut and locked the door, as the security grill screeched. 'Guanyin, protect me!' She threw herself under her bed. Each heartbeat was like thunder. Beads of sweat collected on her brow. She dared not move.

The tiger tore off the grill and flung it aside. Another sweep of its mighty paw reduced the apartment door to kindling.

Splashing through the rising water, Grandma Wong frantically searched for a paper effigy of the White Tiger. So many things she needed had floated away. At the entrance to the storm drain, a single yellow and black tiger effigy had become stuck behind some debris. She plucked it out. She needed blood or some meat to place into the effigy's mouth to appease the tiger. But her husband's blood would not help; the tiger had already tasted it. She needed something else.

Miss Lee heard the tiger pacing around her apartment, claws tap, tap, tapping on the parquet floor. The bedroom door exploded. Heavy bricks and plaster crashed to the floor. Then silence. She peeked up from under the bed. Two black eyes just stared, curious. The tiger's nose twitched; it smelled her. Miss Lee closed her eyes and muttered a final prayer to Guanyin, the Merciful One.

Grandma Wong picked up one of the broken pieces of the porcelain statue of Guanyin. Gritting her teeth, she used a jagged edge to cut her hand. 'Trouble woman,' she muttered as she dipped the paper effigy in the flowing blood. She removed some matches from her pocket and set the paper alight. It smouldered and then burned. She retrieved a dry sheet of red gui ren paper from her bag, which she also burned, and then she fell to her knees in prayer:

> *'I pray to you now*
> *Gui Ren.*
> *Make the Tiger*
> *Return again.*
> *To the shadows*
> *In the night.*
> *Bring us once again*
> *The light.'*

The ritual was not quite complete, but it would have to do. She moved over to inspect her husband. His chest rose and fell weakly. He was deathly pale, and felt cold. Ten minutes later the ambulance finally arrived.

Miss Lee had her eyes clamped shut. Every moment she expected sudden violent pain and death. But nothing. It felt like hours before she slowly opened her eyes. The giant tiger had gone, vanished. It felt like many more hours before she finally had the courage to crawl out from under her bed. Glancing at herself in the mirror, her hair was now completely white.

Four weeks later Grandma Wong met her husband at the hospital to take him home. He was hungry, so they stopped at a yum cha restaurant. As they waited for the food to arrive, Mr Wong noticed a golden locket hanging around Grandma's Wong's neck. 'What's that?' he asked. She removed the locket from her neck, opened it, and withdrew a blood soaked piece of paper with his name on it. 'This is my life insurance,' she said and smiled.

Mr Wong blanched and tried hard to regain his composure. For the rest of the meal, he assiduously placed food into her bowl and made sure her cup of bo lei tea was never empty.

Tattoo Me

Simon Berry

'I WISH I COULD GET A TATTOO.'
Terry contemplated the ice that served to chill his single malt –
shiny amber in the weak lighting. He'd let the ice melt a bit before
finishing and ordering another.

It was a small bar into which the owners had invested the absolute
minimum necessary to avoid being shut down by the Food and
Environmental Hygiene Department. Even so, Terry assumed that
part of the proprietors' investment had been in the form of red packets.
The bar was popular with people who preferred to step away from the
mainstream. People whose idea of being fashionable was to be non-
conformist and to pretend they didn't give a shit about appearances.
Tucked away down a flight of cracked steps, the bar was not the sort
of place people walked past and stepped in for a drink. For customers
it was somewhere you could talk without shouting and where conversations were interesting and prices were reasonable compared to Soho's
more salubrious establishments.

Among those who frequented the establishment it was called 'the
bar' because it didn't seem to have a name. If it did, it wasn't displayed
anywhere not even on the hand-written bills that read CASH ONLY. The
patrons were regulars; people who didn't wear suits, didn't complain
about cigarette smoke or the occasional rat scurrying along the gutter
and who weren't averse to buying more than just alcohol.

'Yours are pretty damn good. What is that? The four horsemen?'

The girl was talking to him? He looked up. Eurasian. Long black
hair cut in a bohemian style. High Slavic cheekbones, wide eyes and
long limbs packaged in tight jeans and a low-cut leather top. He

wondered how tall she would be when she dismounted from her bar stool.

'Yeah. The four horsemen. I had it done in Macau back in the nineties when we were building one of the new casinos.' Terry angled his arm to give the girl a better look. He flexed his bicep and was gratified to see she noticed.

'Casinos? Big construction sites have their uses. You're not a lawyer are you?'

'No,' said Terry. The girl *was* talking to him and she looked like she'd had a few. He didn't have a problem with either proposition. His girlfriend had again been a no-show. In his world that gave him licence for the evening.

'That's good because lawyers are dumb, they just don't know it. Of course you're not. A lawyer wouldn't be into tattoos. Don't go with the gowns and wigs thing.'

'Can't argue with that. Can I get you another?'

'You're hitting on me? Bad call, but go ahead. I could do with a man right now.' She slid across from her bar stool to the empty one between them, nudging her nearly-empty glass along the heavily scratched counter.

'Another, C.Y.,' she said to the bartender. She drained the last of the dull red mixture of tomato juice and something. She placed the empty glass a few centimetres further away and angled her body towards Terry.

The scrawny man with the goatee on the other side of the counter was moving at a speed that didn't suit this place.

'Bloody Mary?' asked Terry.

'Yeah. Dad named the drink after me. My very own drink.' She laughed as she spoke. A quiet cynical laugh.

Terry laughed. 'I take it your name's Mary?'

'Got it in one my well-inked inebriant.'

They watched C.Y. add ground pepper and salt. 'You can skip the celery,' she instructed.

'Same again, please.' Terry tapped his own glass to make sure the bartender didn't give him what the girl was drinking.

'War is my favourite,' she said.

'Favourite?'

'Horseman of the apocalypse. War. He was the red one. Famine, all dressed in black and Pestilence with the extremely monotonous white wardrobe. Very dull imaginations they have. They're all men of course, although I've never been too certain about Pestilence. Not sure anyone else is either.'

She was, thought Terry, as drunk as she was exotic.

'I missed one,' she said.

'Death. The pale rider.' Terry pointed to the largest of the figures inked into his skin. It didn't look pale against his olive complexion.

'Death. How could I forget Death? Funny guy once you get to know him. Dad used to hang out with him. He's a bit taller than the others. Of course there's more than four now. Hammurabi was the fifth – that bastard really earned it – and what's his name Marx. Yeah Karl Marx was the most recent.' She sneered.

Terry thought this was getting a bit silly, taking the Goth lifestyle too far, but he did have an old Cure CD back in his apartment. In his youth he'd seen them live. Maybe she'd be interested.

The bartender placed the drink in front of Mary.

'I said to skip the celery. Never mind.' She deftly transferred the offending stick of green from the new glass to the old one. A few drops of the red liquid ran down the stalk and onto the scratched and stained wooden counter. She absently mopped them up with her forefinger and licked it. C.Y. snatched the glass with the red-stained celery from the counter.

'Who's Hammurabi?' Terry felt stupid as soon as he'd asked the question.

'Babylonian king. Inflicted the world with laws, regulations and red tape and the legal profession. And you know Marx. I mean, look how badly his so-called economic theories did when those despots applied them in the real world. Death, pain and misery to the nth degree. Thanks.' She raised her glass in Terry's direction, sipped the drink and grimaced.

'You wanna know something? One shit-faced drunk to another?' She leaned closer, giving Terry an opportunity to look down her top. 'It sucks being me – pun intended.'

'I'm sure.'

'You don't believe me? Carry on and you will. Nobody ever does until it's too late. It'll be a shame about your tatts.'

Terry took delivery of his latest. He'd find out how many he'd had when he settled his tab for the night. Whatever the tally, it had to be less than the girl sitting next to him.

'It's not like I'm the only weirdo around here,' Mary said. 'There's too fucking many of us for comfort. Not many of my kind of course. We're the solitary type. But look around you. How many of these people are normal, nine-to-five types with mortgages, affairs and holiday plans and Facebook pages and ingrown toenails?'

'Are you that good at reading people?'

'Prick someone,' she said. 'I mean, pick someone.'

Terry nodded towards the nearest table. The young Chinese woman pulled a cigarette from a black-label package and neatly pinched the filter off. Placing the shortened cancer stick between her lips, she allowed her date to light it with practised nonchalance and drew heavily. The tip glowed in the poor lighting.

'Who? Her? Druggie. I can smell her. Even over the booze and the cigarette smoke and the armpits I can smell her addiction from here. Crystal meth. In the lab, they call it methamphetamine hydrochloride.'

'You're a chemist?' Terry asked.

'Nah. Not even close. I just mix with interesting people. Writers. Arty types. Pick another.'

Terry looked at the bartender, lugubriously pulling handles for a small group in the back corner.

'Him? C.Y. He owns this place. Well, not technically. His wife ran off with his partner, business partner that is, and kicked him out. His partner still owns half of it, at least until they find the bodies, which they won't. As I said, construction sites have their uses. C.Y. and I understand each other.'

Terry was beginning to wonder if there was more to her than alcohol and an over-developed imagination.

'So what do you do?'

'I asked you first,' she said.

'If you're not a chemist. . . .' Terry prompted.

'I teach creative writing at night school. How else is a loser like me going to earn a living? Regular jobs are out but unless I want to spend my days hiding under six feet of dirt and my nights robbing clothes lines for something clean to wear, I have to pay my bills like everyone else. And you? You're not a banker, are you?'

'Hell no. Why'd you think that?'

'I did a banker last month. Thought it would be fun to do something popular, but she bled red just like everyone else. I was half expecting it to be green like money.'

'Wait up. You said "bled"?' The girl had to be taking the piss.

'Yeah. I told you, didn't I? Or not. Anyway, I'm a vampire. A very drunk vampire with an ethnically inherited shortage of ethyl dehydrogenation enzymes, that's my mother's side of the gene pool, but still a vampire.'

'Read too many Anne Rice novels?'

'Yeah. They're pretty good, but nope, I'm the real deal. That's not exactly tomato juice C.Y.'s been pouring for me.'

Terry was starting to wonder just how far Mary, if that was her name, was going to push this.

'A vamp, huh.' Terry felt stupid saying it.

'That's not polite. Not at all. Makes me sound like some cheap low-life.'

'Sorry. So . . . er . . . how did you . . . end up like. . . ?' Terry was happy to play along so long as the possibility of more physical forms of fantasy was on the table.

'Born this way. Dad is or was the big guy that everyone talks about. Mum was normal. A strange kind of normal by all accounts but just a run-of-the-mill warlord's daughter who fell for the wrong guy.

'Some days I feel like I'm the oldest person on the planet and other times like I'm gonna be a teenager for ever. Of course, I'm neither.

Dad you know about. My mother . . . whatever they called blue blood and fashionable in Shanghai in the twenties. My grandfather was a warlord. I said that already, didn't I? A failed warlord by all accounts, but is there any other kind? So Mum smoked like a chimney and seduced the man with no heart, no soul and no conscience. Somehow she got through to him. Didn't change him though. No chance. She died when I was eleven. Couldn't breastfeed me anyway, not that I needed it. I didn't feel anything when she died. I've always been a Daddy's girl.'

Terry just looked at her.

'Mum was his second wife; that I know of anyway.'

'And his first wife?'

'Countess Erzsebet Bàthory. Elizabeth. Romanian bitch, or maybe Hungarian. Anyway, she tried to impress Dad by, you know . . . anything for eternal life, but fat chance. And she actually believed that bathing in the blood of virgins would keep her young. Female virgins only, of course.'

'Well, some people will believe anything.'

'She certainly did. Dad was pretty underwhelmed, but once he got rid of Count Ferenc – her first husband and a right murderous bastard – Dad got to live the high life in a castle and all that and didn't have to worry about disposing of the leftovers. It was all good until too many people found out. Dad just quietly slipped away and left her. She spent the last few years of her life bricked up in Cachtice Castle.'

'Sounds like a very unpleasant woman,' said Terry, feeling he had to say something.

'Oh she was. She most definitely was. The castle's still there. It's mostly ruins but worth a visit if you're in Slovakia. Dad showed me around in the 1940s. We did something of a European tour after the big war. He was going through a nostalgic phase. It didn't last long.'

'Is your father still around?' Terry asked.

'Oh, Dad's been dead for a while now. I haven't seen him since, when was it . . . oh yes, the Gulf War. We hung out together in Iraq for a bit. Good bonding session but the curfew was a downer. It would have been nice if he'd bothered to tell me how long he was planning on staying dead this time but, no, not him. One day he'll just resurrect himself and turn up and expect to see a birthday present for every year he's been out of my life.

'Speaking of which, what do you get a man who is 712 years old for his birthday? It seems to get harder each year. Last year, I brought one of Bela Lugosi's capes at an auction. Actually, I stole it. I don't have that kind of money. Stealing wallets can only get you so far. But pretty cool, huh? The definitive vampire gets to wear what the definitive vampire actor used to wear. It's not in very good condition, but neither is Dad's favourite coffin. I'm really stumped for this year. Maybe another Ferrari, they're not easy to steal, people notice, but they do come in the right colour.'

'Sounds difficult. How about a first edition of the book?'

'Stoker's? That's not a bad idea. I bet they're expensive though, not that it matters. I'd be stealing it anyway. Dad appreciates those little touches.' She sipped her drink and frowned. 'Where's the best place to find a copy?'

'London I'd imagine. Or New York. There are some good rare book shops in Midtown.'

'Travelling's a pain, though, getting forged papers. And airport security's a total bitch. Fucking sniffer dogs freak out and I get patted down by 300 pounds of TSA-enabled French fries and soft drink every damn time I try to board a plane. I wouldn't mind so much if they were Keanu Reeves or Jet Li. I'd prefer Jet Li. He's seriously cute.'

Terry couldn't think of a response to that, not one that was rational anyway. She'd moved on anyway.

'I used to hate killing people because of Mum but it didn't take long to realise that it was a lot better to kill someone properly than leave them wandering around like extras on the *Walking Dead*. After a while you don't care anymore. I don't. I don't want to. And that's the whole problem. I don't like hurting people, well most of them, but I don't have a choice. I just don't. It really sucks being me. I already said that, didn't I?' She inched her bar stool a little closer.

'What about *True Blood?*' Terry could quote from TV too if it might lead somewhere.

'Nah. I tried raiding a blood bank. It's not as easy as it sounds. Too many cameras and security guards and people working late. Not that it matters. Drinking blood that's been processed is the kind of thing you only do once. It's like drinking vodka that's been through someone else's kidneys. Puke city.'

'I'll take your word for that.'

She rotated her glass on the counter, the absent motion of someone who might have run out of conversation.

'Engineer,' he said.

''Scuse me?'

'You asked what I did. I'm a construction engineer.'

Mary ran a finger down the condensation on her glass before replying. 'That's okay, I guess.'

'Not when you have to be out on a site when the weather's bad, it isn't. A few years ago I worked on a convention centre in Harbin. Being up on the scaffolding when it's ten below is not fun.'

'Winter is the best time. It's cool and the nights are longer. I like winter.'

'What about Shanghai? Go back to your roots?' Terry asked.

'Nah, I stand out a bit in China. Not as much as I did in the sixties and seventies when foreigners were as rare as reality but it's easier to blend in here. Besides, it's depressing. The communists built a fucking building on top of my maternal ancestors' graves. A police station, would you believe it? A fucking shithole of a police station. If I want to go to Shanghai to worship my ancestors I have to get arrested. It's not consecrated ground so I suppose I could, but why? Hong Kong is good. Actually, most Western countries are okay too – it doesn't really matter what you look like, you can blend in. You married?'

'Briefly,' he said.

'She dumped you?'

'In a manner of speaking. Chantal died. Cancer.'

'And you still love her?'

'I suppose I do but I have to force myself to remember and it bothers me that it takes more effort than it should. I suppose it was a long time ago now. That's why I came out here. . . .'

'Yeah, I tried the whole relationship thing. It worked for a bit in the sixties. Insomniac. He slept most of the day so we had something in common but that was about it. He wanted kids and . . . do you see me as the maternal type?' She laughed, conveying a sense of absurdity. 'It was pretty cheesy but he said I was to die for. Big mistake there. Sometimes I can't even remember his name.'

'But you fell in love with him anyway.'

'Fell in love? No. I don't fall in love, not if I can help it. It just means more pain later. As I said, being in a relationship was a bit of a lifestyle experiment. I made sure that it was someone I didn't really like all that much so that when the time came . . . like having to put down the family pet. It hurts for a while but you pick yourself up after a bit.'

She paused.

'So how do you deal with it?'

'Well, . . . I thought therapy would help me. Needless to say I was living in the States, reading all these self-help books, *Chicken Soup for the Soulless,* that kind of crap, trying to accept who I am. They worked to some extent but draining my therapist was the best. Oh g . . . g . . . god, I hated her. But at least I got to say 'g . . . god' without puking. Small g, of course. I still can't do the big one. But it's more than Dad ever managed.

'And then there was this one time I actually tried to get religion. Me! One of my more morbid phases. It was kinda hard when you can't even cross the threshold of the local church. I can't visit the graves of all the people I've killed either, well the ones that have graves, not that I'd want to. Navel gazing has its limits.' She leaned closer and ran a finger over the four horsemen. Her touch was surprisingly firm.

'It does,' Terry said. 'Sooner or later you have to move on.' There was something erotic about the lacquered fingernail moving against his skin.

'Get a good look? Just remember that my tits and my fangs are a package deal.' She signalled for another drink.

Terry averted his eyes. It wasn't easy.

'Do you have any idea how hard it is for a vampire to get a tattoo?'

'It never came up when I was doing biology in high school,' he said.

'I'll tell you. It's fucking impossible. The needle breaks the skin. The ink goes in and then what? The body heals itself. Two days tops and the ink begins to fade. By the end of the week I'm back to looking like an advertisement for skin whitening products or a corpse in my coffin.'

'So you have a coffin?' He thought about calling her on that.

'Several actually, but I usually sleep in a freezer. It's quieter and cooler, Mid-Levels is bloody noisy and it uses less electricity than air-con. Saving money and helping the environment. Who said I don't have a conscience?'

'Not me.'

'Not you. No, you didn't. You know something? I tried being all ethical. I'd check people out and make sure they weren't rare blood types. Well, it was a pain. Even for me, it's not easy to steal someone's wallet and see if they have a donor card. Here they don't put the blood type on driver's licences anyway so it's basically impossible. Then there's CCTV, damn security cameras, and not everyone's as dozy as they look. Anyway, I gave it a go for a couple of years but it was more trouble than it was worth so I gave up. Life was easier once I got past all that doing the right thing shit.'

'Are you happier now?'

'Not really but, after that, I understood why people keep saying life's too short. Well, not for me, but you know what I mean? You know, right?'

'Yeah. Like when. . . .'

'Exactly!'

'C.Y. ? Yo, C.Y.! Add some more vodka, will ya? This is getting pretty rancid.'

'Sure, Mary.' The unshaven barman applied the bottle without regard for details like quantity. The resulting mixture faded from deep red to a dull uneven pink. This time the drink was mostly alcohol. 'Jus' about out.' He squeezed a measure of tomato juice from the container. 'One more, maybe.'

'Shit.'

C.Y. hastily poured another single malt and pushed it in front of Terry. It must have been at least a triple. 'On the house,' he said without making eye contact.

'Thanks,' said Terry.

The girl looked at the drink and then at Terry. 'Unless you walk out of here now, you know how this is going to end, don't you?'

He shook his head.

'Yeah, you do. So we'll have a nice date. You can have the best burger Soho has to offer or whatever and we'll get even more pissed and you'll get horny and I'll get thirsty and then we'll go somewhere quiet and fuck and when we're done I'll kill you. Not at my place, I hate cleaning up afterwards but at least you'll die happy which is more than I'll ever be able to do. I can't even get a tattoo.'

The Queen of the Mountain
Juan Miguel Sevilla

The Rules

'Try not to look into her eyes, Dad,' Oliver said. 'You won't like what you'll see.'

What if we could decide the last memory we would ever have of someone? This thought didn't cross my mind when Oliver said it to me but why would it? We rarely think to say goodbye or imagine never seeing that person again. That was it for me, unfortunately. If I knew it would be the last time, I would have thought of something better to say.

'Just stay where you are and don't come out until it's all over.' Usually, I'm very good with words.

It's past midnight and I haven't had a single bite to eat since I woke up. It's part of the ritual, apparently. If you summon the Queen and she smells food inside you, she'll take it as a sign of disrespect and not grant you your wish. That's why when I was scattering soil from the hiking trail around our small one-bedroom flat, my stomach acid felt like it was slowly dissolving my insides.

I admit, this is quite an image – an American in his thirties, emptying a sack of soil into a shoebox of an apartment. Whatever empty floor space I had in the living room now resembled a muddy dirt path. I've pushed all the cheap Ikea furniture I had to one side and in the centre, I placed a chair, a mirror and two candles. I switched off all the lights and waited until one a.m.

I consider myself a rational man. As an atheist, superstition and the supernatural have no place in my life or in anyone's for that matter. That was until I realised my son's life was in danger. Now I may not be good at my job as an English teacher, or being a son or even being a husband, but I thought I was okay being a father. I liked it. I liked it a lot. So, that's a good start.

When unusual things started happening to Oliver, my mother-in-law, an old, unpleasant woman that could barely speak English, told me that his life was in danger. We should have never gone on that hike last August. That was when she believes a mountain spirit called the Queen took a liking to Oliver and decided to take him as her own. The only thing left to do was to summon her to our house and ask for him back.

She detailed the instructions to the ritual very clearly with my wife translating for me.

'You must have everything prepared by midnight. Sprinkle soil from the mountain around the room where you want to summon the Queen. This makes her comfortable. In the middle, place a tall, narrow mirror big enough to reflect your whole body when you stand in front of it. Next, place two candles side by side and a chair in front of the mirror. Also, have a bag of salt beside you. Turn off all the lights and wait there until it is exactly one o'clock. It should be pitch dark.

'When the clock strikes one, light the two candles. This should be your only source of light. Once the candles are lit, say "I wish to speak to the Queen" three times. After that, prick your finger and smear a drop of blood on the mirror. Sit down facing your reflection and wait. If any of the candles go out from this point on, this means the Queen is displeased and it's absolutely vital that you abort the ritual altogether and leave the room immediately.

'If the candles stay lit, you will feel a light breeze. You will hear footsteps around you, sometimes in front, sometimes behind, sometimes right beside you. Under no circumstance, should you ever leave your chair. When the footsteps stop, the Queen will appear in the mirror. Never, on any account, make eye contact with her. If you are to speak to her, keep your eyes just slightly below her chin and keep them there. Never let your sight wander to see her face.

'Now, this is when you make your plea. State your reason for summoning her and then as slowly as you can, sprinkle the salt around your chair. Beware that this will anger the Queen but since you've bound her inside the mirror with your blood, she will have no choice but to stay. All you have to do now is stay inside the circle of salt until sunrise.

'However, be cautioned that she will do everything to get you off the chair and outside the circle. So, be strong and do not show any sign of fear.'

I've heard a lot of urban legends in my time – my hometown back in the States practically functioned though them – but my mother-in-law insisted this was something different. Villagers by the foot of the mountain had practised this ritual for hundreds of years. This was a last resort, for people at the end of their rope.

I wasn't too far off.

They even had a nursery rhyme to go with it that they used to scare their unruly children. Roughly translated, it goes:

> *Scratch, scratch, put out the light*
> *There is a shadow hiding in the night.*
> *Whisper, whisper, a wish to the mirror*
> *And see the old lady drawing nearer.*
> *Knock, knock, the Queen is here.*
> *She'll make you face your darkest fear.*

The Soil

Getting the soil wasn't easy. It had to be from the trail where Oliver went missing. I remember that August hike. I'd had a big fight with my wife Helen and we decided that weekend to do something together as a family. It was a sweltering day, the air stagnant. The rain from the morning dampened the soil, which was now being slowly cooked by the sun. The steam rising up from the earth was unbearable. All manners of insects and bugs joined us on our hike.

Two hours in and we hadn't said a word. Oliver followed closely behind us. The trail cut through a small village. Mahjong tables, stray dogs and the constant smell of something being stir-fried welcomed us as we made our way through. Some villagers would be friendly, some would be rude and some couldn't care less. Soon, the paved concrete trail faded into dirt.

'Have you fixed the balcony railing yet?' Helen asked, breaking the silence.

'I'll get it done next weekend,' I said.

'That's what you've been saying the past few months. Those three loose bars are a hazard.'

'It's no big deal, Helen. I've talked to the building management already.'

She kicked a stone, which bounced on a tree and fell off the side of a shallow cliff. That was a sign. She was itching for a fight.

'It's not just the balcony, John. Do you think I can ever rely on you for something again?' Shots fired.

I'd like to say that it was love at first sight when I met Helen. We first met when I was trying to get my feet on the ground in Hong Kong, blasting my CV to any opening that had the words 'native English speaker' on the requirements. It was a preschool called Blossom House where we first saw each other. She worked the front desk, and I spent my days keeping up with kids.

It was probably convenience that brought us together, not romance. The city, while exciting, can also be the loneliest place in the world. I knew no one in Hong Kong, which was part of the plan. The idea was to get as far away from home as humanly possible, leaving everything behind. I didn't work my way to get here. I just went. I had nothing. I had no one. So when a beautiful Chinese lady showed the slightest interest, who was I to say no?

We were married in a ceremony that put Las Vegas to shame in terms of efficiency. Soon after, we had Oliver.

Years later, on that August hike, we felt so far removed from the day we met. The argument on who did this and what evolved into a proper shouting match. She wanted to be right and I wasn't strong enough to let her be. When we turned around, Oliver was missing. We retraced our steps, cursing each other for not watching more carefully.

A couple of hours turned into several. We asked the village residents, still at their mahjong tables, the smell of stir-fry still lingering in the air, if they had seen a five-year-old boy. They hadn't. The sun was getting ready to set when we spotted a silhouette by the beach. We both ran down.

'Ollie! Don't you ever do that again!' I said as I grabbed him.

'What happened? Are you all right?' Helen asked.

Oliver looked oblivious, as if he was just on the couch watching TV. He was smiling. He had no marks on his face, legs or arms. His shoes weren't even dirty despite the distance he must have hiked by himself.

'I wasn't alone. I was just playing with the old lady,' Oliver said.

We looked around but there was no one. The wind howled and the sun now dimmed. At that time it was already too late to hike forward and we had no choice but to head back home.

Things didn't seem to be that bad then. Now, in retrospect, as I sit here getting ready to meet that old lady, or the Queen, as I know her now, things couldn't have been worse. I stare back at my reflection in the mirror and try to see my face in the dark. I feel secure that Oliver is hiding somewhere safe. I listen to the ticking clock, waiting for it to strike one.

The Mirror

The mirror was the last thing we ever bought together. We bought it off an old couple from Chai Wan at a very reasonable price. It was old too and it felt like it knew more about Hong Kong than most of the people that lived here. I remember lugging it back to Discovery Bay where Helen wanted to live, a place carved out by white housewives and white absentee husbands who don't want to deal with what Hong Kong has to offer.

We had a pretty good set-up. For a time, things were happy. Discovery Bay allowed us a bit of distance from everything. Whatever my day was like in the city, somehow knowing I'd come back to something quiet was comforting. Things were pretty uneventful. Even days after Oliver went missing, nothing out of the ordinary happened.

It was only when Linda, his nanny, told us that Oliver had been very quiet since we got back that I became concerned. Whenever we were away, he insisted on sitting in the corner and drawing in his notebooks. When Linda would ask to see them, he would growl at her, something Oliver, normally cheerful and quiet, never did before. When she saw him napping, she was able to grab a sample of Oliver's sketches.

The hair on the back of my neck stood on end. It was filled with faces of an old woman. The drawings weren't very detailed but all had the eyes scratched out. One of the sketches looked like Oliver holding the hand of the old woman who, judging by the proportion of the drawing, was nine feet tall. On the bottom half were thick vines where her legs were supposed to be.

It was the night of the new moon when I realised something was really wrong with Oliver. It must have been three in the morning when I felt a presence at the foot of our bed. I opened my eyes and to my shock, he was standing there looking at me, smiling. He was sketching something in his notebook. I tried to ask what he was doing there and he simply replied, 'The Queen wanted to know what you looked like.'

The clock finally strikes one and I light the candles in front of me. I stare at the mirror and keep an eye on the candles, praying they'd never go out. I see my face staring back at me. The Queen already knows what I look like. It's time I introduce myself properly.

The Salt
Oliver would be the first one to tell you, the Queen will respond when provoked. After that early morning incident in our bedroom, we took Oliver to a therapist. He found nothing wrong with him. His nanny, however, was adamant that something supernatural was happening to Oliver. She insisted on staying beside Oliver even when he slept. We found this unusual and forbade her to do so. Soon after, we allowed it when we'd see her crumpled up in the corner of Oliver's bedroom door with a rosary and prayer book.

At that time, I was growing distant once again with Helen. Discovery Bay is a small community. I would hear of stories in and around the building. There were whispers from the helpers walking the dogs, bringing babies out to get some sun. Someone was visiting Helen when I was out. Some said it was a pilot, some said it was some businessman. I didn't care enough to ask who it was, or if it was both.

It wasn't long after our wedding when we realised we wanted different things. We stayed together because it was the easy thing to do, not because it was the right thing to do. That's why when tensions flared up during that August hike, we both realised that the broken balcony was just the trigger. I never asked who it was that visited her or made any effort to repair the balcony because I never wanted things to work out. I was waiting for a reason to end things with her.

Soon after though, this small community would be rocked by more than just news of infidelity. One morning, sirens blared through the main road. There was something going on by the beach. Our front door was open and a breeze was slowly leaving our flat. Linda was nowhere to be seen.

When we got to the beach, a crowd had already gathered. The police had cordoned off the area. The bloated corpse of Linda was rocking back and forth on the beach.

'It's the first time anyone has drowned here,' one of the security guys said. 'Such a shame.'

When we got back to the flat, we saw Oliver standing there waiting for us. 'Linda wanted to play with the Queen, but she lost.'

Now, I know what the Queen is capable of. So now I tread with the utmost care. I look at the candles, still lit. I clear my throat as silently as I can and break the silence.

'I wish to speak to the Queen. I wish to speak to the Queen. I wish to speak to the Queen.'

Just then, I hear very faint footsteps. I see a shadow run fast at the corner of my eye. The footsteps seem to be not only coming from the floor but also climbing through the walls and the ceiling. There's a sudden earthy smell, much like the cooked soil from the August hike. On the mirror, something is changing. My face is fading ever so slightly.

The shadow that ran past me seems to now be occupying the mirror. I take a deep breath. I bow my head. I hear a clicking sound, almost reptilian.

It's finally happening. The Queen is here.

The Blood

When Helen gave birth to Oliver, we soon noticed that he was a precocious child, more than most. He would crawl everywhere and explore every nook and cranny. We lived on the eighteenth floor of one of the high-rise buildings in Discovery Bay, with a view of the sea and the more expensive low-rise flats down below.

Raising Oliver brought Helen and me closer than ever before. If at that point we didn't have a reason to be together, Oliver came in at the right time. Even before things went sour between us, he brought us together and made us do things we never did as a couple. The only dates we ever went out on were with Oliver. It was the only time I felt happy. We might not have the ability to be a happy couple, but we could be happy with our child.

When the incident with his nanny happened, I slept beside Oliver and watched over him. It was then I realised the nightmares he had almost every single night. He would wake up sweating and screaming. I cursed myself for missing it all those nights. One night, as we slept, I felt a slight breeze coming in. I checked the windows to see if they were open. Through the glass, I could see a shadow by the trees. It looked like a person, sitting by the branches. I looked closely and I could've sworn it was an old woman, staring back at me.

The nightmares continued for many nights and Oliver was getting very thin and not getting enough sleep. He looked weak as the days went by. Helen's mother then told me this was something they experienced in the olden days. We should have never gone on that August hike, she said. It was the worst day to challenge the mountain. The mountain opens and closes at certain times, and when it's closed, it takes something from you.

In the States, you conquer mountains. Apparently, here, they only allow you to pass. Helen's mother told me that my son would just get weaker and weaker until the Queen took her payment. It had to be done. I embraced Oliver one night, whispered in his ear, 'Daddy's not gonna let anything take you away from me.' I needed to summon the Queen. I needed to make my plea.

Now, the figure on the mirror slowly materialises. This is my cue. 'Leave my son alone. Leave Oliver alone,' I said. The clicking sound stops. Now I'm reaching for the salt beside me, knowing I have limited time. I slowly sprinkle the salt around me creating a circle. I hear a snarl. The clicking sound intensifies. The room seems like it's shaking but I can't tell with the darkness. My heart is pounding but I'm here now and I'm not leaving my chair.

The mirror cracks. Everything falls silent. I think the Queen got my message. I am not leaving this chair until sunrise.

The Endgame

The room goes pitch dark. The candles go out. I don't know what to do. As detailed as the instructions were, they didn't include this part. I feel suddenly warm – too warm. I feel I'm being choked by someone but I can't see. I'm coughing and wheezing and I can barely inhale.

I feel something slither up my leg. In my surprise, I almost fall off my chair – almost. I fix myself back on to the chair and hold myself down as hard as I can. I just keep imagining Oliver sleeping somewhere in the flat. I imagine him cosy up in my bedroom or maybe his. Or perhaps sitting out in the bathtub, waiting for his dad to finish talking to the Queen.

I gasp for air. Something is crushing my lungs but I don't know what. I hear laughter. The door to the bathroom swings open and I see an old lady hunched forward. I look away, avoiding eye contact. On the balcony, I see a small, ghostly figure watching me from the door. I look away again. She's everywhere.

'Try not to look into her eyes. You won't like what you'll see,' I remember Oliver saying.

I hold my chair down and continue to gasp for air. The old lady starts to crawl towards me. I can hear her nails digging into the floor and the soil. I dare not look. I keep my eyes down and hold the chair.

She begins to crawl right by me. I see her cracked skin, like bark. Her tangled black hair hides most of her face. I can only make out her black teeth. She turns to me all of a sudden and I manage to look away without catching her eyes.

I vomit, but my empty stomach feels like emptying itself more. Beside me, I can hear the old lady breathe. The warm air from her mouth smells like death. I am shaking. I am sweating profusely. My eyes begin to water and I feel like fainting. I hear something snap. I hear a scream. I turn to look around but just then, the old lady stands in front of me and tries to look into my eyes. I close them right away. I can't see but I know she's right there in front of me, and she's not going away. I gasp once again. The air has completely left the room. The room spins. I hold onto the chair as I slowly fade away.

I open my eyes to a faint light outside the window. It is quiet. I peek out and see shades of blue in the sky.

Is it over?

I look around and see that I'm still sitting in the chair. I'm still inside the circle of salt. I check the clock and it's already six o'clock. I can hear a bus stirring outside. I turn on the lights and in the dull, fluorescence of my flat, I see the remnants of the ritual: an imperfect circle of salt, the soil scattered everywhere – it all seems mundane now. I can breathe normally. Everything is exactly as it should be. But I can't shake the feeling something is off.

I hear a faint scream from eighteen floors down. My soul wants to leave my body. *Just stay there and don't come out until it's all over.*

No. It couldn't be – the ghostly figure on the balcony. I run to the door and open it and see three bars missing, enough to fit a child through.

I drop to the floor and hear the sirens come closer and closer. There is another scream from below. I do not dare look down. The lights of the police and ambulance hit the curtains. Soon after, I hear a knock on the door.

'Police,' someone said.

I should've listened to Helen. I should have fixed those bars when I had the chance.

. . . the candle snuffs

Sylvia

Stewart McKay

'Extract from the Diary of Sylvia _____,

'*14 August, 1871.*
'*Oh, the heat. This awful heat. Before this God-forsaken rock I had never once thought of heat as a tangible object. It was ethereal, untouchable: hot, cold, love, hate. . . . Yet here, I look around the room – there's my writing desk, my ottoman, my journal, and the heat. Right behind me. At my shoulder. I'm sure that were I to reach behind me I could touch it.*

'*I should ring my bell, have someone come with a fan. The exertion may be too much. Besides, I desire solitude. An impassive Chinaman, silently fanning in the corner, would be one person too many.*

'*'Tis day three hundred and thirty four of three hundred and thirty five. Such long numbers! Tomorrow my darling returns. Let me savour that last sentence a while. . . . China has had him for the past eleven-month; soon he will be mine. The two letters I received from him were full of tea, and trade, and other dull trifles. I forgave him, after a mild burst of frustration, as it is his first foray into this new world and 'twas bound to fill his mind. He is a man, and thus incapable of multitudinous thoughts. Yes mama, I did listen to your endless lectures on the male sex!*

'*I took tea with the dreaded Mrs Winthrope this afternoon: my one regular social engagement. And yet today it was bearable, as she allowed me to talk of David without interrupting once. She is "so very looking forward to meeting him". And yet she wonders if*

208

I am at all nervous about finally starting married life, as if the past year of solitude has been a luxury to me. Unaware as I am of the marital relations she enjoys with Mr Winthrope (though the amount of time he spends in his club does hint . . .) I answered politely. That David and I are childhood sweethearts. That I followed him to this outpost of Empire as readily as I would have followed him to Hampstead. That tomorrow marks, I truly believe, the start of my new life. That of a loving companion, wife and, someday soon, mother!

'*Each time I open this diary the day draws closer* – six months, three months, a fortnight. . . . *From* tomorrow *our marriage can truly begin! Eighteen months since the ceremony, near one year on from the end of that interminable voyage, at the end of the longest, hottest, most vexing year imaginable, David shall be mine. Mine!*

'*I really would write more, and yet perhaps this is the perfect sentiment on which to end. I must lie down; it is simply too hot to do otherwise.*'

Will, the tour guide, raises his eyes from the book. One member of the small audience, Jessie, wonders if he couldn't have picked a more atmospheric spot to tell a ghost story. A garbage truck reverses past them, beeping angrily, forcing Will to wait before resuming.

'*15 August, 9 a.m.*
'*I am sure I must have written this countless times previously, but repetition is symbolic of my limbo here, and thus: from our veranda one has the most superb view of the harbour. Beyond the rooftops of Victoria the sea shines and sails flutter. Oh, how I wish I were better able to describe a scene like this . . . "shines" and "flutter" are poor choices, I'm sure. Behind me stand the verdant slopes of the mountain, with all manner of strange and eerie insects thrumming in the morning sun.*

'*Our little abode may not be the best situated (I do feel for the rickshaw-men struggling up the slopes, though I daresay they are quite used to it), yet I have slowly come to call it "home". Perhaps with a husband by my side I can face society here a touch more readily.*

'No, this table and parasol have been my constant retreat these months, away from the stench and noise of the street. And at this time tomorrow, David and I will breakfast here in the delicious morning breeze. I shall remain all day, not beating my usual retreat from the midday sun, as I wait to spot David's ship. It will arrive from the west with sails of deep red, this much I know. And yet, half the ships in the harbour have deep red sails. It seems to be quite the fashion in these parts. I'll content myself with watching the vessels and imagining all the fantastical places they've seen and are yet to see, imagining that each and every one is carrying my priceless cargo.

'Already I am beginning to sweat, and itch. D___ this climate! Unladylike of me, I know, but it does vex me so. However, I am brought some solace by an unexpected memory. David's birthmark. Imagine if he were here now, as he will be so soon, out in this heat. The silly blotch on his neck, which I love as much as any other part of him, would be turning red while he scratched at it, cursing. I miss everything about him. I can't wait any longer to see him and all his tiny imperfections. . . .'

Jessie notices that the three girls in front of her are holding hands, determined to be terrified by the slightest noise. She rolls her eyes.

'3 p.m.
'My how weather can turn. The afternoon has blown away every trace of the morning's glory. Now it is all wind, and rain. The trees creak higher up on the mountainside. I was desperate to remain on the veranda, but Mrs Winthrope pleaded with me to return indoors and I am sad to say she was correct.

'I do hope my dearest can dock before the worst of the storm hits. The rational side of my brain, such as it is, assumes he has been delayed in Macau. One last agonising pause on the journey

home. The romantic side envisions him riding the storm, astride the deck, straining to get home to his beloved wife. . . .'

'Oh my God, is that what happened? Did her husband die in the storm? And now her ghost, like, haunts the building?'

One of the girls asks this in a high-pitched whisper. Her two friends put hands to their mouths and shiver.

'Ah, no, not quite.' Will lowers the book from which he was reading. Jessie waits for the punch line. 'No,' he continues, 'the truth is much more sinister. . . .'

Jessie's husband, Lucas, puts an arm around her shoulders. 'Man, he's a bit. . . .'

'A bit much?' He delivers his lines with such emphasis that, rather than lending drama, it feels as if he's addressing a kindergarten class. She likes that – it'll work in the article – and she jots it down. 'He sounds as if he's reading from a script.'

'Probably is.' Lucas moves to take her hand. She instinctively flinches; but allows the gesture.

'God I'm exhausted,' Jessie sighs. 'I really can't be bothered with this tonight.'

'Running this morning?'

'Yeah. And I didn't get out the office 'till seven. *And* I've got a breakfast interview tomorrow morning.'

'You know, I think you're pushing yourself too hard. It's only been two months since. . . .'

'Since what? Do you think I've forgotten, Lucas?'

Instantly she regrets it. His face crumples for a second. She reminds herself, yet again, that it affected him as well.

'Sorry. Just . . . look, we're moving.'

Their small group turns off the main street and into a stuffy alley. Restaurant bins give the air a sweet, nauseating smell. It's December, but it's warm. Will explains that their next stop is up here, 'somewhere among the shadows'.

Lucas pokes her in the back. 'If you want to turn back now, I'll understand.'

She looks at him side-on. 'Please. This has been one of the least scary nights ever. So far all we've done is walk through Wan Chai. We just stopped at a 7-Eleven, for God's sake!'

'Well, I get the feeling that things will get really terrifying now.'

Jessie half-laughs at his attempt to lighten the mood. She's become inured to them over the past few weeks.

'Remind me why we're here again?'

'I'm reviewing this ghost walk. That is, believe it or not, my job.'

Jessie feels something in the pit of her stomach, as she recalls that conversation with her editor.

'Look, Jess,' he had said, motioning for her to sit down. 'I know something's going on. At home. In your private life. Whatever. And you reserve the right not to tell me a thing.'

Her throat was dry; she knew when a 'but' was coming.

'But . . . to put it plainly, as I always do, your writing's suffered. I mean, when you started here, you were fresh, new, a kick in the ass for half the staff here. But since. . . .'

They sat in silence for a minute. Jessie stared at the floor, her editor at the ceiling.

'Look, I don't need to spell it out. You're a smart girl. And I gotta great piece for you to get your teeth in to. To get you back in the swing.'

Months earlier, several writers at *HKLife* had conducted some research into their family trees for a piece called *Hong Kong in the Blood?* Most of the local writers traced their families back to post-WWII immigrants, but Jessie managed to follow her family tree much further than anyone else – way back to the early years of the colony. Her family had always spoken of having 'mixed' blood, early memories of wizened great-grandparents at family gatherings speaking cryptically. None of the younger generations, especially not her parents, had seemed particularly interested. Hong Kong was that kind of place, no?

Yet, by the end of her research, Jessie was shocked at how true these whispers had been. Although the archives became more blurry and harder to pin down as the dates receded, it appeared that Jessie's family had arrived in Hong Kong in the early 1870s. From the snatches of information that remained in the records her ancestors had had something to do with an old hospital, now the site of an apartment block in Wan Chai.

'Okay, Jess,' the editor continued. 'Look. I want to *give* you one more chance.' The electronic cigarette he had taken to waving around looked ridiculous, Jessie thought, but his words hit home. 'One more chance.' He must have noticed her expression.

'But, look, no, don't think of it as a last chance, or anything like that. This isn't a warning.'

'Sounds like one,' Jessie mumbled.

'No, no, no. Just go out there and write. Like you used to. Until . . . whatever happened . . . happened. And remember, the offer's still there: talk to me about it. Anyway, let me get this right. For the *Blood* piece you uncovered the fact that your family went way back into the mists of time.'

'Well, in Hong Kong terms, yes.'

'And when you tried to get hold of the hospital records, it turned out that you couldn't access them. They'd been bought by, of all things, a tour company. A *ghost* tour company! Now, what does this magazine specialise in?'

Jessie reels off the familiar mantra about 'presenting an informative, unbiased view of Hong Kong's rich and active social goings-on'.

'Exactly, so you review this new tour: *Haunted Hong Kong,* or whatever the hell it's called. Tie it in to your family. Lift the final stone from in front of the tomb. . . .'

Jessie sighed.

At the end of the alley stands the Anniversary. Not the swankiest apartment block on the island; but attaining a certain standard of tackiness in the ornate iron fence running a ring around the first floor wall. It's starting to flow now, thinks Jessie, as she scratches this line in her notepad.

'Are you ready to enter one of the most haunted locations in Hong Kong?' Will attempts a mysterious-cum-sinister look and Lucas almost snorts out loud.

Jessie's thinking about her family: faint outlines of people from two centuries previous. She repeats the words aloud:

'. . . faint outlines from two centuries previous . . . two centuries ago. . . .'

She writes it down, then scores it out violently. Lucas again touches her shoulder.

'Woah, Jess, calm down. It's just an article. . . .'

'It's not *just* an article – It's. . . .'

'What?' Lucas sighs. 'I do wonder, sweetheart, why you don't just tell them what happened. They'd understand, and go easier on you. Not send you out on assignments in the middle of the night.'

'You know, my aunt worked here,' Jessie says, determined to talk about something else. 'Years ago, when it was a hotel.' It was reassuring to make mention of her 'real' family, her modern, living relatives, ones she could call on the phone.

'Really?' says Lucas. He hesitates. 'Is that the one you told me about – that had a nervous breakdown?'

'Yeah, she was a cleaner. It happened on her first day in the job. She's. . . .' Jessie leaves the sentence unfinished. Strange how, in such a big city, her family seems intrinsically linked to this plot of earth.

The group enters what looks like the bin-man's entrance and gathers in an orange-lit basement. As they endure another of the guide's now expected pauses, a fire door opens and a security guard passes through. Jessie catches a glimpse of faux-marble lobby, and the tinkling strains of a water feature.

'So,' begins Will, 'Sylvia's diary ended abruptly on 15 August, 1871. Having studied over two hundred entries, historians have worked out that the house she describes in the journal was located somewhere around modern-day Caine Road. When the diary resumes, however, some three months have passed, and everything has changed.'

One of the girls sneezes in the stuffy air and her friends jump nervously.

'This block of apartments was constructed in 2003. The Anniversary is just the latest in a long line of buildings to occupy this space, dating back to a hospital built in the 1860s. As we'll see, you can still find nineteenth-century brickwork deep under this building.

'Ten years ago, in preparation for the new project, the foundations were strengthened and, covered in decades worth of dust and grime, workmen uncovered a box. Inside of which they found . . .' one of the girls gasps '. . . Sylvia's diary.

'Follow me, below. . . .' They file down a flight of metal stairs. The air becomes even more close, and warm, and Jessie opens her collar wide. Her neck itches. Lucas takes her hand. At the foot of the steps there is a click. Will emerges again in the light of a torch.

'So . . . we left Sylvia impatiently waiting for her returning husband, delayed by a tropical storm. Then nothing. Silence. No new diary entries. Until November of that year.' Will sets the torch down on a plastic chair, from which the colour has almost faded, and picks up the diary. With the light at a new angle, the group's shadow is re-imagined, distorted, on the far brick wall.

> '*23 November.*
> *"Tis done, 'tis done, 'tis done. I have submitted and they have relaxed their grip. True to their word, I find this book awaiting me on my dresser when I return from Doctor Montgomery. I am loath to even glance at my last entry – that was a different life, a different woman. But, ultimately, I began writing this on the very next page – the fresh ink defiantly staring back at August's foolish author. When I think back . . . oh, how I don't want to but I must . . . when I think of* him *stepping out of the rickshaw. Running blindly to his arms. I see the basket, over and over I see the basket, and the half-bred* thing *it contained. . . . Stop Sylvia! But perhaps to write it down, to commit it to paper, will be a boon? Can I bring myself to do so?*'

Jessie scratches at her neck and coughs uncomfortably. She turns to Lucas but he is listening intently, apparently unaffected by the heat.

'Sylvia is now writing from her room here, in the hospital. All we know from the records is that she was admitted in mid-August 1871 with "an hysterical disposition". Her medical history, diagnosis, even her surname were omitted. The world, remember, was a different place. We're talking the best part of 150 years ago. A wealthy husband with a wife in an embarrassing state of mind. The stigma attached to madness was huge. . . . As for the diary, there's another break of several months before the next entries:

> *'February.*
> *'I am released. I am free. I can roam wherever I choose. So long as it is within these four dusty, plastered walls. The good doctor maintains that keeping a diary helps me, although I know the others are sceptical. To hell with them. To hell with* him. *To hell with them all.*
>
> *'16th Feb.*
> *'I asked the good doctor today if I might be taken to the balcony. He acquiesced. I could see the harbour. Hundreds upon hundreds of red sails. Tonight I shall dream of them. All the red sailing boats carrying all the devoted husbands back to the arms of all the blind wives. Yes, the wives shall be blind. Red ribbons tied around their eyes. Like a painting of Anne Boleyn I saw as a child. Kneeling, awaiting the axe. Or perhaps they shall have had their eyes gouged out. Yes. Hollow black holes searching the horizon for their loves.'*

Will's pauses grow longer and longer. When he stops, the silence is loud. Pounding in everyone's ears. Jessie presses her fingers to her temples, a sudden headache wracking her skull.

> *'February.*
> *'Today I had a visit from mama. She sat at the end of my bed and told me what to expect after I marry. What to anticipate from my husband. I positively squirmed when she spoke of what lay under my petticoats.*
>   *'But how silly of me. I must have dreamt it – as I am already*

happily married. I'm all the way out in the Orient, and mama is not. Mama is dead.'

The headache passes, but Jessie's discomfort increases. Is nobody else as hot as her? She can feel pricks of sweat forming in the hollow of her back. Her neck is still irritating, scratching against her collar. Lucas notices her fidgeting and offers his hand. She bats it away. Will reads on.

'I have lost count. Silly woman. I had but one task to fulfil and I have made a terrible mess of it. I no longer know how many days my darling has been away. I had been keeping such a meticulous count . . . I simply must get out of this room, and keep a look out for David. Perhaps he has returned and cannot find our house.

'He has been away so very long . . . I hate to think of him wandering the streets of London. Lost. My darling. . . .

'After this, the entries become undated, scrawled, one-word blotches on the paper. Some are illegible. Prominent among them are the words *betrayed* and *betrayal*, as are references to *it*.

'When the diary was discovered, it was circulated amongst several local historians. They all came to the same conclusion regarding Sylvia: what she discovered that fateful day when her husband finally returned home. Perhaps you all have too. . . .' Will no longer sounds as if he is reading from a script.

'One of the strangest aspects of the diary is this: following page after page of rambling and ink stains, the final entry is written beautifully, in lucid prose:

'30 March, 1872.
'The sun floods into my chamber this morning. I haven't felt quite so alive for months. I know what to do. I have made a pact that gives me peace of mind. When the good doctor arrives I shall ask, politely, if I may visit the balcony. I'm sure he will acquiesce. He has gone several weeks now without having had cause to

*reprimand me. I simply must be allowed outside. I simply must
make contact with this world, with which I have finally made
peace.*

'And that's it. We know from the hospital records that the doctor
agreed to Sylvia's request. Because we know that that morning, after
gazing out over the harbour one final time, she threw herself from the
balcony.'

Will closes the book. Even he is unnerved by a strange noise he
hears in the gloomy silence. Is it someone breathing?

He continues: 'In this spot, over the decades, there have been
reported sightings of a young woman dressed in a nightgown. Just last
week a night porter in these apartments told me that he saw her. She
does nothing to those who see her. People report that she never looks
at them. She looks through them, as if searching for something in the
distance. Then she fades away. . . .'

Will's voice retreats down his throat. The torch has tumbled off the
chair and cast a new shadow across the vault. He realises that the noise
he can hear, from behind the girls, is someone retching. Gasping.

'Hey, hey!' Lucas is shouting. 'Help. She's choking!'

One girl turns around and screams. Behind her, Jessie is on her
knees, grabbling in the dust. One hand clutches at her throat; the other
hand squeezes sand and dirt out like an hourglass. Lucas tries to raise
her with arms under her shoulders, but she shoves him off leaving with
dirt on his face. Will's skin tingles when he sees the look in her eyes:
pure malevolence.

Will and the girls manage to shepherd Jessie back up the steps.
Growls roll from deep within her, as she forces breath down her throat.
Lucas tries to approach but she hisses and spits. He remains a pace or
two behind, holding the torch.

As they bundle in to the apartment foyer the staff take a step back
behind their desk.

'Call an ambulance. Now!'

Jessie sprawls on the tiled floor, creating a puddle of dust and saliva
by her head. It seems that she is breathing more easily, just. Her breath

still rasps and rattles. Her husband approaches cautiously. Will notices something that he hadn't seen in the gloom of the vaults: a bright, angry red birthmark on Jessie's neck.

By the time the ambulance arrives she has almost got her breath back, slumped on a leather stool by the fountain.

The paramedics check but find no reason to take her in to hospital. They diagnose a panic attack, and recommend that she visit a doctor as soon as possible. One of them, small and rotund, seems annoyed by this false alarm.

He asks Will: 'Don't you have medical disclaimers before people go on these tours?'

'Well, everyone signs a sheet saying that they know what's coming, that it's not suitable for people with heart conditions, pregnancies. . . .' He points to Jessie. 'She signed one.'

'Should be more careful if you ask me. Getting people all worked up, scared silly.' He makes his way towards the door.

The other, taller, paramedic is silent as he packs up their equipment.

Lucas smiles. 'Thanks guys. Look, I guess I should mention that . . . two months ago . . . my wife and I lost a baby. Our baby. . . . Do you think this is related?'

For the first time, the smaller paramedic's face softens. 'I see. No, I shouldn't think so. This is just a routine panic attack. She'll be fine in an hour.'

Jessie sits, still breathing heavily, and stares.

'You sure you're okay?'

'Yeah, I'm fine.'

'You were really choking down there!'

'It was just the heat and the stuffy air. . . .' She turns to him, as if just remembering something. 'You shouldn't have called an ambulance. It was completely over the top! Seriously!'

Lucas looks at his wife, and is taken aback by the fury behind her eyes. 'Jess, you couldn't breathe. I thought you were. . . .'

'Jesus, Lucas. Just . . . I just wanna go home.'

The taller paramedic smiles politely, turns to leave and then hesitates.

'Actually, may I check something?' He approaches Jessie once more, and peels back her collar. It's wet with sweat. The birthmark is still a violent shade of red, throbbing with her pulse.

'It's just a birthmark,' Lucas stands up to see. 'It can't have anything to do with this, surely?'

The paramedic softly presses the red blotch with his gloved hand. Jessie flinches, silently.

'No. Like we said, it's probably just a panic attack. Stuffy air. Maybe a touch of claustrophobia.'

Minutes pass, but he shows no sign of leaving. His partner is already waiting in the ambulance.

The tall paramedic has been considering whether or not to say what's on his mind, glancing awkwardly at Jessie. She shields her eyes with a trembling hand.

'Mind you,' he begins, 'I dealt with a pretty similar case a while ago. In this very building. Ten years or so back.'

'Another ghost tour?'

'Nah, just a cleaner. Back before these fancy apartments went up. It was a hotel. She went down the storeroom for something, and collapsed. Funny thing was. . . .'

He pauses. He remembers the woman sprawled out in the corridor, dragged as far as she could be, gasping for air. He recalls the manager tugging at his tie, explaining that it was her first day on the job, that she must have had a reaction to one of the cleaning products. . . . With a frown he remembers what he saw on her neck.

'Yeah? Was what?' Lucas looks confused.

'Nothing. Forget it. She was okay in the end.'

Nothing seems quite as frightening in the morning.

Jessie thinks this as she lingers in bed. Although their apartment is cramped, sunlight manages to reach every corner of the room.

Her phone has rung twice now; her editor wondering where the hell she is. She could just make up an excuse: flu, stomach bug, burst pipe. . . . She knows she could. But she doesn't. The vibrations on her bedside table get angrier, then stop.

She simply lies there, staring not at the ceiling but beyond it, until she forgets where she is.

The vibrations begin again. This time it's Lucas. Jessie looks at the screen, and then calmly, methodically, she turns her phone off.

She wades through bed sheets to get to the far wall. She looks out of the small window. Twenty-five floors below runs a crowded North Point street. She considers how odd it is to watch the scene in silence, until she imagines that she can hear every single sound. She's never taken the time to stand and look out this window, not once in two years. In the distance, between gaps in buildings, she can see the harbour.

Jessie slumps backwards and returns to her bed. She remains there all day.

That evening, Lucas emerges from the MTR exit closest to their home. He's left work early, concerned by his wife not answering her phone. As he steps out on to the pavement he again notices how warm it is for December.

An ambulance wails past and precedes him around the corner towards the apartment block. He sees the crowd gathered outside the front entrance, accompanied by two more sets of flashing lights. When he looks twenty-five storeys up, and sees an open window, a gaping black square amid the twilight, he understands.

Daggers

Bernardette S Sto. Domingo

M IA'S CHEEKS WOBBLED as her face hit the cold, hard wall. She bit her tongue. The taste of blood, which reminded her of a penny she tried to eat when she was a kid, filled her mouth.

Chris wasn't done yet; he raised his fist and hit her in the abdomen. She curled into a ball; her eyes bulged, forcing the tears out as she gasped for air.

'Don't you ever do this again,' he said.

She was on the bedroom floor, hands trembling around her foetal position. She didn't hear Chris' words, not that it mattered, but she nodded just the same. She covered her mouth, careful not to let a single drop of blood fall on the floor; nothing upsets her husband more than a filthy house.

Mia shut her eyes tight and thought about her plants, waiting for her on the balcony, anticipating their nightly talk. Her Chinese Evergreens, her Dracaenas. The English Ivy that she has just started to grow, the Money Tree in the right hand corner, the Birds of Paradise that she transferred to a bigger pot just today. She had been meaning to concoct a home-made fertiliser for them.

Air slowly filled her lungs and the metallic taste in her mouth receded; she smiled as her mind relegated her to a dark place where pain could not reach her.

She was on the bed when she came to. She was wearing clean clothes, and her wounds were tended to while Chris read a book beside her as if nothing happened.

Mia turned her back to him, her mouth twitched. How many days and nights would she have to spend waiting for her wounds to heal, or for the sting to die, only to be punched in the head or kicked in the knee again?

She had to behave.

Good wives don't get punished, her husband would always say.

Then she felt Chris' arm envelop her, his touch a block of lead on her body, his breath searing the back of her neck.

'Never say no to me, Mia. It's for your own good,' he whispered as he slipped his hand under her nightgown.

It was still dark when Mia woke the next day. There was a long list of chores, which would require more energy than usual after last night's incident.

She watched Chris eat his breakfast of noodles, eggs and luncheon meat as he blabbered about a shirt that he wanted ironed, the tiny drop of blood on the bedroom floor that he wanted cleaned, the vase broken when Mia was hurled into the wall that he wanted replaced.

'Yes, Chris,' she heard herself say.

There were only two rules in their two-bedroom flat in Sai Wan Ho – clean the house and always do what Chris says. Mia had learned to live with these rules for the last five years.

She would make sure that all the magazines were in the rack, the pillows on the sofa arranged symmetrically, the walls and the floor spotless, and the blankets folded on the bed before her husband came home from work.

It was the only way to be safe.

She was lucky he allowed her to keep her plants. They added beauty and provided fresh air in the house, he said, but if their leaves start to wither, or they made the balcony dirty, they would have to go.

That was fair enough. She should try harder not to upset him. Yes, he was good to her, and leaving him was a bad decision. Stupid. Really stupid. Her husband was right all along.

Where would she be if Chris had not married her? She'd still be working as a server in that old dai pai dong in Kowloon, earning just enough to afford a small room in a dingy shared flat and two meals a day, while trying to save money for her cheap government-run night courses.

Chris and his friends were regular lunch customers back then. They wore freshly-ironed long-sleeved shirts, ties, polished shoes – they worked in an office nearby. He would come back after work to buy dinner every night. Sometimes he would ask Mia to eat with him, or go for a walk.

After a few months, they married. He was twenty-seven; she was nineteen.

Mia could not remember when she had first misbehaved and upset Chris. Most of the time, she forgot the circumstances and even the manner by which she was punished, but she always remembered the pain. It's a scar on her left cheek; a dead toenail; a missing tooth. A pained smile, or a limp – they all stare back at her in the mirror to warn her that breaking the rules has its consequence.

Mia was slicing fresh pork meat in the kitchen when Chris charged towards her. He threw a white cotton shirt to her face; she soon found the small scorch mark on the right side.

She tried to explain that it was an accident, that the phone had rung while she was ironing, and that Chris never liked it when his calls were not answered immediately; her voice was rattling in her throat.

Chris looked at her without saying a word, and she knew she had said too much. The slap was so hard that she thought she heard her own eardrum rupture. She fell on the floor, the knife still in her hand. Gripping the handle with both hands, Mia stabbed Chris' left thigh and pulled the blade down to his knee. He wailed and looked at his wife with bulging eyes. Mia stood up and struck again, this time puncturing his chest. One. Two. Three. Four. Five times. She couldn't stop. If she stopped, Chris would take the knife from her and kill her.

Who's going to clean all this mess?

Chris fell on the floor, hands on his wounds, trying to staunch the blood.

A smile curled at the side of her mouth.

'Is there something funny? You ruin my shirt, you ruin our dinner, you ruin everything with your stupidity and here you are, smiling? You're worthless!' Chris yelled, yanking Mia back to reality, to her crushed position on the kitchen floor. He kicked her in the groin before disappearing into the living room.

I've done it again, Mia murmured to her plants. It felt good, she added, but realising it hadn't really happened she felt even better. She could never hurt him back, surely? What good wife would?

She carefully examined her plants as if waiting for a reply. Her Chinese Evergreens, with their smooth green leaves bordered by a bright, blood-like colour, stared back at her.

Mia opened her eyes as strips of sunlight slipped between the partially-drawn curtains in their bedroom. She struggled to hear her husband snoring beside her, or the alarm clock that she had set for six a.m. She touched her left ear, and realised she couldn't hear.

Her fingers were red and sore; calluses hardened the palm of her right hand, probably because she had cleaned a lot yesterday.

She sat up, and realised she was alone. She jumped out of bed and headed straight to the kitchen. She opened the fridge, took out the eggs, and poured orange juice into a tall glass.

'I'm so sorry, Chris. I . . . I overslept. Don't worry, it will only take a few minutes to cook an omelette,' she said.

Silence.

'Chris?'

Mia checked the other room, the two bathrooms, the balcony, the kitchen. She went back to the bedroom, her wobbly hands searched for her husband underneath the pile of white sheets on the bed.

A chant filled her head. 'Where are you? Where are you? Where are you?'

Some of his clothes were not in the closet; two pairs of shoes were missing from the rack. Even his laptop was gone. His mobile phone was turned off.

He has left.

He has left his worthless, misbehaving wife.

Mia went back to the living room and collapsed on the sofa, disrupting the order of the small square pillows.

For days, she ate alone, took care of her plants, watched television, and slept whenever she felt like it. She could reshuffle the pillows as she saw fit without getting slapped; or choose not to sweep the floor without getting smacked in the head.

But Mia would always put the pillows back in order after rearranging them, or scrub the floor twice or thrice a day, after leaving it dirty for a few hours. No, she could not falter. What if Chris comes home and finds the house in disarray?

She could have been in serious trouble the other day when she found ashes – grey and feathery, some black and crushable – in the laundry area. She scrubbed, and brushed and washed until her hands cracked and peeled.

Mia would feel guilty lying on the bed without Chris so she ate, slept and rested at the balcony, sometimes watering her plants, talking to them, or wiping their leaves with a white cotton cloth.

Her plants have become healthier and more robust, as if they were coming alive. Sometimes Mia would imagine seeing their elongated leaves reach out to her like lanky, fretful fingers longing for a touch.

How could they have outgrown their pots in such a short time? Mia took out her gardening tools and knelt on the floor of the balcony. She chose a pot and dug into the side to loosen the dirt when something clinked against her trowel.

She poked and ploughed and unearthed it, gold and round. A ring. Just like her own wedding ring; but attached to a severed finger. Mia reburied it and carried on re-potting her Dracaena.

Egg Tarts
Phillip Y Kim

A WILLOWY YOUNG WOMAN approaches the old man.

How can we help you, Uncle? Are you lost?

The old man blinks to clear his vision. She is dressed in a beige pantsuit and holds one of those skinny computer slabs. All the young people seem to have them these days, cradling them like spoiled lapdogs. She is smiling at him, but her face is tight and unwelcoming. She doesn't conceal that he is distracting her from things she'd rather be doing.

Before he can gaze at her any longer, a familiar voice barges into his head, harrumphing.

She's just some young tramp. Don't waste our time on her. Let's get going.

He wants to ignore the instruction. The young woman reminds him of his daughter the way she looked twenty years earlier, the daughter he hasn't been with in the same room – or even country – for five years. He wants to continue enjoying the sight of her – how she tucks her chin to make her sharp eyes look rounder, how she wears a pink and yellow daisy hairclip to soften an air of detachment that comes from, what? Self-assuredness? A hidden inadequacy? He's not sure. But he suddenly worries that his leathery face with its ochre blotches might seem repulsive to her.

This girl looks nothing like our Esther! She's probably not very smart or well educated, either. Come on!

He walks around the young woman and makes his way towards the conference room.

She hurries forward and blocks his path. He notices that she smells of oils wrung from foreign flowers. Ah, that's what she wants to appear to be – an expensive import.

Sorry, Uncle. But you can't go in there.

Her smile is gone, replaced by a frown. He's not bothered by it. On the contrary, that reproving expression is one that is oddly comforting in its familiarity; it could have been lifted straight from his daughter's face during those occasions in the past when he, or more often her mother, nagged her about spending too much of her evenings burying her nose in travel magazines, being wasteful about food, or some such complaint. Stubborn one, Esther always was.

Each day of the five years of absence from her have been marred by blots of loneliness. During some stretches, it has enveloped him like dense smoke, paralysing him from reaching out towards any part of his day. During others, he has been overcome with claustrophobia and panic, suffocated by the pressure of constantly having to fend for himself. But he hasn't been willing to force himself back into her life. Distance is what she has demanded of him, to accumulate experiences unhitched from his and the drudgery of bakeries, to put down roots in a place where decisions made – good or bad – are her own.

At least she has just sent him a card in the mail. 'Happy birthday, Bah. Hope you are well.' Below her name were scribblings by his grandchildren: 'Hi, Ngoi-gung! We miss you and your delicious tarts.' He feels happy for this crumb of affection. But there remains a gnaw for things long absent. Despite having several shoeboxes full of pictures of Esther, other imprints of her – the occasional bump of her shoulder against his when she helped run errands, the frantic rummaging noises around their tiny apartment when she had misplaced something important – had begun to fade long ago.

What's wrong with you? Did I marry such a daydreamer? Get on with it.

The old man proffers the box tucked under his arm. I have brought these for Mr Kwok Cheng-chung. To pay my respects.

The young woman shrugs. Sorry, but Chairman Kwok is in a meeting now. I'll pass along your regards.

The old man shakes his head. It is our birthday. This is from one old man to another.

He pulls a worn wallet from his trousers. She bends forward to look at his ID card, which shows him as a younger man, still with a bit of light in his eyes and a few teeth that have since abandoned him like dying friends.

Yes, yes, I see. Congratulations, Uncle. But, you. . . .

Tell this girl to piss off!

The command hits him like a slap against the back of his skull. He jerks the sleeve of his nylon jacket from the young woman's grasp and then turns towards the conference room door. He takes hold of the gold-coloured handle and swings it downward.

Earlier that day, the old man's two zebra finches were hopping around their bamboo cages hung from the metal pipes above the dank mattress.

You've already been fed, he grouses at them. Stop being greedy. These tarts are not for you.

They're just noisy little shits. Why'd you bother getting them in the first place?

To give me something to focus on besides you all the time, he mumbles under his breath.

So ungrateful! Where would you have gotten to without me all these years? You, who have as much backbone as a baozi.

Okay, okay, so you always say. Now, shut up. I need to focus on this batch.

The old man whisks the eggs. He then pours in the caster sugar and evaporated milk, and beats the custard until it glows a bright, confident yellow. The motion, the one he has used for thirty years, now makes his wrists ache. He wishes he still has staff to mix for him, to help make his Gam Tai Yeung Golden Conure egg custards, known for their light flaky crust and luscious filling. Once finished, he spoons the mix into the moulds and places them into the counter-top oven. He hopes that the unfamiliar contraption will do better this time around than with the previous three batches, which came out with the crust too doughy or the custard too firm. He longs for the reliability of his shop's old pastry oven.

As he waits for the custards to bake, he steps out of the dingy kitchen and over to the wooden crate of clothes next to his mattress.

Wear the blue plaid shirt, the special one I bought for you. It hides your stomach.

No one's going to care how I dress.

I do.

As he pulls his arms into the shirtsleeves, he looks up at the finches. Well, I guess I should look good today, nah? I'm seeing one of the richest men in Hong Kong. Mr Big Lucky. I have to impress him on our birthday. Isn't it funny that we're practically twins?

Twins? He's a pig-dog. He's a bastard who destroys lives. That's why we're doing this.

He himself sniggers at the absurdity of comparing himself to the billionaire, but for entirely different reasons.

The two subordinates flanking Kwok Cheng-chung stand as the old man enters the room. A middle-aged woman closes her portfolio and rises too. She gives the trio a deep, reverential bow and scampers from the room. Kwok Cheng-chung – Mr Big Lucky himself – remains seated.

The old man nods his head towards the tycoon.

He looks older than in the newspapers, doesn't he? That jolly smile of his can steal away the years, but it's a bad thief. The wrinkles keep getting returned to him. Hah!

The young woman has followed the old man into the room. Very sorry, sirs. I tried to stop him, but he insisted on coming in. I'll have security remove him at once.

What do you want? Mr Big Lucky asks, amused at the old man's brazenness.

Happy birthday, Chairman Kwok, replies the old man. It is mine, too. I thought that we could celebrate together. We're practically the same age.

I'm sorry, but you're interrupting, replies one of the subordinates. We're in the middle of receiving business proposals.

The old man nods. Yes, I know you're running a contest on your seventieth birthday. Are you really going to give 500,000 dollars to someone with the best idea for a small business?

Mr Big Lucky smiles. Yes, but what concern is it of yours?

The old man takes a deep breath. He then walks up to Mr Big Lucky's desk and sets down his box.

Be confident. Stand tall.

Please have an egg tart. I baked them myself.

WE baked them. It was originally my recipe, don't forget.

Kwok Cheng-chung hesitates, then chuckles. He picks out two tarts, gives one back to the old man and one to a subordinate, and invites them to eat. As they chew, the suspicion in the subordinate's eyes disappears, replaced with a flush of pleasure. His cheeks relax.

Quite good, he proclaims. Excellent, even. The old man should get a Michelin star for these!

Kwok Cheng-chung now bites into a tart. His lips break wide with delight. He calls forward the young woman and hands one to her. As she nibbles, she throws back her head as if in a swoon. Her shoulders go slack. Heavenly! So rich!

Right, like you would really know! You're just a child.

These are perfection, Mr Big Lucky says. This is your recipe? Where did you learn to make these? Can you repeat it?

The old man tucked the box of freshly baked tarts under his arm and slipped into his unlaced Adidas. He then stood in front of the TV and VCR silently playing his favourite movie, Alfred Hitchcock's *Rebecca*.

Come on, you've seen this movie fifty times.

I really like this scene, when the heroine is saved by the shipwreck.

Still? Aren't you tired of it?

He keeps his eyes fixed on the screen until the heroine backs away from the window ledge and out of immediate danger. He then clicks the power button and watches the screen grow dark, as if burying a fond memory.

He gazes at the faded snapshot of his wife, mounted in a dented metal picture frame on top of the TV. Her face is partially hidden by a large red visor that also keeps her permed hair away from her face. She is reclining against a large polka-dotted deck chair. She smiles at the camera but looks uneasy about the cost of this Mediterranean cruise. The vacation had been Esther's idea, a treat that she said her parents should have after countless years of toil. Esther had even gone so far as to book the trip with her own savings, convinced that her mother would not have otherwise allowed herself such an indulgence. It was the only time her mother had ever left Hong Kong, and the only time in years Gam Tai Yeung had closed for longer than a single day.

You know that Esther only wanted us to go to Greece because she wanted a break from working at the bakery.

That's not true. She saw how exhausted we were all the time. She was thinking about us, not herself.

Anyway, what does it matter? It's all gone now. They've taken it all. There's nothing left.

Isn't there?

As soon as the doubts form in his head, he braces for the bludgeoning he is sure to receive over his inadequate manliness. And on cue, his wife's visage in the picture begins to transform. Her eyes narrow into a glower, and the shadow from her visor moves downward to obscure the rest of her face, as if the overhead sun itself is cowering behind a bank of clouds. He steps back and averts his eyes and up towards his blissfully ignorant finches.

However, the reaction he hears this time is surprisingly mild, soothing almost. *I know it's hard to leave. But you have to do this.*

He looks again at the picture of his wife. The light has returned to her face, and she looks calmer. In fact, beyond simply offering sympathy, she looks like she actually shares his fear. That's something new. But then, why not? This tiny apartment has been the only place she has called home for four decades. Who wouldn't feel uneasy about walking away from it? Perhaps she now recognises that the only way to leave behind such a large slice of her past is together with him, arm-in-arm.

And you're doing it for both of us.

Yes, I guess so.

When he steps out onto his flat's landing, the fat, creamy smells of the egg tarts wrestle with the tinny stink of rusting metal, old newspapers and rats' piss. He padlocks his front door and walks down the three flights of stairs. He encounters Mrs Lam, returning from the wet market. A bunch of leafy dou miao pokes out of a white plastic bag. She stiffens when she sees him.

Hello, Mr Ho, she says haltingly. Are we having a nice day today? Did you eat lunch?

How patronising! She's always so smarmy.

He stops to face her. She looks at him askance, as if wondering whether she has done anything wrong.

Don't I owe you money? he asks.

Eh? Why on Earth are you asking her that?

Mrs Lam is startled at the question, but then nods slowly. Yes, for paying for those repairs last month. Three hundred dollars, if I recall.

Wun bun! That's outrageous. It wasn't more than two hundred.

This city has gotten so expensive, he grumbles. He reaches into his pocket, pulls out a fistful of bills and hands them to Mrs Lam. Count out what I owe you.

She carefully extracts three red notes and hands the others back to him. Thank you for remembering, Mr Ho.

Without acknowledging her gratitude, he pushes past.

What the hell was that about? Why were you so charitable? You don't even like her and she knows it.

YOU never liked her. I never had a problem with her.

She can be such a nasty, small-minded shrew.

No more than you, he mumbles. Beside, no more debts. Not after today.

He heads down the alley towards the post office to mail a reply letter to his daughter.

The assembled crowd in the hotel ballroom applauds as Mr Big Lucky turns to introduce the old man.

And this is Mr Ho Keung-suk. He introduced himself to me earlier today while I was receiving business proposals for my competition. Though he will not be our winner, he is the maker of the finest egg tarts that I have ever tasted. I hope that everyone here will have a chance to try them one day. And funnily enough, today is also his birthday!

The room erupts in more applause as a photographer snaps a photo of the two old men. Only Mr Big Lucky smiles.

Okay, say what you came here to say.

The old man shuffles forward towards the microphone. No one stops him. He stares out into the banquet room. Along the back wall, there is an enormous cake, an ice carving of an eagle and a chocolate fountain being assaulted by children with marshmallows on skewers. The old man thinks of his own grandchildren, how much they must have grown. How old are they now, six and eight?

He then looks at the bejewelled, dolled-up ladies around the room.

They're so unlike me, aren't they? Who do they think they are? They're like old plastic flowers pretending to be young and fresh. But they're just fake.

The old man clears his throat to speak.

Talk loudly and clearly.

You know, Chairman Kwok and I are almost the same age. We might have once played as children in the same playground. But now, he is rich and powerful. He can probably ask Hong Kong to name a whole district after him, ha ha. But me, I've had a small life. I've only ever liked making egg tarts. Maybe too much, as you can tell by my belly. I had a shop. Perhaps you know it? It was in Causeway Bay. Gam Tai Yeung. It was a little cha chaan teng serving my egg tarts, pastries and milk tea.

A few knowing murmurs stir through the crowd.

Of course they knew Gam Tai Yeung. And it's their loss now.

My teahouse was forced to close two weeks ago, after Chairman Kwok raised the rent to three times what it used to be. Some fancy

European jewellery store will appear on the ground floor, where my shop once was.

The crowd grows silent. The old man looks at the tycoon, who resembles the eagle ice sculpture with its cold, hard smile.

I just want to make an honest living, Mr Kwok. I think someone like you and your rich foreigner friends should understand. I just want to get up in the morning and do what I have always done and bring a little happiness to the people of Hong Kong. But what can a simple old man like me do now? Nothing. How can I start again? I cannot.

Mr Big Lucky makes a slight hand gesture towards the young woman. She begins to march towards the old man, while coaxing the crowd into an awkward final round of applause.

Do it now, before it's too late!

I can't! He's an important and powerful man. . . .

You must! Just as you promised you would! Hurry, you idiot!

Gritting what remaining teeth he has, the old man turns towards the tycoon. He reaches into both pockets of his nylon jacket and pulls out two eggs with each hand. Ignoring the stiffness in his shoulder, he raises an arm and hurls two eggs at Mr Big Lucky. They strike him on his cheek and forehead. White and yellow explode across his face. His bifocals somersault away as he recoils back towards the side of the stage. The crowd cries out in collective alarm.

These are for you, Mr Big Lucky, the old man yells out over the hubbub. I don't need them anymore!

He throws the other two eggs, but the young woman steps between the two men. The eggs strike her outstretched hand and wrist and shatter against them. She squeals at the impact and turns her face away, but remains standing tall and straight.

You damn bitch! Get out of the way!

The old man is grabbed from behind by two pairs of large hands. Before he can offer any resistance, he is lifted off his feet and carried roughly from the stage. Faced backwards as he is dragged out of the ballroom, he sees that the young woman is chasing after him, flapping her soiled hand in the air to shake off the remnants of the shattered eggs that cling to her fingers. Behind her, half the crowd watches slack-jawed while the other half rushes towards the stage to attend to Mr Big Lucky.

Once outside the ballroom, he is dropped onto his side against the carpeted floor. He grimaces as pain shoots up his lower back and through his throwing shoulder. One of the men who has carried him out gives him a sharp and swift kick to the ribs, momentarily taking away his breath.

As he gingerly turns onto his back and opens his eyes, he finds the young woman bending towards him, her outraged face inches from his. Her breath smells faintly of wine.

How dare you be so rude, Uncle! She slaps his face with her egged hand. He tastes raw yolk mixed with trickles of blood on the inside of his upper lip. She then stands up and jabs a finger down towards his face. She continues to berate him, but he cannot make out the words because of the indignant hissing in his head.

The old man leans against the marble rail of the balcony overlooking the harbour. From there, he can see across to the hotel's other wing, where Mr Big Lucky's party has clearly resumed. Occasionally, he spots the young woman as she works the room, preening, prancing and generally carrying herself like the day's hero.

She *is* just like Esther, he decides.

Are you blind? Esther has nice cheekbones and a dimple. That girl's face is like a mooncake! How dare you think this hao po looks like our daughter. Come to your senses! We have more work to do.

The old man tries to shoo away the haranguing by jamming a finger into an ear. No! I've done enough! It's finished.

No it's not. We have to go back in there and. . .

Stop! We've made our point, haven't we? I'm done. Now leave me be! This is MY life.

It's mine, too.

No, no. It *was,* but not anymore. Go mind your own business.

How dare you. . .

I'm ignoring you.

Egg Tarts

The old man tries to focus on something else to prove his resolve. But all he can think of is Esther. She hadn't said anything about herself in her letter. He wonders whether she is happy, whether she has figured out life, just as she had set out to try to do. Has she deciphered the recipe to tease out its flavours, to unlock the sweetness inside its crust? Does she carry the same steely look of certainty as the tycoon's young woman when she works a room full of strangers or if she ever feels the need to strike a man's face?

He remembers his daughter's pleadings before she left him and flew off to Vancouver.

Bah, how can you stand to keep going to the bakery where that delivery van killed Mah? Doesn't the place remind you of her? Isn't the business partially to blame for what happened? Anyway, didn't you once say you wanted to do something else with your life? I can't take it. You need to close the place and let us all move forward.

She didn't understand him then, and he doubts she would even now. Esther, you were always free to choose your own way, despite what your Mah said to you from time to time. And yes, I also had other dreams. But not Mah. That shop was all she could focus on. And when she died, she was destined to remain there forever. I could touch her in every mound of flour. I could smell her in every batch that we baked. I heard her in every clanging pan. How could I possibly abandon her?

That's right. You couldn't.

But at least he has now written his apologies to his daughter, and in the only way that he knows how – simply and categorically. And he has passed to her his sole remaining possession of value.

Yes, MY recipe.

His thoughts turn to his finches. He hopes that they have fallen asleep by now and that he has ensured them a peaceful, permanent slumber by placing enough charcoal briquettes into the counter-top oven contraption before locking up the flat.

Noisy little shits. . .

Aiya! will you please just shut up! Why don't you leave me alone now, after everything that has happened and all we've been through today? Don't you understand that you don't get to live on like this through me?

What did you just say?

You heard me. Get away.

A pause. Then, *Fine. Try doing things your way.*

Sighing, he turns towards the balcony's railing and looks out at the harbour. He spots a Star Ferry and watches it chug a return route from Tsim Sha Tsui in front of an approaching tugboat and behind a speeding jetfoil. He then peers down at the courtyard five stories below. A silver sedan is pulling away after a young couple has emerged from the back seat. The young man wipes his hands against the back of his suit trousers and then leads his date into the hotel lobby.

Other lives are carrying on, oblivious to an old man's troubles. Just as always.

What should I do now?

He waits for a reply.

Are you there?

His question is met with silence. It's as if all that he knows has suddenly fled, and he is standing out in a barren field. He cannot remember when he has been this isolated. Is this what real freedom feels like? Is he now liberated from the walls that have always confined him? Can he really make his own choices? He thinks that he should feel calm. But instead, he is unsettled. Without care or worry, without anything, he feels abandoned. He peers out again over the balcony at the gaping space below him. Another car pulls into the courtyard, this one a taxi. From it emerges a stout elderly woman. When she removes her visor and peers up at him, he is taken aback by a face which is featureless and ghost-like. She neither smiles nor scowls. But then he sees her wave a hand. He leans further out towards her. The rising air feels as welcoming as from a warm, familiar oven.

Lavender Song

Nancy KW Leung

She

Today is 23 March. It has been three months, fifteen days and seven hours since he left me. I hug his sweater to my face and fill my lungs again. I can just barely smell him and desperately want him to be a part of me. He watches me from his perch on the dresser, frozen and forever smiling. His favourite baseball hat is askew and his eyes lovingly piercing.

We had promised each other to never be apart. He would not lie, so I can't help but search for him every day. Some days I feel him and know that he is close to me.

It takes all my strength to get out of bed and leave his gaze, but I know that I must. If I don't, how will I ever find him? I light a lavender scented candle. It is our secret signal that we are thinking of each other. Now the dancing flame gives me hope that it will be a beacon for him.

My eyes are instinctively drawn to his and I can't suppress a smile, but then I remember. When Mom told me the news, I asked her to repeat it over and over again because I couldn't understand the words. The look in her eyes told me it was true, and that was the moment my heart died. His funeral was a closed casket so I couldn't see him one last time, not that I could have seen him clearly through my tears. Mom said my last memory should be of how he was. He deserved better than to be remembered as a victim of a hit and run. The newspapers said he was thrown ten metres into a shop window and his bike was mangled under the tyres. At his gravesite, all I could do was tell him that I loved him and cry out, asking him why he left.

Mom finally pulled me away as I gasped for breath and my body convulsed with the reality.

On the walk down from my home, people quickly look away when our eyes meet in the stairwell. I can sometimes hear their whispers, 'It's not natural, she's taking it too hard,' 'She's young, there'll be others,' 'She's becoming a ghost, too skinny and pale.' I don't care what they say. They don't understand what I am going through. I automatically lower my head so strands of my straggly hair fall to cover my swollen eyes as I hurry away.

The bus sways up Stubbs Road towards the Peak. With each scrape and bang I get shivers. I close my eyes and imagine that it is not the rapping of branches, but his spirit telling me that he has found me. As I walk towards the old banyan tree, my breath catches as I see my hopes and dreams, now billowing under the cascading golden-tipped whiskers. The aged tree, a sentinel to the prayers of the city's residents, welcomes me like an old friend. At the iron gate next to the wishing tree, I search frantically for my tag with my message to him. It is the heart-shaped one with the lavender tie. My heart beats fast with anticipation. I close my eyes and inhale. 'Please,' I whisper, before turning it over. My face and hopes fall. He has not written back yet. *When? When?* I wonder as my vision begins to blur.

No longer am I able to tell what is real and what isn't. I think of him constantly, fearful of forgetting each moment we spent together. Sometimes without warning, I see him across the street, but when I run and embrace the broad shoulders of the young man to surprise him, it is me who is surprised. It is never him. I shudder when I am no longer sure of the feel of his hands. Even his face seems to be changing in my mind, and it frightens me. My bedroom is the only place where I know I can see and be with him. There is nothing to do, but wait. It is agonising. My love, hopes and dreams keep his spirit alive in me and for the moment it sustains me.

Rainy days have become my favourite. When the wind howls or a light rain falls, I imagine that it is my beloved whispering and tapping my window to let me know he loves me.

Why my soulmate was taken away consumes me. I replay everything in my mind and wonder what I did that was so evil that caused him to be so violently wrenched away from me. I have stared at the mole under my eye in the mirror, and wondered. I heard Mom and Auntie talking one day after his funeral. Mom was asking if my sadness was her fault. When I was born with the mole, Mom took me to see a face reader. He said heartache and sadness would follow me in life. The mole, like a tear drop, would mar my happiness. However, Mom said she had also heard that the birthmark was a beauty mark and it was a blessing, so she never got the mole removed. She didn't want to risk it if it might bring me luck and fortune. I don't and never have blamed her. It's too late now and it won't bring him back.

He

It has become a ritual. She pounds her fists on her chest, beating herself until she has no more energy. Her wails haunt the night and ring in my ears. Sometimes it is more than I can bear. I am there to comfort her. I wrap my arms around her, but she does not stop. She cannot feel me. Hours later she finally cries herself to sleep and I can take my leave.

I never had the intention of leaving her the way I did, but who does? It has been difficult for me also. It torments me to see her in despair. I drift away but I cannot stay away for very long as her thoughts and grief call to me and draw my spirit to her. My promise to never leave her drives me on and propels me in my quest.

The hospital seems to be going through a slow period and there is nothing to do. I wander the halls and wait. After the first few days, the antiseptic smell of the halls no longer bothers me. Most of the people here cough or have young feverish children. Like me, a few patients are here for heart problems, but the cause of my aching heart is unlike theirs. Spirits linger above some hospital beds unable to make a clean break from this world. They remain until their loved ones are ready to let them go. Sometimes it takes months. Like everyone else, I have come to wait until it is my turn. I am not here to make friends although there are a few wandering spirits, some in better shape than others. Seeing a spirit in torn service uniform with ghastly injuries relentlessly wandering the corridors saddens me. I have called to him but he ignores me. He is on a quest of his own. He is searching for his comrades and commanding officer to get his next orders. I imagine he will continue until he finally realises that he has died. I look up as the lights flicker and I smile. I'm sure it is little Ah Yan being her mischievous self again. I met her when she was running through the halls laughing. She left her body when she was eight, leukaemia. She, like the other departed children, always finds something to entertain herself with. I assume they don't want to leave their friends until their parents are ready to join them.

I turn my head at the sound of running footsteps. The double doors slam open as a stretcher speeds towards the emergency room. Surrounded by nurses, doctors and IV pumps, I catch a glimpse of a young man. He is still alive, I think. I can't help but wonder if he could be the one, and follow.

Nurses cut his clothes off and attach more monitoring devices to him, while doctors work on stopping his bleeding.

In a calm voice I hear the EMT tell the staff, 'Motor vehicle accident victim. Witnesses say he got hit square in the chest. Luckily the car was slowing at the crosswalk so he didn't get the full impact. We found him sprawled on the hood and windshield.' The EMT looks at the motionless and bloodied face and slowly shakes his head, 'The driver may have been distracted by his mobile phone.'

A shrill continuous beep cuts through the air. Everyone turns to the source of the noise to see a flat-line. The medical team jumps into action. A doctor pumps his chest while nurses quickly inject liquids into his body.

'Echocardiogram, stat,' demands the doctor as he continues to pump the young man's chest.

I watch in awe as staff wheel in more machines. I float over to the young man's face. It is serene.

'He has fluid around his heart. Get me a syringe!' the doctor yells into my face.

Three feet above the body I see him, a luminous form. He looks at me, then at the commotion around his body. He is not sad. With one last look he floats higher, then disappears. Just like that and he is gone. I start to go after him but then stop. I look back at his body just as the doctor plunges the needle into his chest. A minute passes before he withdraws it. The syringe is filled with a bloody froth.

'Give him another shot of epi,' the doctor orders.

The heart monitor is still flat.

At the far end of the room I notice the disembodied head hanging from the wall. I had seen this reclusive spirit before, roaming the hospital corridors. He was probably drawn to this room by the energy of the staff and wanted to have a peek at the commotion.

'Let's defib him,' says the doctor. The medical staff takes a step back from the body. 'Everyone clear.'

I turn back to view the scene below me just as the lifeless body jerks. Out of the corner of my eye there is a movement. My eyes meet the spirit's menacing gaze. They are not friendly, but determined. With his injured leg he is lumbering towards the stretcher. My heart is pounding. This may be my only chance. I turn to the body and race towards it.

Beep, beep, beep. . . . 'We've got him back,' I faintly hear.

She

The bars on the windows of the tong lau are like my prison, they prevent me from being with him. Leaping from the third floor would not guarantee that I will be with him and I need a guarantee. I reach for his picture and gently touch his cheek. 'We will be together again, my love,' I whisper.

The blade glistens as I stare at my reflection. I move the cold steel slowly against my wrist but not deep enough to cut, as the scars can't be obvious. I run my finger over the healing ridges on my thigh and position the knife above the smooth, unblemished skin. I inhale and then stop. With a sharp pain it feels as if the dagger has been driven into my heart. A vibrant stream of red spills and trails down my thigh. I let the searing pain carry me. It allows me to forget the anguish I feel, but only for a moment. Without my beloved, my protector, my everything, this is the only way that I know that I am still alive, and it too tortures me.

Every week I sit at his gravesite. As usual I have brought his favourite, a cup of instant noodles. I tell him about the past week as I pour hot water onto the noodles and set a pair of wooden chopsticks in front of his tombstone. Today, it is curry seafood flavour.

My time with him is always too short, but it is getting dark and I am no longer able to make out the words of the book I am reading to him. As I get up, I remember to pull my skirt down to hide the marks on my thigh. Early on I had made an unspoken deal with God. If I suffer enough maybe he will return.

He

I worry that when my beloved sees me for the first time, she will not know that it is me. I have had to acquaint myself with family and friends familiar with this body. It has helped that the doctor has explained to them, how I have lost some of my memories from the trauma, and that they may never return. Having been freed from the physical body for so long, I have had to accustom myself with being confined again. The weight and limitations will take some getting used to, but it will allow me to hold and touch her again. How I long for that moment. I am now no longer able to see the wandering spirits and that confirms that I am back in the land of the living.

Almost six months have passed since we were separated and I hope my darling will recognise me. I have cut my hair and dressed like my former body. I even brought my favourite baseball hat and wore it askew to help her know that it is me. I reach up and feel around the rim of the front gate. My heart trembles as I fumble with the key. I hold a sprig of lavender so that she will know that I have returned to her, just as I had promised. As I near her room, lavender fills my head and confirms our love for each other. I can hardly contain myself knowing that we are finally to be reunited. I watch my hand grasp the doorknob and I slowly open her bedroom door. I see her for the first time and smile. My love for her wells up in my chest as I bite my lower lip. She lies still, she looks peaceful. 'My dearest, I am back,' I whisper. I kneel by her bed and gently brush the hair on her forehead. I take her hand and pull it to my chest. It is cold. I gently pull the blanket to cover her. An empty pill bottle rolls to the floor. My heart skips a beat and my throat constricts. My eyes dart desperately over her body and my brain works frantically to make sense of it all. The cold skin, the blue lips, the motionless chest. I search for any slight movements of her chest. 'No, this can't be happening. Pleeeaase. . . .' I sputter. I run my hands over her body and try to shake her awake. Her arm falls over the edge of the bed, motionless. I grasp her hand to my lips and urgently kiss her fingers. 'Why? Why? I was coming for you,' I plead between my convulsive sobs. With clenched fists, I throw my head back. A scream pours from me as it fills the building.

On the Other Side of the Fire

Reena Bhojwani

A DARK CLOUD MOVED AWAY from the moon above, and the roofless tent brightened. As soon as the last of the group had entered, the doorway of the tent sealed itself, blocking out the rest of the world. The three old men allowed their eyes to adjust. They could finally see the objects around them which were bathed in moonlight. The colours of their surroundings were vibrant, so stimulating and lively that they had to shield their eyes. They were at a banquet.

A chair screeched as Lee sat down at the table. To his right was Wang and to his left, Hui. Resting their hands on their kneecaps, the old men enjoyed the gentle brush of the silky tablecloth against their calloused knuckles. Hui smiled his approval with his thick lips, and the others nodded in agreement.

Looking around, they realised all the other tables were filling up with their group mates. Matted hair and skin glistening with grimy sweat was a frequent sight. Other than that, everyone was behaving as if this was an important gathering. The tattered clothing of the men and women didn't seem to concern anyone. Their bony bodies sat in dignified postures, waiting to be served. Hui, Lee and Wang straightened their backs too.

The trio felt confused. Their surroundings perplexed them, and their hosts were nowhere in sight. And yet, this place, wherever they were, seemed a welcome change from the place they had come from, wherever that was.

The sharp sheen of the cutlery from their table was jabbing at their eyes. They felt unaccustomed to the fancy setting. As Lee observed this, a memory crept into his mind. In it, he watched himself being married to a very beautiful woman, but he couldn't remember her. Hui and Wang seemed to be experiencing similar flashbacks of their own. Each of them had nostalgic smiles on their faces. For a little while, they would allow themselves to forget the simple truth: they were all dead.

A crumpled house stood on a hill, drooping from the weight of poverty. Ying-yi was busy making preparations for that evening. From the way she moved, one would never guess she was the grandmother of a teenager. Despite her greying hair and the wrinkles around her small eyes, her face had a radiant glow.

Next to her was a wooden table with a missing leg. On it were a bowl of fruit and an incense holder full of short sticks. The used joss sticks were in position, anxious about being lit again.

Ying-yi didn't hear the loud clang. She only looked up because the door had moved a metal container into her line of vision. Her grandson, Tim, had just entered.

'Po-po, you'll be so proud. I got a great bargain today!' he said, looking at her so she could read his lips.

'And how is that?' she asked, tucking a stray strand of grey hair behind her ear.

'You'll see!'

'We don't have time for games, Tim. Quick, we have to make our offerings before the sun sets.'

Tim was scrawny, but he walked into the house confidently with his purchase dangling in a clear plastic bag from his hands.

The men hadn't thought about their appearance in a long while. Their dirt-encrusted strands of once-silver hair had clumped together over the years. Scrubbing the charred depths of Hell with their bare hands didn't require them to be well-groomed. The gap under Wang's chipped fingernails had collected plenty of caked soot. His fingers looked like fat sausages that had been forgotten in a pan, sentenced to burn slowly.

Lee was skinny, with flesh that had barely covered him when he was alive. His hollow eyes resembled those of carved pumpkins Westerners lit up at the end of October.

Hui's stomach jiggled slightly as it rumbled. Before they had been given permission to leave Hell for the night, they had been warned to be on their best behaviour. This was the first time since they had died that they would get to revisit their former world. Most dead beings resorted to their primal instincts once they were placed on Earth again. It was a test to see if they could contain themselves; if they were ready to move on to the next phase of their Hell sentences or if they needed to serve more time.

Tonight was the one night Lee wouldn't need to worry about being tossed around with burning pieces of coal like a roasted chestnut, or bathed with hot, fetid oils that leaked from the sweaty, slaughtered necks of rotten animals. No, tonight was the fifteenth night of the seventh month. It was the Hungry Ghost Festival. And these men, seated within the large banquet tent, suddenly found themselves to be ravenous.

Ying-yi waited as her grandson moved the three-legged table into their backyard. *He's so much like his grandfather, stronger than he looks. I really wish he had gotten a chance to know him better.*

Tim's parents had kept him away from Ying-yi for many years so that she could 'rest'. The real reason, Ying-yi forced herself to admit, was that they were worried. They expected insanity would have encroached her when her husband had gone missing, but this year when Tim insisted on visiting, his parents, who had run out of excuses, succumbed. They were reassured when Tim reported no extraordinary behaviour upon his arrival.

It had been over thirteen years, and she had yet to hear what really happened during the accident. That was the last time that she had seen her husband. More than twelve different people had given her the same report that day: that three men were still unaccounted for. The case had been closed at the end of that month, but Ying-yi was still waiting for answers, hoping against all hope that her husband was still alive, or that they would find his body and confirm his death. Hanging in between the two possibilities was a fate she hoped her husband would not have to endure.

Outside the house, the pores of the joss sticks were starting to release their powdered sweat. Ying-yi used a match to light the fire within the metal container. Grey smoke swirled into the air, mixing with the fiery colours of the sunset.

Hui, Lee and Wang pinched the empty air with their chopsticks. A collage of smells mounted in their nostrils, and they had a hard time keeping themselves seated. This was the only night since they had died that their appetite had somehow returned, magnified. Cravings gnawed at them from the dry pits of their stomachs, slowly threatening to crawl up and take control. They waited for onion cakes, pork chops, chicken feet, beef bellies and red bean cakes to dance on their tongues and satisfy their appetites.

In Hell, they had only been able to sense pain, sorrow and suffering. Among those chapped walls, joy and happiness didn't last very long. Now, the aromas of freshly cooked, succulent meat made their mouths water. They tapped their chopsticks impatiently, craning their necks to see if a dim sum cart was nearby. It was.

This banquet was peculiar. Carts full of bamboo baskets whizzed around like lightning, filling empty tables with delicacies they didn't even know existed. Porcelain platters clattered together as greedy hands grabbed at them.

Soon, Hui, Lee and Wang realised that they were the only ones that didn't have any food. A light breeze wafted various smells of flavoured oils their way. That's when Lee noticed it. The sight before him reminded him of how his broken television used to have trouble receiving transmission signals. Fragmented pixels of the black and white image teased him. Then, slowly, a coloured object started to take form. It was a silver dish with a cover on top. Lee licked his lips as his friends stared at him with jealousy. It was time for his feast!

With the fire burning bright, Ying-yi was ready to start the prayers. She walked into the house and called for her grandson. 'Okay, Tim, where are the paper offerings?'

She found Tim sitting cross-legged in a corner, drawing. He smiled as she approached him, revealing his uneven front teeth. Ying-yi noticed a black marker and a booklet of wax paper balanced on his lap.

'I have them, Po-po!' he said, holding the booklet. 'The shopkeeper assured me that the spirits will be very pleased with whatever I draw!' he said, facing away from Ying-yi, knowing she didn't hear him. He closed the booklet of wax paper before she could see what he had drawn.

She sighed and turned to go back out, beckoning for him to come. He got up and followed her out of the house where the hungry fire waited.

Under his grandmother's watchful gaze, Tim tore out a drawing and threw the first offering into the crackling flames.

The deep laughter of Wang and Hui echoed in Lee's ears as he put down his 'food'. The hard object could not be considered a form of nutrition. It would have served better as a paperweight.

Lee had tried to eat the lower portion of the rectangular object after seeing the half-bitten white apple. In return, the lustrous metallic surface put all his remaining teeth to shame. He tried sucking, chewing, biting and tearing, but nothing worked. Against the china crockery, the object simply protested, *tink, tink* when he put it down, defeated. Lee reddened and wanted to caress his gums. Then another pixelated object started to form. This time in front of Hui.

'Tim, what are those pictures? Don't just throw them into the fire! Show me first!'

'The one I just threw in was a shoe and the one before that was a smartphone!'

Ying-yi shook her head. 'Now, the spirits will finish us for good! We might as well set the house on fire ourselves!'

'What are you talking about, Po-po? Who wouldn't want a new mobile phone or this cool bike?' he asked, showing her the picture of a motorbike he had drawn.

'I really wish your grandfather would come back!' she said, more to herself than him.

The orange flames licked at her arms, demanding more food. Sighing, Ying-yi shook her head as Tim continued to offer the rest of the pages in the booklet.

The round moon stood naked, right above their heads, like the open mouth of a face in shock. The barking behind the trio provided a momentary distraction from the plastic and metal buffet stacked high in front of them. The table was so full that the men could only see each other through the gaps in the piles. Hui plucked out a silver Rolex watch and chucked it at the dog. The canine howled.

Sniffing his new find, the dog considered the object, listening to the ticking noises of the moving hands. Finally, uncertain of what to do, he raised his leg, relieved himself on the expensive metal and darted away to another part of the tent.

'See,' said Hui, sighing, 'even *he* doesn't think much of these things.'

'I don't care what the dog thinks! I want food!' growled Wang, banging his fist on the table, rattling the china.

Lee was silent.

With the final page of the booklet torn and not a single piece of food offered, Ying-yi panicked. 'Tim! This festival is not a joke! I told you to buy traditional offerings! Where are the pictures of the food?' she demanded, her face becoming paler by the second.

'I . . . I don't have anything else, Po-po,' Tim said, hanging his head.

'Tim, your grandfather doesn't seem like he's coming back anytime soon. I don't know what happened to him, but I'm quite certain that it's bad. We'll have to assume the worst. Now, I'm counting on you to become more mature and do your duty as a grandson!'

The colour in Tim's face drained slowly. It was the first time he had seen his grandmother so upset.

'I'm just a simple cook at a restaurant,' she continued. 'I'm growing old. I can't do this forever. Without the blessings of the spirits, we'll be finished! Now that we've started feeding the fire, we'll have to continue. Start offering these fruits,' she said, handing him the chipped bowl. 'I was saving them for our dinner, but you've left me no choice. I'm going to go and search for other offerings inside. Wait until one fruit has completely burned before offering the next. If you throw them all inside at once, then you won't get dinner!'

Tim stood rooted to the spot, holding the bowl in his hands as he watched her go. He noticed for the first time that his grandmother's back was slightly hunched.

As Ying-yi walked into the house, she wiped the tears welling in her eyes. She knew that if Tim could please a spirit by feeding it, then in return they might be able to ask for some information about her husband. More importantly, if he really was dead, then this was the only chance Tim had to help him prepare for the afterlife. The grandson of the deceased was expected to make the offerings, and this was the first time Tim had visited her since her husband had gone missing. Her careful plan now seemed like an under-boiled egg, runny and formless. She'd have to think fast.

Hui, Wang and Lee were about to get up and break all the rules. *How were they expected to be on their best behaviour in a situation like this?* This torture was almost worse than all their duties in Hell put together. The large sand glass at the entrance of the tent had almost run out, and they still hadn't tasted a single morsel of food! Their teeth hurt from biting all the hard objects that had appeared on their plates. Much to the protest of their chairs, they stood up and scavenged for food on the other tables nearby.

Walking around, all they could see were empty dishes stacked up on top of each other, with oil drizzling down onto the floor like a weak waterfall. Lee wondered if his friends would laugh at him if he stuck his tongue out to intercept the fragrant, tasty-looking liquid, leaking from a plate near him. He turned back and was just about to suggest it when he noticed something. 'Look, you two! Something else is coming!' he exclaimed.

They all took a step back. The previous item that had appeared was a large motorcycle, and they weren't sure if the table could handle the weight of anything more. What appeared however, surprised them. A gigantic orange, the size of a baby elephant, fell onto the table, scattering the previous offerings pell-mell. The table was now empty, except for the single fruit in the middle, which had split into three portions from the impact.

The men didn't use their hands. They each charged at the fruit, face first, attacking it with their mouths. Moments later, they emerged from the citrusy paradise, their faces covered with specks of orange, juice trickling down their chins.

'Heaven!' said Wang, grabbing a large chunk of the fruit and stuffing it into his mouth.

'Whoever gave us this!' said Lee, with his mouth full. 'Give us more! Take all these things with you!' he said pointing at the mess around him. 'They're of no use to us.'

'Hmmm. . . .' the others agreed, each in their own states of bliss.

Ying-yi came out of the house holding her most prized possession, her recipe book. Within it, she had collected her best recipes that had won the restaurant she worked for much praise. She hoped that offering one of these would suffice, but she was already resigned to the fact that her collection was about to perish.

When she stepped over the threshold, however, she gasped. Surrounding Tim was a pile of treasure: a motorcycle, a fridge, a washing machine, a smartphone, a pair of expensive shoes and a Rolex watch that Tim was trying on for size.

'Where did you get all this, Tim?' she asked.

'It just . . . appeared, Po-po,' he told her. 'After I put the orange into the fire, I waited like you said. As soon as the whole orange disappeared, the fire started crackling. Then, it suddenly threw all these things out!'

For a split second, Lee experienced a strange sensation. His friends vanished, followed by the banquet hall. The tent he had been in moments ago was replaced by tall trees and a hunched house. He was floating inches above the ground. He felt a jolt in his head and realised his memory had returned. He recognised his surroundings. He knew where he was.

A large smile emerged on Ying-yi's face. 'You've made me proud, Tim!' she said, enveloping him into a big hug. They spent the rest of the evening lugging their new fortune into the house, except the motorbike, which they hid under a tarpaulin.

Later, when Ying-yi was about to close the window, she noticed wisps of smoke whirling and twisting in front of the house.

As a shape formed clearly, Ying-yi's hands smacked against her open mouth.

'Lee!' she screamed, running out the house with Tim behind her.

'Ying . . . Ying-yi!' said Lee, recognising his wife, noticing she had aged beautifully.

'What. . . ? How. . . ?' she started but was unable to go on. 'Tim! Can you see . . . your grandfather?'

Tim's eyes were open wide. He had never met his grandfather. He had only seen a few photos over the years, yet he was able to recognise the apparition in front of him. 'Ngoi-po?'

'Is this. . . ?'

'He's Tim. Your grandson,' explained Ying-yi.

'Thank you for feeding me. . . .' said Lee, smiling. Then he noticed the watch on Tim's wrist. He recognised it. Everything that had happened in the roofless tent started to make sense now.

'Wait . . . so this means. . . .' started Ying-yi.

'Yes, I'm no longer alive. I'm a ghost.'

'And . . . the others?' asked his wife, shakily.

'Hui, Wang and I died that night when part of the bridge collapsed.'

'Wha— What happened?'

'It was our fault, Ying. We wanted better lives. I wanted Tim's parents to come back and live with us, and they wanted their children to go to proper schools and learn English. To fulfil those wishes, we needed money.'

Ying-yi nodded slowly, realising.

Her husband continued, 'Hui, Wang and I were working late that night. We were waiting for someone to come and pay us for stealing some papers from the site that were going to delay the construction of the rest of the bridge.'

Ying-yi flinched slightly as he said this, hoping he wouldn't notice.

'We didn't see the cracks in the new section that had just been built. While we were waiting . . . the bridge . . . collapsed on us.'

Ying-yi closed her eyes, imagining the gruesome sight of her husband and his best friends being pulverised under the heavy chunk of concrete. 'And your bodies?'

'We must have been crushed completely.'

Ying-yi reached out to try and touch her husband's cheek, her thin fingers tracing the contours of his wispy face. He had sacrificed himself to try and give his family a better life. She wished she could hold him and let him know that she still loved him but just as she came close, the smoky figure of Lee started dissipating.

'Lee?' Ying-yi shouted.

'I think I have to go now, Ying. . . .' he said, his voice barely a whisper before he dissolved into the air.

Ying-yi turned around, searching. She looked around the whole backyard, jumping at every sound the wind blew in her ears, but he was gone. 'Come on, Tim,' she finally said, leading her grandson back into their house.

They cried in each other's arms that night mourning their loss. Yet, they were also relieved. At least they knew the truth now.

Back inside the furnace-like belly of Hell, Hui and Wang had no recollection of what had happened. Each of them held onto their tools and set to work. They didn't even know to think about how the fire in their stomachs had been satiated. For now.

Hui turned to Wang and asked, 'Have you seen Lee?'

The Authors

Joy Al-Sofi teaches English in Hong Kong and is finishing her MFA in Creative Writing at City University. Her USA life included being a single parent, a lawyer and in the high-tech world. She is a published poet and has contributed to the Hong Kong Writers Circle anthologies for the past several years.

Simon Berry is a recovering lawyer who has graduated from writing creative legal opinions to writing creative fiction while studying for an MFA at City University in Hong Kong. His stories have appeared in HKWC anthologies, *Of Gods and Mobsters* and *Another Hong Kong*. He was co-editor of *Another Hong Kong*.

Reena Bhojwani teaches creative writing to kids at Elephant Community Press by day and conjures up her own magical, mystical, mysterious tales by night.

Bernardette S Sto. Domingo moved to Hong Kong from Manila in 2011 to pursue a writing career. She has worked as editor of a community newspaper and a leading trade magazine. A perfect day for her consists of just three things: a nice movie, tomato-flavoured potato chips and yellow plum.

Ian Greenfield was born in England but has been teaching mathematics in Hong Kong since 1998. He has had ten stories published in previous HKWC anthologies and has also been published in *Hong Kong Culture*.

Sophia Greengrass studied creative writing in Norwich, and has lived in Hong Kong for four years, most recently on Lamma Island along with her dog Coco whom she is writing a children's book about. She currently teaches public speaking and English exam preparation for UK boarding schools.

Kate Hawkins is co-editor of *Hong Kong Gothic* as well as co-editor of *Another Hong Kong*. She holds a degree in Creative Writing from Queensland University of Technology and has also studied writing at the University of Leeds. Kate has a love of creating poetry and writing scripts as well as viewing and reviewing art.

Peter Humphreys is a senior editor at a Hong Kong educational publisher. His short stories have appeared in *Of Gods and Mobsters* and *Another Hong Kong* (HKWC), *Cha: An Asian Literary Review* and *Far Enough East*. His website is *peterjohnhumphreys.com* and he blogs at *theworddiver.wordpress.com*

Véronique K Jonassen has been living in Hong Kong for six years, working in the banking industry. She enjoys writing, especially urban fantasy. She completed a course in Creative Writing at UCLA in Los Angeles in 2012. She travels a lot and loves writing about how cultural differences impact on people.

CM John has lived and worked in Hong Kong since 2000 and is trying to write his first novel, which is much like pulling teeth. He enjoys bushwalking and hopes to encounter Bigfoot, or at least a guy dressed in a monkey suit.

Phillip Y Kim is a Korean-American who has been a long-time Hong Kong resident and finance professional. He took up creative writing a few years ago, drawing inspiration from his wide-ranging experiences in Asia. He has published three short stories in the Hong Kong Writers Circle's previous anthologies. His first novel, *Nothing Gained,* was published by Penguin in March 2013. He is a part owner of the *Asia Literary Review.* He blogs about rich and infamous Asian money-grubbers at *www.asiaonepercent.blogspot.com.*

Nancy KW Leung left Toronto and brought her voracious appetite for reading to Hong Kong. She has published in scientific medical journals and has broadened her interests to creative writing. *Lavender Song* is her second published short-story fiction. Her previous story appeared in the HKWC anthology *Another Hong Kong*.

Marc J Magnee is a writer and tutor who found himself in China over a decade ago, a teacher, green and mystified, a stranger in the strangest of strange lands. He soon moved to Hong Kong, where he now lives with his beloved wife, a water view, and his stories. His website is *marcmagnee.net*.

Stewart McKay has been an English teacher, and writer, in Hong Kong since 2012. He would describe his entry to this year's anthology as gothic with a capital 'G', borrowing (heavily, yet lovingly . . .) from the classic eighteenth Century gothic writers. His website is *st.mckay.wordpress.com*.

Anjali Mittal moved to Hong Kong three years ago from the UK. She writes children's fiction and has just had her third book, *The Boat Race,* published. Anjali believes in encouraging children to read by making books stimulating and by presenting at schools around the world. Her website is *www.anjalimittal.com*

Flora Qian currently lives in Washington D. C., where she is studying for her MFA at the University of Maryland. Born in Shanghai, she lived in Hong Kong for seven years working as an investment communications professional. She holds a BA in English and an MA in Translation. Her translation of Sophie Kinsella's book *Shopaholic & Sister* has been published in China.

Vaughan Rapatahana enjoys the perspective granted from having homes in Hong Kong, the Philippines and Aotearoa (New Zealand). He has been published widely internationally in a variety of genres, including *Expand Your Mind with Poetry* (2014) and *OutLoud Too,* an

anthology of Hong Kong poets (2014). Forthcoming work includes
Atonement (poetry, 2014) *Why English? Confronting the Hydra* (2015).

Luke Reid is a writer of fiction both in prose and screenplays. With a
large body of (currently) unfinished novels and scripts behind him,
this is his first foray into short stories. He enjoys writing science
fiction, drama and comedy.

Juan Miguel Sevilla moved to Hong Kong in 2012, currently working
as a copywriter. He worked as a screenwriter and film director in his
native Philippines, where he has, to date, written six produced screenplays. His website is *juanmiguelsevilla.com.*

Elizabeth Solomon is an amateur writer, teacher and peace activist
who dabbles in poetry and prose. Life is her writing muse. Raised
between Bombay and Jerusalem, she is a proud post-colonialist who
speaks four languages, badly. Elizabeth is working on her first novel,
set in the Parsi neighbourhood of her childhood.

Sharon Tang is from the UK, where she worked as a pharmacist in
various locations in and around London. Writing has been a long-time
hobby of hers. She now lives in Hong Kong with a husband and two
children and teaches pharmacy part time.

Marnie Walker is a professional harpist, singer and composer. A
co-editor of *Hong Kong Gothic,* Marnie's short fiction is published in
Imagine This: An Artprize Anthology. Her poem 'My Mind is Nowhere'
recently won a prize in the 2014 David Burland Poetry Competition.
Marnie is currently editing her first novel, which she hopes to publish
in 2015. Her website is *marniewalker.net.*

CPSIA information can be obtained at www.ICGtesting.com
Printed in the USA
BVOW01s2018181214

379556BV00002B/2/P